ALL NIGHT LOVER

Cassie's eyes followed Adam as he moved rhythmically to the beat. *Wow. He is good. No. He is better than good.* He turned his back to her as he continued to dance.

Nice buns! What I wouldn't give to touch them. He must spend hours in the gym, working out. Look at those abs, those thighs, that chest. Okay, stop, before you hyperventilate. Get a grip, Cassie. Oh, I'd love to get a grip! Just one touch. What can it hurt? It's been three long years.

She followed his gyrating hips in appreciation. Her heartbeat accelerated when he began to unbutton his shirt.

Is it getting hot in here, or is it just me? Okay, it's undoubtedly me. This is ludicrous. I'm getting all hot and bothered over a stripper. Okay, a gorgeous, sexy stripper with bulging biceps and a stomach so ripped, I would love to lick whipped cream from it. It's okay for someone to wake me up now. I'm ready for the dream to end and reality to set back in. Men like this are only in my dreams, and if they aren't, they aren't worth the trouble.

Also by Sylvia Lett

Take Me Down

Like Never Before

Perfect for You

Published by Kensington Publishing Corporation

All
Night
Lover

Sylvia Lett

Kensington Publishing Corp.

http://www.kensingtonbooks.com

DAFINA BOOKS are published by

Kensington Publishing Corp.
119 West 40th Street
New York, NY 10018

All Kensington Titles, Imprints, and Distributed Lines are available at special quantity discounts for bulk purchases for sales promotions, premiums, fund-raising, and educational or institutional use. Special book excerpts or customized printings can also be created to fit specific needs. For details, write or phone the office of the Kensington special sales manager: Kensington Publishing Corp., 119 West 40th Street, New York, NY 10018, attn: Special Sales Department, Phone: 1-800-221-2647.

Dafina and the Dafina logo Reg. U.S. Pat. & TM Off.

ISBN-13: 978-0-7582-3479-7
ISBN-10: 0-7582-3479-1

First mass market printing: August 2010

10 9 8 7 6 5 4 3 2 1

Printed in the United States of America

*This book is dedicated to
my family and fans!
I hope you enjoy reading*
All Night Lover
as much as I enjoyed writing it.

Acknowledgments

Thank you, God, for the talent you bestowed on me. I am doing what I love to do in my writing.

My wonderful children, Michael Louis Lett II and Courtney, you guys continue to amaze me. Michael, you made varsity football in tenth grade. You are also on the path to becoming an Eagle Scout next year. Keep up the great work. Courtney, you made the National Junior Honor Society. Yes, you are a brain like me. You both rock! You inspire me to be a better person and a better mother. I love you both, and I am very proud of you!

Special thanks go to my mother, Mattie Willis. You always support me, even when you don't necessarily agree with my genre of writing. I love you, Mama.

My gratitude also goes to my siblings, C. Earl, Johnnie, Liz, Val, Sam, and Bessie. Your continued support and encouragement keep me grounded and focused. I love you guys.

Melanie Lee Singh, you are my number one fan. I love you, Mel. Thanks for always getting the word out about my books.

Chapter 1

Cassie Mancini sat staring blankly out her bed-room window. It was snowing again. The ground and rooftops were all covered in white, glistening snow. She shivered at the draft and closed the blinds and curtains.

When she looked into the mirror, her tired re-flection stared back at her. Her brown eyes had lost most of their sparkle. Her small, heart-shaped face was perfect and free of blemishes. When she smiled, her cheeks dimpled and her twinkling brown eyes lit up her beautiful face. She rarely smiled these days.

She wore very little makeup to cover her natu-ral beauty. Her small, heart-shaped lips held a slight pout. Beside her bottom lip was a small black mole. Long sandy brown hair hung down her back in a single braid. At twenty-five she looked more like seventeen. The only difference between then and now was her petite figure was better than it had been eight years ago. Her breasts were fuller, and her hips were rounder.

She had developed both while pregnant and hadn't lost either after the birth of her son.

Giving herself one last critical look, she stepped away from the bureau and walked to her bed. She looked down at her watch, and it registered nine o'clock. It was bedtime. She had the first shift at the hospital in the morning.

She was picking up the remote control to turn off the television when something flashed across the screen and stopped her cold. Trent Mancini! Trent smiled brightly for the cameras.

"Today in a press conference, the president and CEO of Mancini Industries, Trent Mancini, announced his candidacy for mayor of New York. The New York native has issued a challenge to the incumbent for a debate."

She stared openmouthed at the TV screen. She had known her ex-husband had political aspirations, but she hadn't been sure if or when he would finally throw his hat into the race. No more guessing. Trent had made his intentions known to the world.

Cassie got up and paced the room. *Okay, this doesn't bode well for me. This could explain why Trent wants to get back together. He wants to play happy family for his political career. Been there, done that. I'm not going through that farce again.*

The phone rang, and Cassie walked over and picked it up. She saw Trent's number on the caller ID. Against her better judgment, she took the call.

"Hello," said Cassie, walking over to the window. Looking out, she saw bright lights and heard the distant hum of the subway.

"Hello, sweetheart. How are you? Have you heard the news yet?" asked her ex-husband hopefully.

"I'm fine. Your son is fine also. Thanks for asking. Yes, I heard the news. Good luck with your political career. I hope it works out for you."

"Aw, Cassie, don't be that way. You know I love you and TJ. You are my family. I'll be tied up in meetings tomorrow, but I'll be by next week. There's something I want to ask you."

Her heart was filled with dread. She knew what he wanted to ask her, and she wasn't about to give him the chance. "I'm busy next week. Trent, it's been three months since you've seen TJ. He's been asking about you."

"That's your fault. You took that right away from me when you blackmailed me into giving you full custody. This is on your head."

"If you had wanted to see him, you know I would have allowed it. I'm not going to argue with you about this. I know you never wanted a child and it's my fault for getting pregnant. I've heard it all before, Trent. You gave him up without a fight. The information my lawyer had on you wouldn't have stood up in court, and you know it. It was a cop-out on your part. You got exactly what you wanted. No wife, no child, and no child support. I also got what I wanted, you out of my life." Cassie slammed down the phone. The phone rang again, and Cassie snatched it up. "I'm done, Trent. Leave me alone."

"Cassie, it's not Trent. It's your father. What's going on?" her father asked, his voice filled with concern. "Is Trent harassing you?"

"Dad. Hi," said Cassie, breathing a sigh of relief. "Nothing's wrong. I'm fine. How are you?"

"Missing my little girl," he answered honestly. "Honey, I think it's time for you to come home. You are alone in New York with no family."

"It's not that simple, Dad."

"Yes, it is. You are alone with a small child in New York. Honey, your family is here in Dallas. We can help you with TJ. I worry about you. Okay. I'm done with the lecture. The other reason I'm calling is your sister. Monica is getting married next weekend. I know you received the wedding and shower invitation. Honey, I want you to be there. Your sister misses you, too. It's time to put this family back together. Trent Mancini is not worth what he put this family through. Come home, Cassie. Not just for our sakes, but for yours and your son's. I love you, sweetheart."

"I'll think about it. I love you, too, Dad, and I'll talk to you later," said Cassie sadly, then replaced the receiver. Once the receiver was down, the dam broke and she dropped down to the floor in tears.

Cassie had seen her family only three times in the past six years, since she'd left Dallas. They did not like or approve of Trent, and Cassie had sided with her husband over her family. They had all warned her about him, and she hadn't listened. She had been young and in love and had thought Trent was her Prince Charming. After their marriage, she had soon realized how wrong she was.

At last, she dried her eyes and came wearily to her feet. Her father was right. It was time to go home.

After checking in on TJ, she took a shower and

went to bed. Closing her eyes, she prayed sleep would soon come, but alas, it would not be that easy. She had too much on her mind to sleep. She sat up in bed and lifted her laptop from the nightstand next to the bed. She turned on the computer and waited for it to boot up. Cassie began searching the Web for flights to Texas. Once satisfied with the price, she booked one-way tickets.

Getting ready for work on Monday was always hard for Cassie, but today was especially hard. She had decided that it was time to go to Dallas, and that meant turning in her resignation.

She hit the alarm button twice before drowsily climbing out of bed. After taking a shower, she proceeded with her morning ritual of getting ready. Turning on the coffeemaker, she went into TJ's room to get him ready for day care.

She looked around the room with regret. The wallpaper was blue and white with clowns and balloons. It had taken her so long to find the right wallpaper for this room, and now it didn't seem to matter so much.

TJ was fast asleep in his toddler bed. His chubby little arm was curved around his favorite teddy bear. Cassie couldn't resist touching his dark, straight hair. She dropped a kiss on top of his head. He moved slightly under her light touch.

"Honey, wake up. It's time to get up, sweetie."

His brown eyes popped open, and he sat up, rubbing his sleepy eyes. At four and a half years old, he already had his father's good looks. He had his father's hair and build. He was a small replica of

Trent. The only things he had inherited from his mother were her stubbornness and her eyes.

TJ rolled out of bed and ran into the bathroom. A moment later he came back in the room with his toothbrush in his mouth. He smiled at Cassie, then left the room again. Upon returning three minutes later, this time without his toothbrush, he picked up the Superman sweat suit his mother had laid on the bed, then proceeded to dress himself. Cassie watched him with pride and smiled when he walked over to her for help. He was growing up so fast.

Forty-five minutes later Cassie dropped him off at day care and made him promise there would be no more fighting. He was very stubborn and only wanted to do what he wanted to do. TJ was missing out on a man's influence in his life. His grandfather would soon remedy that.

After waving good-bye to TJ, Cassie hopped back in her car and headed to the hospital. She arrived at the nurses' station a few minutes early. She quickly logged in to the computer and typed up her letter of resignation. She would work through the first shift on Wednesday. That would give her time to get everything in order for their flight out on Friday.

The hardest part was saying good-bye to her best friend, Laura. She and Laura had started at the hospital on the same day. Laura had been the one to laugh and cry with her through her good and bad times.

On Friday morning Cassie was up bright and early, loading suitcases into her car. She moved quietly around the apartment to keep from waking the sleeping imp. But TJ soon woke up, and she took the sheets and covers off his bed and packed them while he got dressed. Then they went out to pick up breakfast and brought it back to the apartment.

TJ was unusually quiet during breakfast. Cassie knew he was a bit scared and edgy about moving away from the only home he knew. She and TJ were finishing breakfast when the doorbell rang. TJ jumped to his feet.

"I'll get it," said Cassie. "You finish eating." She waited until he was back in his chair before she went to answer the door. Looking out the peephole, she saw Laura.

"Where's my favorite little boy?" asked Laura, looking around the room for her godson.

"He's eating breakfast," said Cassie, closing the door behind her. "He's a bit nervous about leaving his home."

"That's understandable," said her friend, setting her purse on the coffee table. "How are you doing? Having any second thoughts?"

"Do the words *terrified* and *petrified* mean anything to you? I know in my heart that I am doing the right thing, but I know Trent is going to freak when he finds out I'm gone."

"Aunt Laura," said TJ excitedly. He ran into her open arms, and she hugged him, planting a kiss on his dimpled cheek.

Laura frowned. "I still can't believe you are leaving. Now who am I going to tell all my deepest, darkest secrets to?"

"I'll only be a phone call away. You have Dad's number and the address. I will call and write often," Cassie assured her.

"We'd better get going if I'm going to get you guys to the airport in time." Laura took one of the large rolling suitcases, and Cassie took the other one.

Cassie looked around the apartment one last time. This was it. Laura was making sure all her furniture was donated to charity. Cassie didn't want to take anything with her. She wanted a fresh start.

They shared a tearful good-bye with Laura at the airport. She couldn't bring herself to go inside the terminal to see them off.

Cassie watched her son shift nervously in his seat. This was TJ's first airplane ride, so she had let him sit by the window so he could see out.

When the plane landed in Dallas, they made their way to baggage claim. Cassie took the bags off the conveyor belt and rolled them outside to the curb. TJ was by her side as she nervously waited for her father to pick them up.

A few minutes later the silver Mercedes pulled up to the curb. Peter Randall got out of the car, and Cassie had only a few seconds to appraise her father before he pulled her into his embrace. Cassie returned his hug. Peter released her and kneeled down and hugged TJ.

Peter Randall was tall, well over six feet, and athletic. His short brown hair was parted on the side and tinged with gray at his ears. His face was handsome, though he had a few worry lines on his forehead. His eyes were a striking gray. He was dressed in a pair of black slacks and a gray-and-black sweater. Even though he was casually attired, everything about him screamed money. His walk, talk, and mannerisms all spoke volumes about how he had been raised.

"It's good to have you home, sweetheart, both of you. Here, let me get your luggage." He clicked the button on his key chain, and the trunk of the Mercedes opened. Peter placed the bags in the trunk and then opened the front passenger door for Cassie and then a back door for TJ. "You made it just in time. If you're up to it, I can drop you off at the club for your sister's bachelorette party. It's at a local jazz club called Have Hart."

Cassie nodded. "I'd love to surprise Monica. You don't mind keeping an eye on TJ?"

"I'd love to spend some time with my only grandchild. I had the cook prepare a special meal for us. So, is this a visit, or are you home to stay? Where does Trent fit into this picture? Please tell me you are finished with him."

"You don't beat around the bush, do you, Dad?" Cassie asked, looking over at her father.

"There's no point in it." He looked over at his youngest daughter. "So which is it, Cassie?"

"We're home to stay. Can we talk about this later? I really don't want to get into this in front of TJ." She did not want to discuss her failed marriage or her ex-husband with her father.

Cassie saw the sign on the door, CLOSED FOR PRIVATE PARTY. She knocked on the glass door. A security guard unlocked it.

"Hi. I'm the bride's sister. I'm a little early for the party. Can I wait inside?" She waved to her father and watched him drive away.

"Sure, come on in," said the hulking bodyguard as he let her inside. "The caterer is still setting up the food. The DJ is here, but the entertainment has not arrived yet. He should be here any moment."

Cassie looked around the nightclub in appreciation. It was very upscale. She sat down at the bar. She couldn't wait to see the look on Monica's face.

"Hi," said a voice behind her. "You're a little early for the party."

Cassie twirled around on the bar stool to face the man behind the voice. Her eyes lit up as she took in the handsome man standing before her.

In the words of her best friend, *really yummy.*

He was a little over six feet tall, with broad shoulders, a flat stomach, and long, muscular legs. He was definitely an athlete. His hands were medium sized and well groomed. His nails looked almost like they were manicured. His skin was coffee with a hint of cream. His hair was black and short, and he had a neatly trimmed goatee.

Strong, muscular biceps bulged beneath the short sleeves of his black silk shirt. The first few buttons were open, and a sprinkling of dark, curly hair peeked out. Around his neck was a thin gold chain. His legs were encased in a pair of snug black leather pants. A matching leather jacket was thrown casually over his shoulder.

Her eyes moved down his body in appreciation. He was quite appetizing, although overdressed, unless he was the entertainment.

That's it. He has to be the entertainment.

Dark, penetrating eyes raked over her in appreciation. His eyes moved from her red chiffon blouse down to her black slacks and matching high-heeled boots and back up again. Her sandy brown, long hair was pinned up on top of her head. She wore minimal makeup on her heart-shaped face. Her lips were outlined with a soft plum lipstick. He found himself getting lost in her sultry brown eyes.

Adam was definitely impressed by her. He couldn't tell how tall she was from her position at the bar, but he could see enough of her. Her legs were slim, and so were her hips. He could easily make out the outline of her breasts beneath her blouse. Red was a good color for her.

There was something familiar about him, but she couldn't quite put her finger on it. She frowned as he strode past her and went back behind the bar. She watched him scoop up some ice and squirt water in a glass. He placed the glass on the counter in front of her.

"Thank you," said Cassie. Recognition dawned on her. She remembered where she'd seen his smiling face. She's seen him on a billboard as they were leaving the airport. "Now I know where I've seen you. You're the billboard guy. You do the strip-a-grams."

"Excuse me?" Adam laughed, facing her. *Is she for real?* If she wasn't, she was a great actress. She thought he was a stripper. He didn't know if it was a compliment or an insult. Should he play along with her, or tell her who he really was? His first instinct was to tell her.

"The bodyguard said the entertainment should be here shortly, and you are definitely dressed for the part," she said matter-of-factly.

He stared at her in silence, not bothering to correct her.

"I can't believe my stepmother has a stripper at

Monica's bachelorette party. I can see I've missed a lot. If you need to practice, I won't disturb you. I'm really not into that kind of thing, but knock yourself out."

"Have you ever been to a strip club?" he asked with raised eyebrows.

"No, I can't say that I have. My idea of fun does not include stuffing my hard-earned money into any man's pants."

"You don't know what you're missing. Private showings are my specialty. I'll make sure you enjoy your first dance." Merriment lit his dark eyes as he laid his jacket on the bar beside her. "What's your favorite song?" Still smiling, he walked across the dance floor. He'd give her a show she wouldn't soon forget. "Tony, do you have "Pony" by Ginuwine?"

"Sure do, boss man. Give me a second and I'll spin it," said the DJ, smiling. "She is a knockout."

Cassie's eyes followed him over to the DJ's booth. She hopped off the bar stool and moved to a table near the dance floor. She hated to admit it, but she was looking forward to seeing him dance. He looked great clothed. She couldn't wait to see what he looked like without clothes. "You look a little old to be working your way through college. Are you a lifetime student?"

"Ouch!" He winced. "You don't pull any punches, do you? So tell me, do you like it slow and easy or fast and hard?" His eyes locked with hers, and he almost laughed aloud at her expression. Her eyes were wide as saucers as she stared mutely at him.

Bringing the glass of water to her lips, Cassie choked on the sip she took. "Excuse me?" she spluttered. Her hand was shaking, and she sloshed water on the table as she set the glass down. She was positive he wasn't referring to dancing.

This time Adam did laugh out loud. She was actually blushing and very flustered. This was going to be more fun than he'd had in a long time.

"I was referring to dancing, of course," he replied. They both knew he was not. "This is an oldie but goodie." He started dancing to the slow beat of the music.

Cassie's eyes followed Adam as he moved rhythmically to the beat. *Wow. He is good. No. He is better than good.* He turned his back to her as he continued to dance.

Nice buns! What I wouldn't give to touch them. He must spend hours in the gym, working out. Look at those abs, those thighs, that chest. Okay, stop, before you hyperventilate. Get a grip, Cassie. Oh, I'd love to get a grip! Just one touch. What can it hurt? It's been three long years.

She followed his gyrating hips in appreciation. Her heartbeat accelerated when he began to unbutton his shirt.

Is it getting hot in here, or is it just me? Okay, it's undoubtedly me. This is ludicrous. I'm getting all hot and bothered over a stripper. Okay, a gorgeous, sexy stripper with bulging biceps and a stomach so ripped, I would love to lick whipped cream from it. It's okay for someone to wake me up now. I'm ready for the dream to end and reality to set back in. Men like this are only in my dreams, and if they aren't, they aren't worth the trouble.

Mr. Strip-a-gram danced over to Cassie. She could feel the heat radiating from his body. Cassie let out a startled gasp as he caught her fanning hand and pulled her out of her seat. Still dancing, he brought her hands to his chest. His hot flesh seared her hands as his chest muscles moved beneath her sweating palms. Heat engulfed her body as her hands had a will of their own and moved over his chest.

Okay, Cassie girl, inhale and exhale slowly. I think I'm in trouble here. Common sense, where are you when I need you?

Despite the warning bells going off in her head, she began to move with him to the beat of the music. He shrugged off his shirt, wrapped it around her waist, and used it to pull her even closer.

Her hands moved from his chest to wrap around his waist. Against her will, her hands slid down and covered his buns of steel. Cassie was in heaven and hell. His buns felt as good as she imagined they would.

God, help me out here. I think I'm in trouble. I am touching a complete stranger, and I'm enjoying it. Am I losing my mind? This is totally out of character for me. I swear it is.

His butt had muscles on top of muscles, and she felt them all as her hands moved over him. Regaining her senses, she removed her hands and tried to move away from him.

"Okay, that's enough touching and gyrating," she said, her voice breathless. Her face was flushed, and she was breathing heavily. "Please let go. It's time for both of us to cool down."

"But we're just getting to the good part."

Her brown eyes were huge as they followed his hands to his pants. He unsnapped the snug-fitting leather pants and then slowly slid the zipper down. Adam was enjoying himself immensely at her expense. He hooked his fingers in the belt loops and began to slide the material down.

"Stop!" She turned her back on him and closed her eyes. Visions of the half-naked stripper flashed across her mind. "I think I've seen more than enough skin for this evening. You can save the rest for the party."

Adam could hardly contain his laughter as he watched her. He had no idea who this beautiful creature was, but he wanted to get to know her better. Noting her embarrassment, he snapped and zipped his pants, then picked up the shirt and slipped his arms into the sleeves. When he finished dressing, he walked up behind her. His body was close but was not touching hers.

She applauded and took several steps away from him, putting some distance between them. Cassie turned to face him. "You were great." She took a ten out of her purse. Moving toward him, she dropped it down the front of his shirt and stepped back from him.

He crooked his finger at her. Cassie eyed him warily and shook her head. He took two steps toward her and stopped.

"At least meet me halfway," he challenged. Mr. Strip-a-gram took another step forward and crooked his finger again.

"Three steps are not exactly meeting you halfway, but from a man's point of view, I suppose it is."

Laughing, he took three more steps. "How's this?"

Smiling, Cassie took two steps toward him. He closed the distance between them by catching her hand and drawing her to him.

He had held more sophisticated and beautiful women than her, but he had never danced like this for any of them. He found the whole situation slightly erotic. Adam found this woman way more appealing than he wanted to.

His hand reached out and brushed a strand of hair from her flushed cheek. They both felt the spark as they gazed at each other, and his hand lingered longer than necessary against her skin. His head lowered slowly to hers.

Cassie couldn't breathe as she watched the descent of his head. *He's going to kiss me. Correction. He's going to kiss me, and I'm going to let him. Cassie, snap out of it. He's a stripper. You don't know where his mouth has been.* She could feel his breath on her skin as she anticipated the feel of his mouth.

"Looks like Adam is up to his old tricks," said a female voice behind them. "Sorry for the interruption, but I have the place for tonight, remember?"

Cassie froze at the sound of her sister's voice. The connection between them was broken, and Adam's hand fell away from her face.

"And he brought a date," teased Karen Randall.

Adam released Cassie and moved away from her. "Hello, Mrs. Randall. Monica. I just dropped by to make sure everything was set up for the party."

"Uh-huh," teased Monica. "Sure you did."

"Well, I also had the opportunity to work on my dancing skills and make a few bucks in the process," Adam pointed out.

He isn't a stripper! Cassie was so embarrassed, she wanted the floor to open up and swallow her. *If he isn't a stripper, then who is he? Monica called him Adam. Is he the manager of the club? He obviously has some ties to it if he came by to make sure everything was set up.*

Gathering her composure, Cassie pasted on a smile and turned to face Rachel, her sister, and her stepmother, whom they called Karen. "Surprise," she said.

Both Monica's and Karen's looks were incredulous. "Cassie!" they chorused.

Amid laughter, tears, and hugs, Adam watched warily.

"I'm so glad you came," said Monica, hugging her younger sister. "I missed you. Does Dad know you're here?"

"Yes. He picked me up from the airport, and he dropped me off. I wanted to surprise you. I have to admit the look on your face was worth it," said Cassie.

"Welcome home," said Karen, hugging her again.

"So, if Dad just dropped you off, then how do you know Adam?" Monica's eyes moved to the man Cassie knew only as Mr. Strip-a-gram.

"I don't know Adam," said Cassie, too embarrassed to go into the details. "We just met, actually."

"Then one of you is a fast worker, and my guess is it isn't you, little sister," said Monica, looking from Adam's startled face to Cassie. "So you didn't know she was my sister? That alone will save your life, Romeo." Monica sat her purse on the table. "Okay. One of you better start talking and fast."

"It's not what you think. Or what I thought," Cassie explained, then laughed nervously. "It was a stupid mistake on my part. I thought he was the entertainment for the night."

"What?" Monica asked, confused. "The entertainment?"

Adam took the ten-dollar bill from the front of his shirt and showed it to Monica. A smile split her lips as he caught Cassie's hand and placed the money in her palm.

The room was filled with laughter from all three women. Cassie sat down at the table and picked up her glass of water. When Adam moved toward her table, her look stopped him in his tracks.

"If I were you, I wouldn't come any closer," she warned, taking a sip of water and setting the glass back on the table.

"You thought Adam was a stripper?" Monica asked, wiping the tears from her eyes. She looked him up and down. "I can see why you made that mistake. Wait a minute." She turned to Adam. "Did you dance for her? You did. Didn't you?" Peels of laughter filled the room again. "This is priceless. It must have been some dance for Cassie to tip you ten dollars."

"Okay, that's enough teasing," said Karen. "Since you two haven't been formally introduced, Adam Hart, owner of Have Hart, meet my stepdaughter Cassandra."

"Hello, Cassandra," said Adam, smiling and holding out his hand to her.

She was slow to take it and regretted it the moment their hands touched. They both felt the jolt as his hand closed over hers. Shaken, she quickly pulled her hand back.

"My pleasure," Adam added, winking at Cassie. He saw her hand move and dodged the ice and water that flew in his direction. He moved just in time as the liquid hit the floor. "I guess that's my cue to leave. I'll have someone clean that up. Ladies, have a wonderful evening. I intend to."

Cassie glared at his retreating back. *Insufferable man! I hope he had a good laugh!*

Chapter 2

Adam went home to change clothes. He had never been mistaken for a stripper before, and to him, that was not a compliment. He changed quickly into a pair of black slacks and a black silk shirt before heading over to Shawn's place to pick him up. They were meeting Shawn's brothers, Derek and Mark, at one of the many gentlemen's clubs they planned to visit before the night was over.

On the way to the club, Adam related the events of his meeting with Cassie to his best friend. He didn't think Shawn would ever stop laughing.

"You stripped for Monica's sister. Wow! That's a new low even for you, Casanova. So tell me, how hot is Cassie? I vaguely remember her. She has to be pretty hot for you to take off your clothes for her."

"Smoking," said Adam, pulling into the parking lot of the club. "I guess it's lucky for me that I was dressed when your bride and Karen Randall walked in."

"You know, when my future father-in-law finds

out about this, he will be out for your blood. He may uninvite you over for the annual Randall Christmas dinner."

"Just what I don't need, a hospital board member pissed off at me. Although, I must admit Christmas dinner at the Randalls holds more appeal this year than it did last year."

"I'm sure it does, but wipe that look off your face. Don't even think about it."

Adam pulled up to the valet. "Get out of the car, Counselor. Let's go toast your impending doom. Oh, I meant nuptials."

"You are so sad. I can't wait for you to fall and fall hard," said Shawn, getting out of the car and closing the door.

"Not gonna happen," Adam vowed to the closed door. He got out and handed the valet the keys to his Porsche.

They were at the second gentlemen's club when an idea formed in Adam's head. "Let's get out of here."

"And go where?" asked Shawn, setting down his tequila shot glass.

"Trust me," said Adam, getting to his feet. He tossed money on the table to cover their bill. "Have you ever crashed a bachelorette party?"

"Ain't nothing to it, but to do it," agreed Derek, downing his beer.

"I'm in. Let's go turn the party out," Mark said.

Shawn shook his head. "You guys are trying to get me in trouble before the wedding. Monica will kill me."

Three pairs of eyes dared him to spoil their fun.

"Okay. Let's go crash the party," Shawn groaned.

"This is turning into a night of firsts for me," Adam noted with a chuckle, putting his arm around Shawn's shoulders and leading him out of the club.

Monica's party was in full swing. About twelve women were admiring a sexy negligee.

Monica placed it in front of her and danced around. "Shawn is going to love this."

"Shawn is going to love taking it off," joked Jessica, the maid of honor.

"Shawn loves it right now," said the groom, coming farther into the room, followed by Adam and company.

"What are you doing here?" asked Monica, walking into the arms of her fiancé.

"I couldn't stay away from you a moment longer," replied Shawn, planting a passionate kiss on her parted lips.

"Get a room," said Adam as his eyes met and held Cassie's.

"I bet I can guess whose idea it was to crash the party," said Cassie, still looking at Adam.

"Shawn, do you remember Cassie?" Monica pulled her fiancé over to her sister.

Cassie and Shawn embraced. Cassie remembered the tall, suave, handsome attorney.

"It's good to see you again, Shawn," she said.

"I'm glad you could make it. Cassie, these are my brothers, Derek and Mark. Adam, my best man, I hear you've already met," Shawn replied.

"Believe me when I say my homecoming has been very eventful. One surprise after another."

Cassie shook hands with both of Shawn's brothers. They were both nice-looking men. Derek was in his midtwenties. She guessed Mark was in his early to midthirties. "It's nice to meet you both."

Around ten o'clock, Karen and some of the older guests left the party. Adam instructed the DJ to pick up the beat of the music. Adam was the first to make his way out to the dance floor. Immediately four women flanked him and danced around him. Cassie watched him walk over to a table and pull several women out to the dance floor. He knew how to work a room. Pretty soon everyone had joined in the fun. Derek caught Cassie's hand and pulled her out to the dance floor. They danced to several songs before Mark cut in.

Adam watched Cassie out of the corner of his eye. She was laughing at something Mark had said. He twirled her around, and she twirled him. After a while he walked her to a table, and she took a seat. Adam was disappointed when Mark sat down with her. *So much for joining her at her table. I'm a patient man. My time will come.*

Cassie leaned back in the leather seat of her sister's BMW. She had thoroughly enjoyed the party. She had almost forgotten what it was like to laugh, sing, and dance. Tonight she felt carefree and happy.

"So," Monica said, interrupting her thoughts. "What exactly did Karen and I intrude on earlier? You and Adam looked pretty intense for two people who just met. He was about to kiss you, and I didn't see you resisting."

"It was nothing," Cassie assured her. "We both got caught up in the moment."

"Cassie, I'm going to play big sister. Adam is a very handsome, charming, sexy, and very persuasive man, but he's not someone you want to become involved with. I say this with love, because I love both of you, but I know him and I know you. He's not the 'happily ever after, white picket fence' type of guy. He's more the 'love them and leave them' type of guy. Please don't even think about going there."

"Monica, it was harmless flirting, nothing more. It's been a while for me, and my hormones got a little out of control. I've reined them in now."

"There is nothing harmless about Adam Hart. Cassie, please stay away from him. I'd hate to have to beat down my future husband's best friend for hurting my sister."

"You can relax, sis. I have no intention of getting involved with Adam or anyone else in the near future."

"I know things didn't work out the way you had hoped with Trent, but don't let it sour you on men. There are a few good ones left. I'm marrying one of them. They may be hard to find, but they are out there. At some point, you will open your mind and heart to love again. Okay. I'm finished with the lecture. I'm so glad you're here."

Cassie slept in the next morning. When she went down for breakfast, Monica was there, making eggs and bacon.

"Morning," said Monica, dropping two waffles in

the toaster. "I thought I was going to have to send TJ to get you out of bed. How did you sleep?"

"Like a baby," Cassie confessed. "It's good to be home. Where is TJ?"

"He went with Dad and Karen to run a few errands. Have a seat, kiddo. I made enough for two."

"You seem rather calm for someone who is getting married today. What's your secret?" Cassie asked, sitting down at the breakfast bar.

"It's called unconditional love. Shawn and I have been through a lot in the past couple of years. It's made us stronger, and it's made our love stronger. I can't imagine my life without him. He's my first thought when I get up in the morning and my last thought before I fall asleep."

"Wow," said Cassie, smiling at her sister. "You guys should have written your own vows. That was very Hallmark."

Monica balled up a paper towel and threw it at her. "You just wait Cassandra Renae Randall Mancini Mancini. I still can't believe you married that jerk twice. It will happen for you again. Mark my word."

"That's me," Cassie said, laughing and pointing at herself. "I'm the jerk magnet. I attracted Trent and now Adam." Cassie could have kicked herself at the knowing look on her sister's face. "Forget I said that, and please don't start with the lecture. Trent is out of my life, and I'm not letting Adam into it. See, I've learned my lesson."

Monica placed the tray of bacon, eggs, and waffles on the breakfast bar. She took the bar stool next to Cassie. "I really hope you mean that and it's not just lip service to shut me up."

In lieu of answering, Cassie picked up a slice of crispy bacon and broke off a piece and popped it into her mouth. She refused to fight with her sister on her wedding day.

Over breakfast Monica shared a secret with her. She was four months pregnant. She swore Cassie to secrecy. Monica didn't want their dad and Karen to know until after the wedding.

Adam picked up Shawn at his house, and they arrived at the Randall house around one o'clock. The wedding was at two o'clock. The two men took refuge in one of the downstairs bedrooms, where Adam paced back and forth like a caged animal. He hated weddings almost as much as funerals. He never could understand the significance of a wedding and all the trappings. No one would ever put him through this hell that women called a wedding. What was the point, anyway? A justice of the peace would serve the same purpose. And what did it mean to be a best man, anyway? Best man to do what?

He loosened his tie for the fourth time, or was it the fifth time? It was almost like he felt the matrimonial noose tightening around his own neck. He had never before been this close to someone who was getting married. Adam made it a point not to go to weddings if he could avoid them. He was actually sweating.

An hour later, as he stood by Shawn at the altar, he shifted uneasily, until Shawn elbowed him to stop it. His eyes moved uneasily around the house full of guests before coming to rest on the woman in the red dress.

Cassie was seated in a chair next to Karen Randall, who always looked like a million bucks, but then, she could afford to. Her husband was worth much more than a mere million.

The vision in red crossed her long, shapely legs, and Adam groaned in appreciation. Her legs were encased in a pair of sheer panty hose, which hugged her like a second skin. His gaze moved upward to her small waist, to her well-endowed breasts, then to her lovely face. She smiled at something Karen said as she pushed her long hair behind her ear with short red fingernails.

His eyes moved to the child sitting next to her. The little boy looked about three or four. He was fair skinned like his mother. No. Correction. He didn't have fair skin. He was white. At least his father had to have been a white man. His hair was brown and slightly curly, and he had dimples. He wiggled in his seat as he tried to take off his bow tie. His mother caught his hand and held it in hers before he could finish the deed. She whispered something to him, and he stopped squirming for all of two seconds.

Adam's attention was diverted as the wedding march began and Monica came down the aisle. He had to admit, she did make a beautiful bride. His eyes strayed back to Monica's sister. He wondered what she would look like in a wedding dress.

Good God! What am I thinking? Hart, you are losing it! You've seen the woman only twice. Besides, you don't believe in the constitution of holy matrimony. Remember!

Cassie watched curiously as Monica and Shawn

exchanged vows. They made a striking couple. She stared at the best man's profile. Adam looked handsome in his black tuxedo. Cassie had to admit, Adam looked good in anything, or nothing at all. *I had to go there.*

When Shawn and Monica were pronounced man and wife, the room exploded in applause. All the wind left Cassie as the best man turned. This man took her breath away. Their eyes locked, and she flushed under his heated gaze. He winked at her before exiting down the aisle with the rest of the wedding party.

Her legs trembled as she got to her feet. As he drew near, Cassie turned on her heels and fled upstairs. Shaking, she closed the bedroom door behind her. Taking a deep breath, she realized how foolish she must appear to him.

Why did I run? He must think I'm a real idiot. I am an idiot.

She sat down on the bed and remained there until her trembling subsided. She had no idea what she was afraid of. Something about him scared the living daylights out of her. She knew what that something was. It was her body's reaction to Adam. He oozed charisma. After a few minutes of solitude, she got up the nerve to leave the room. Peeping outside, she saw that the coast was clear. She left the room and rejoined the party.

The formal dining room was lined with tables and chairs. The bride and groom's table was in the center of the room. Everyone was seated when Cassie entered the room. She took the vacant chair TJ had saved for her at the family table.

They were halfway through dinner when Cassie

heard the distinct sound of a utensil hitting against a crystal wineglass. They all turned to the wedding party's table.

Adam came to his feet, smiling. "As most of you know, I'm a man of few words." He paused for effect, and everyone laughed. He held up his glass. "If anyone had told me I would be standing up here one day for Shawn and Monica, I would have told them they were crazy. I don't do weddings, normally. In this case, I had to make an exception. Shawn has always been my best friend and like a brother to me. Today I gained a sister. I wish the two of you the very best life has to offer." He raised his glass to toast the happy couple, as did everyone else.

Cassie twirled the champagne glass in her hand as she sat at the family table. Thus far, she had been able to avoid a meeting with Adam. Her luck was about to run out.

"Come here, Cassie." Monica stood over her and smiled, catching her hand. "Adam, go dance with my sister." Monica waved the photographer over. "Please get some shots of them for my wedding book. Thanks." Monica walked away to rejoin her husband at their table.

I'm going to kill her! Cassie was filled with apprehension and stark fear. There was something about him that caused her temperature to go up by several degrees. She fidgeted nervously with the glass in her hand. When the waiter came by, Adam took the glass from Cassie and set it on the tray.

"My father, along with half the wedding party, warned me away from you," she admitted.

"Your father warned you because he thinks I'm an unreformed playboy. Would you like to dance?"

"Only if you promise to keep all your clothes on this time," she teased.

Adam laughed. "You have a sense of humor. I like that. You look fantastic, by the way. Red is definitely your color. Shall we? You can't say no. The photographer is waiting." He held out his hand to her.

After a brief hesitation Cassie caught his hand. Adam drew her easily into his arms. Her arms went around him, and she breathed in his captivating cologne. He twirled them easily around the dance floor.

Halfway through the song, Cassie felt a tugging on her dress. She stopped dancing and looked down. TJ was staring up at them with large brown eyes.

"Mom, can I have this dance?" he asked, holding out his hand to her.

Cassie's heart melted as she stared down at her handsome little boy in his black suit and tie. She took his small hand in hers. "Yes, you may."

Adam watched curiously. This was an unexpected complication, but not a deal breaker. Her son was very well mannered. A smile touched Adam's lips as he watched them dance around the room. He could see the love shining in Cassie's eyes as they danced.

After the dance, Cassie's eyes searched for and then found Adam. He was surrounded by a group of women. *Why am I not surprised? He's a handsome man. He looks like he's enjoying the attention. So why does it bother me so much?* She walked over to a waiter and picked up another glass of champagne. Turning to face Adam, she held it up to him in salute and took a sip of the drink.

Adam watched her walk away, with a sly smile on his face. She was more than interested, and so was he. *Let the games begin.*

"Whoa. I know that look," said Shawn, watching his friend watch Cassie. "This one is off-limits, my friend. Don't talk to her. Don't flirt with her. Don't go near her. Am I making myself clear? Cassandra is not to be toyed with. Stay away from her, or Peter will declare war on you. If you go after his daughter, the man will go ballistic."

Adam smiled at him innocently and shrugged in indifference. "I'm not afraid of Peter Randall. I give you my word. I will not go near her again, today," said Adam, turning to walk away. "But if she comes near me, it's a different story altogether. If she makes the first move, Counselor, all bets are off," he teased over his shoulder.

"All single women over here," said Monica, smiling down from the stairs. "It's time for me to throw the bouquet."

Cassie took two steps backward and moved off to the side. Twice had been enough for her. She had no intentions of going through hell again. She took one last sip of champagne and then sat the glass down on a nearby table.

Monica turned her back to the crowd and gave the bouquet a toss. A hush fell over the crowd, and Monica turned around to see the bouquet lying in Cassie's hands. Cassie knew from the smile on her sister's face, it was not an accident. Monica's hand flew to her mouth to stifle her laughter at the look on Cassie's face.

Cassie looked down at the object in question and didn't know whether to laugh or cry. She laid the flowers down next to the champagne glass and walked gracefully from the room. She could not imagine anything more horrible than being married again. True, all men were not like her ex, but she wasn't ready to test the waters again. Cassie had not dated since her divorce. It was hard to meet people with an ex-husband always looking over her shoulder and interfering in her life.

"Okay, guys. It's your turn," said Shawn, sliding the garter down Monica's leg.

Monica's face turned red in embarrassment at the whistles of appreciation as Shawn let the dress fall back at her feet in a pool of white satin and lace.

Adam tried to ease his way over to the side door so he could make an escape. He wanted no part of the toss.

"Where's Adam? Anybody seen Dr. Hart?" Mark asked, looking around the crowded room.

"Grab him. He's by the door," Jeremy called good-naturedly.

Adam shot Monica's cousin Jeremy a murderous glare.

"I got him," yelled Derek, leading Adam back over to the group of single men.

When Shawn tossed the garter, all the guys moved forward except for Adam. He took an involuntary step back. To his surprise and everyone else's, the garter landed around the red carnation on his tuxedo lapel.

"You've got to be kidding me. Can you be a little

more accurate next time?" Adam muttered, not at all amused. He picked up the offensive object, looked at it, and threw it back to Shawn.

"One toss per garter," Monica chimed in, grabbing the garter and tossing it back to Adam. "Looks like you're next in line to get married, Adam. God, I feel sorry for your bride-to-be."

"Dr. Hart," someone else yelled, "you and the gorgeous lady in the red dress could be next to tie the knot."

"Not happening," said Peter Randall, not at all amused by the prospect as he glared at Adam's retreating back.

Placing the garter on his forearm, Adam picked up a bottle of champagne and left the room. Marriage to Cassie was not exactly what he had in mind. What he was thinking about was the coming together of a different, more pleasurable sort. One he knew they would both enjoy.

Rubbing the chill bumps from her arms, Cassie wandered around the rose garden. She felt a few drops of moisture on her hands and looked up. It was snowing.

She turned in time to see Adam heading for the gazebo with the garter on his arm and a bottle of champagne in his hand. Cassie was torn between going to him and running from him.

From this distance she was safe from drowning in his dark eyes. She couldn't help noticing earlier that his goatee accentuated strong, firm lips. His black hair begged to be touched, just as his firm jaw begged to be caressed.

Cassie stared at the handsome best man as he proceeded to get drunk. Adam put the champagne bottle to his lips and took another big swallow. He sat down on the bench, leaned back, and closed his eyes, letting the falling snow coat his body.

Smiling, Adam watched Cassie observe him. He wondered what she was thinking as she stared at him so intently. Did she find him attractive? Why wouldn't she? Most women did. He was a handsome guy, not to mention a doctor. If nothing else, that usually captured a woman's attention. Didn't every mother want her daughter to marry a successful doctor?

He watched her slowly approach the gazebo. His eyes fluttered shut as he waited for her to move closer. His heart quickened as he heard her step up into the gazebo. She was close now. He could smell her perfume. It was a light flower scent, which was uniquely her. As she moved closer, he could feel the heat from her body. His body tensed, and he had to breathe deeply to control his own rising body temperature.

Cassie stared down at Adam's form. He certainly didn't look like Prince Charming reclining there. He looked more sinister than any prince she'd ever seen. His brows were knotted together in a frown, as if he were contemplating something serious. His features began to relax as she leaned down to see if he was actually sleeping or just deep in thought.

Adam's eyes flickered open, and he pulled her down on top of him and kissed her. Startled at first, she shoved him. But as heat speared through her body at the feel of his lips on hers, her lips parted at the hungry pressure of his probing tongue.

Strong, capable hands molded her to him. Cassie tried to pull away, but he held her tightly and deepened the kiss. Her body had a mind of its own as his kiss drew a response from her. She returned his heated kiss. Her tongue met his in an erotic dance again and again.

Oh, God, what am I doing? Have I lost my mind? I don't even know him.

Finally breaking the kiss, Cassie scrambled off him and straightened her dress. Gasping for air, she glared down into Adam's amused face. He sat up and rubbed his eyes several times before returning her stare. Cassie shivered uncontrollably as sultry dark eyes undressed her.

Adam came to his feet and gazed down into her flushed face. He made no comment. Instead, he brought the bottle back up to his lips and took another drink. He held the bottle out to her, and she declined with a shake of her head.

"Was there something in particular you wanted, Cassie?"

Her eyebrows shot up in question.

"Possibly a black man?" Adam asked sarcastically, once again reclining on the bench. "Are you curious about what it's like to be with a black man, sweetheart? So tell me, Cassie. What was it like being married to *Ken*? Have you ever been with a black man, Cassie?"

"I'm sure being married to *Ken* was no different from you dating Barbie. And as for black men, I'll refrain from commenting."

"Maybe it wasn't the right man. You know what they say. The blacker the berry, the sweeter the juice. Once you go black, you won't go back.

There are a couple more I can think of, if you're interested. Care to give it a try?"

"Maybe someday, Adam, but I'm sort of particular about whom I try. You know the sayings. You knew he was a snake when you picked him up. Lay down with dogs and you get fleas. You play with trash, and you'll get it in your eyes. There are others, if you are interested," she quipped back.

"I'm more than interested." He smiled confidently. "And it's scaring you to death. You have my undivided attention."

"Oh, really?" She laughed. "I'm sure your undivided attention lasts what? All of two minutes, three at the most?"

"You have three minutes to prove yourself worthy," he retorted, catching her wrist and pulling her down onto his lap. "I've wanted to do this since the first moment I saw you."

Before she could react, his mouth covered hers again. Cassie squirmed in his lap for release and then stopped when she felt him harden beneath her backside. His mouth and tongue teased and taunted her until she gave in to her feelings. Her lips parted, and she returned his sensual kiss.

Adam quickly lost control of the situation, which was something new to him. He was the master of control. Yet somehow she had gotten to him. He didn't like the feeling and reluctantly ended the kiss.

When he released her, her head was spinning and she was breathless. Cassie vaulted angrily to her feet and tried to slap the smirk off his handsome face. He caught her hand in midair and held it. Turning it over, he kissed her palm and smiled in satisfaction when he felt her shiver.

"From my experience, men are pigs, no matter what color they are," Cassie stormed. "And you aren't any exception, you oversexed, brainless, Neanderthal."

She had spirit. He liked fire in a woman. It usually meant they were not timid in bed. Adam came to his feet and advanced on her. Cassie took a nervous step back with each one he took forward.

"I take exception to being called brainless," he said and smiled wickedly. "It's the one thing I am not. You are absolutely gorgeous when you are angry. I especially like the way your breasts heave. I wonder if you look as good with no clothes at all."

Hot color suffused her lovely face as she glared at him.

"I'd love to find out. I'd love to be the one to set that unbridled passion of yours to flames," he whispered seductively, moving toward her again.

Cassie felt familiar warmth spread over her at his practiced seduction. She tried unsuccessfully to shake off the erotic feelings he was causing. "Your three minutes are up," she snapped. "I guess you couldn't hold my attention." She turned on her heels and walked away. His laughter followed her back inside the house.

He was the most egotistical, insulting, and exasperating man she had ever had the misfortune to meet. Cassie prayed she would not see him again, but she knew realistically that she would. How could she not cross paths with him? Adam was Shawn's best friend. She couldn't avoid him forever.

The rest of the evening Cassie watched Adam flirt with every single woman in the room. She was disappointed when he left with one of the bridesmaids.

Adam leaned back in the seat of Gia's Mustang. He had had way too much to drink and was grateful to her for agreeing to drop him home. Cassie was way too tempting, and he had to get away from her or risk the wrath of his best friend. He was hoping Gia didn't think it was more than just giving him a ride home. He didn't want anyone right now, except for the one woman he couldn't have.

When Gia pulled up into his driveway, she killed the engine of her car. She turned to face Adam. "Do you want some company?" she asked brazenly.

"I'm flattered," said Adam, trying to put it as delicately as possible, "but I'm really tired tonight. Maybe some other time."

"I'd like that." Gia smiled.

He caught her hand and brought it to his lips. "Thanks for the lift." He got out of the car and closed the door behind him. That was close, he thought.

Gia was a very attractive woman, but she wasn't his type. She was too bold, and from what he had heard, she wasn't too discriminating.

Cassie asked her father to file the necessary papers with the court regarding her living arrangements so Trent wouldn't be able to say she had disappeared without letting him know where she was.

As much as she was enjoying living a life of leisure, Cassie knew it was time for her to rejoin the working world. She didn't want to be dependent on her father. She was used to taking care of herself and her son. She didn't tell Peter, but she did confide in Monica and Karen that she was ready to start job hunting. Monica suggested County General Hospital. She said she knew a doctor on staff at the hospital. Following her sister's recommendation, Cassie applied for a position at the hospital and was hired on the spot.

Once he found out about the job, her father tried to talk her into taking more time off, but Cassie wasn't used to being idle. Peter wouldn't take no for an answer, and he gave her the checkbook to the account he had set up for her. Cassie had had never seen so many zeros in her life, and she wasn't foolish enough to refuse the account. It was a great nest egg. With her inheritance, she could support herself and her son without having to work at all. The money gave her a freedom and independence she had never had before. Still, she had every intention to keep her job at the hospital. Work would keep her mind off Trent and what would happen when he found them.

Cassie registered TJ for day care. It wasn't what she wanted to do, but she didn't feel like she had much of a choice. She wanted him to be with other kids his age. She had declined Peter's offer to hire a nanny for him. Peter had even suggested she take more time before going back to work so that TJ could adapt to his new surroundings.

She spent the weekend before starting her job just enjoying her son. She and TJ went to the movies to see the new Disney movie and then went out for pizza. They went to church on Sunday, out to eat, and then to the park. When they arrived back home, Mama Rosa, Cassie's nanny from childhood, was waiting for them. Between hugs, kisses, and tears, the older woman explained that Peter had sent her a plane ticket to come stay with them and take care of TJ. She, of course, had jumped at the opportunity to be with them.

Cassie was touched by her father's thoughtfulness. Through tears of joy, she thanked him. Though she loved the idea of having Mama Rosa there to look after TJ, she still enrolled him in a two-day-a-week mother's day off program. She wanted him to have the interaction he needed with other children.

Chapter 3

When Cassie arrived at the hospital on Monday morning, Nurse Cratchard was already there. They went over procedures and forms for about two hours. When they finally finished, Cassie's head was spinning with so much information, she knew there was no way she would remember it all tomorrow.

"Even though I am your immediate supervisor, you will also be working under Dr. Hart," Nurse Cratchard explained.

Cassie's eyes flew to her face at the mention of Dr. Hart.

"Doctors cannot hire or fire nurses. I expect courtesy and professionalism at all times. Dr. Hart has Glenda, Rachel, and you. You will meet them later."

No, it couldn't be. Maybe it was just a coincidence. Surely Adam wasn't a doctor. She remembered her sister's smile when she said she knew a doctor who worked at the hospital. It had to be a coincidence. Hart wasn't that common of a name, but Monica wouldn't do that to her. Or would she?

"Where will I start?" Cassie asked with a sense of dread. "I don't have a lot of emergency room experience. I mostly worked maternity."

"Emergency room. I hate to start you there, but it's where we need the most help. We always seem to be shorthanded in the ER. I'll have Marjorie work with you the first week, to get you up to speed. She's been reassigned to the fifth floor. After that, Glenda will train you for another week. Dr. Hart is not exactly the easiest person to work with. He is a chauvinist and he's a perfectionist. Some may even say he's flirty, but if you let him know from day one that you are not interested, you shouldn't have a problem with him. He is also very demanding and hardworking. If I'm ever admitted to the ER, I hope Dr. Hart is on duty. In fact, he's one of the best doctors we have here at the hospital. I think it's probably why they let him get away with so much. If you do have any problems with him you can't solve on your own, please feel free to come to me."

Cassie's head was spinning again. For some reason all of this was sounding too familiar. She was having a sense of déjà vu. She tried to shake off a feeling of foreboding.

Please, God, please let this not be Adam Hart, nightclub owner, Mr. Strip-a-gram. This can't be my fate.

When the door opened, she felt the hairs on the back of her neck stand up, which was definitely not a good sign. She heard the door close but refused to turn around. Her body refused to move. It was almost like a premonition. She inhaled deeply, which was a mistake. The cologne she smelled could only belong to one man. The scent was as intoxicating as the man.

"Dr. Hart, we were just talking about you," said Nurse Cratchard, coming to her feet. "Come meet your new nurse. Try not to run her off, like you have all the rest. It's getting harder and harder to find good nurses willing to work with you. Be nice to this one."

"I just bet you told her all sorts of juicy tidbits about me," said the deep, familiar voice. "You told her all about me, and she's still here. I'm impressed. She's either very brave, desperate for money, or a glutton for punishment. Which is it?"

Run far away! thought Cassie. *I am finally getting my life back together. I don't need a complication like him in it. Run for your life! I don't need this aggravation. I have a trust fund I can live off of quite nicely.*

Cassie stood up and turned around to face the teasing voice. Adam did a double take when he saw her. The look on her face told him she was not amused or pleased by the situation. Adam could not believe his luck. The beautiful and sexy Cassie was his new nurse. This was going to be easier than he had originally thought. He was planning on seeing her again, and now she had fallen into his lair.

"Maybe it's all three," Cassie offered quietly. She pasted on a smile and stuck her hand out to him. "Hello, Dr. Hart. I'm Cassie Mancini. It looks like we'll be working together."

"Why so formal, Cassie? I'm sure we'll become great friends," said Adam, taking her outstretched hand. Adam's brow arched, and Cassie quickly pulled her hand away.

"Do you two know each other? Am I making a mistake by having her work with you?" asked Nurse Cratchard, looking from Cassie to Adam.

"Yes. No," they chorused. His eyes twinkled with merriment as Cassie glared at him, crossing her arms over her chest.

"As a matter of fact, we've already met," said Adam. "We really should stop meeting like this, or I'm going to start thinking you're stalking me."

"Did you say stalking or staking?" Cassie asked innocently. "Nurse Cratchard, I don't think this is going to work."

"I'll leave you two alone to settle this," Nurse Cratchard said, ignoring Cassie's words. "I'll send Marjorie in to get you in a few minutes. If Cassie doesn't flee in the next fifteen minutes, she's all yours, and I mean that literally."

"Promises, promises." He winked at the older woman.

Nurse Cratchard and Cassie both rolled their eyes heavenward. The head nurse left the room, and Cassie felt like she had been thrown into the proverbial lion's den.

"This is not going to work," she said once the door had closed, leaving them alone. "I can't work with you."

"Why? Because you are attracted to me?" he asked bluntly. "I feel it, too, Cassie. It's stronger than both of us."

She flushed under his heated gaze. His eyes wandered over her slim figure. His exploration started at her flushed face and moved down her breasts to her slim waist, then down her thighs. Her two-piece scrubs hid most of her figure, but nothing got past his probing stare. His eyes came back up to caress her breasts and then rested again on her flushed face.

This is never going to work. I cannot put up with him. Not for all the money in the world. There has to be something else.

"Go take a flying leap, you pig," Cassie said, walking out of the room.

She found Nurse Cratchard in the nurses' break room, having a cup of coffee. Joining her at the table, she sat down. "Nurse Cratchard, surely there must be some other position available. I cannot work with Dr. Hart. We have irreconcilable differences. I don't want to go to jail for manslaughter."

Nurse Cratchard laughed. "I like you, Cassie. I think you can handle him. You will give Dr. Hart a run for his money. I know he can be difficult, but give it a chance. One week, two maximum, and if things haven't worked out, I will try to move you someplace else. The problem is, as I'm sure you've surmised, Dr. Hart is a handful. We have problems keeping nurses wherever he goes. He can be quite charming when he wants to be. He is also very demanding. We need you. He needs someone like you to put him in his place. You can be our champion. None of the married nurses' husbands will let them work with him. Cassie, you are my last hope."

"In two weeks he could very well be hanging from the hospital ceiling," Cassie said seriously. "I don't have the patience or inclination to deal with him."

There was a brief knock on the door, and Adam came in. He looked from Cassie to Nurse Cratchard and back at Cassie. "There is no reason for all this drama, Cassandra. I think we can resolve this to both our satisfaction."

"Are you leaving the hospital?" Cassie asked coyly.

Nurse Cratchard smiled, clearly enjoying herself.

"Please don't use the words *we* and *satisfaction* in the same sentence. It makes my skin crawl," Cassie added.

"Really? That's not the impression I got when you were giving me mouth-to-mouth at the wedding," Adam returned.

Cassie turned beet red, and the head nurse started coughing severely.

"I didn't ask you to kiss me. You forced your unwanted intentions on me," Cassie snarled.

"Not much force was involved, if I remember correctly," he snorted. "You were all over me. Nurse Cratchard, can I have a moment alone with Cassie?"

"Yes," said Nurse Cratchard.

Cassie sighed in exasperation and looked heavenward for some sign from above.

"Just hear him out," the head nurse urged. "What can it hurt? I'll give the two of you a few minutes alone to talk. If you can't resolve your differences, I'll try to find someplace else to put you. Dr. Hart, we can't afford to lose this one."

Cassie looked on helplessly as the older woman left the room. She braced herself and then turned around to face him. "There's nothing you can say to change my mind about you or about working with you," she declared. "Don't waste your breath. This is not the only hospital in Dallas."

"Can we call a truce? I want to apologize for my

behavior. I will be on my best behavior, and I won't do anything you don't want me to do. I was way out of line earlier. I won't hit on you or make a pass at you unless I get some kind of signal from you to do so. I promise not to bite, unless invited to do so."

"I need this job, but not bad enough to put up with your suggestive remarks and sexual innuendos. That's called sexual harassment."

"I've never harassed anyone in my life. You don't need this job," he snickered. "You are Peter Randall's daughter. You're an heiress. You don't have to work. You can sit up on a pedestal like your stepmother and look beautiful all day. Isn't it every debutante's dream to become a trophy wife?"

Her eyes narrowed on him. "Tell me how you really feel. This has nothing to do with my father. Leave him out of it. I worked damn hard to get my nursing degree, and I'm not about to let you or anyone else treat me like I'm nothing but a skirt to chase. If I wanted to be belittled for being a woman, I could have stayed with my ex-husband. I am a professional, and I expect to be treated like one. In the process of doing this job, I don't expect it to be a daily requirement to be chased around the operating room. I want to be treated like a human being, not a sexual object or plaything. If you cannot accept and treat me with the respect I deserve, then we cannot work together. If you can't look at me without imagining me in your bed, then it's your problem. I don't need to hear it vocalized."

"Cassie, you are a beautiful and desirable woman. Why can't you accept it?" he asked, puzzled. "You are the first woman I've ever met who can't accept a compliment."

"Whether or not I am those things has nothing to do with saving a life in the emergency room. In there it doesn't matter much what I look like. It shouldn't matter, because my looks are not important. Saving lives is important, which is why I'm here. I'm not here for your amusement or entertainment. And as for compliments, there is a big difference between being complimentary and being insulting. If you can't treat me as an equal, say so now. If you can't see me as anyone other than the next woman you bed, I don't need to hear it vocalized, because it will only be in your dreams. I have enough problems of my own without you adding to them. I want this job, but I don't need it this badly. I don't have to work. I want to work. I need to work, and whether it's in this hospital or another one is entirely up to you. So, do I have a job or not?"

If I let you walk out that door, I might never see you again. I can play by your rules for a little while. This way I can see you every day and slowly break down your defenses. Cassie Mancini, you won't know what hit you when I turn on the charm.

Adam stared at her for several moments before holding out his hand to her. Cassie refused to shake his hand, so he let it drop to his side.

"Welcome aboard. I'm sure working with me will be like nothing you've ever experienced before. I hope you're up to it. I know I am. I love a challenge." He laughed as he walked to the door. "Let the games begin." He winked at her and walked out the door, whistling.

"I'm sure there won't be a dull moment," Cassie said to the empty room. *God, give me strength.*

Resisting the urge to throw something at his retreating back, she took a seat and counted to twenty. Unfortunately, twenty wasn't high enough.

What have I gotten myself into now? "Out of the frying pan and into the fire" seems to be my motto these days. So what do I have to lose? My mind, my patience? Hopefully not my heart. I think I'm smart enough to stay away from smooth-talking Romeos at my age.

Marjorie Winston was a petite, dark-skinned woman with dancing brown eyes. Her hair was cut short, and she wore wire-rimmed glasses. When she was two months pregnant, she'd requested a transfer from the ER. She had been reassigned to the maternity ward.

"He's really not bad if you know how to handle him. He's just a little cocky and sure of himself. I hope you have plenty of patience and are very open-minded. If not, the guys in the ER are going to eat you alive."

"Why do I get the feeling I've just been thrown to the wolves?" asked Cassie as she followed Marjorie down to the emergency room.

"Because you have." Marjorie laughed. "You're beautiful with brains. With that combination you are going to send the guys in the ER running for their lives. Come on. I'll introduce you to everyone."

Cassie followed Marjorie as she walked into the break room for emergency-room staff.

"Cassie Mancini, meet Roger Harris," said Marjorie. "She's my replacement, so be nice to her.

Cassie, this young Casanova in training is one of our respiratory therapists. He's one of the harmless ones."

"Hey, watch that," Roger joked. His brown eyes sparkled with mischief. He was slightly overweight and wore a pair of faded blue scrubs and white tennis shoes. His stethoscope dangled around his neck. His skin was dark brown, almost black. He held out his hand to Cassie. "It's nice to meet you, Cassie. Welcome aboard."

"Hi, Roger. It's nice to meet you." Cassie took his outstretched hand and returned his warm smile. "It's nice to see a friendly face."

"Wow! Wait until Dr. Hart gets a look at this one," said a dark-headed intern, looking Cassie up and down. He was in his early twenties, and his long hair was pulled back in a ponytail. Cassie often tried not to judge people on first impressions, but she felt an instant dislike for this man. He held out his hand. "I'm Zack Peters."

"Cassie Mancini," she said, taking his outstretched hand. He held her hand longer than necessary, and when he finally released it, she felt like wiping her hand on her pants.

One by one, she met the other ER staff members. There was a total of five nurses, three doctors, four unit secretaries, two respiratory therapists, and four interns. She also met the lab technicians and the two physicians' assistants who were on duty.

When Cassie went into the break room for her break, she found Dr. Hart and some of the guys already there. She poured hot water into a cup and added hot chocolate. She heard someone whisper how hot she was. Someone else asked Adam if he'd gotten her phone number yet. Cassie seethed inwardly at their rudeness.

"Cassie, would you like to join us?" Dr. Hart asked, smiling.

Zack and Rafael, another intern, nudged each other like teenagers.

"No, thank you," Cassie replied coolly, sitting down at a vacant table. She picked up a magazine someone had left on the table. Thumbing through it, she took a sip of her hot chocolate. She saw Adam's shadow and smelled his cologne even before he sat down across from her.

"So what do you think of the ER so far?" he asked pleasantly.

She closed the magazine and looked at him in question. *Why is he trying to make small talk with me? What is he up to now?* "It's fast and busy. It's everything I expected it would be." Cassie mistakenly took the olive branch he held out to her. "How long have you worked in the ER?"

"About two years. I like the pace. It gets even busier on the weekend. It's a madhouse on Saturday night."

"Believe it or not, the pace is a lot slower here than what I was used to in New York. The people here are a lot friendlier, too."

"We can be as friendly as you want us to be." Adam had been waiting for an opening, and she had given him one.

Cassie shook her head in amazement. She knew the truce couldn't last. "I knew it couldn't last," she said, coming to her feet. "Thank you for reminding me who and what you are."

Adam's laughter followed her out

Cassie ignored him and went to check on a patient. When she returned to the nurses' station, Adam was sitting at the desk, looking over a file. He looked up at Cassie and smiled. Getting to his feet, he waved for her to have a seat. Cassie stared at him as he walked away.

By the time her shift was over, Cassie was ready to scream. Adam was driving her crazy. It wasn't anything he said, but the way he watched her every move. She felt his eyes on her whenever he entered the room.

Two weeks! I can do this! No, I can't do this. I can't put up with him for two more days. I know it's not my imagination. I know he's watching me. I feel it.

The rest of the week didn't go any smoother. Adam was a human dynamo. He was dedicated to his patients and gave his all to the job. He worked his butt off and expected everyone on his team to do the same. Adam was the most demanding doctor she had ever worked with. He was much harder on Cassie than he was on the rest of the nursing staff. Cassie had a grudging respect for him.

To her horror, most of the male interns were out of control, and Adam, as the head of the ER, didn't bother to rein them in. Cassie could not believe the nurses let them get away with talking down to them and being not only rude but also crude at times. On several occasions, Rachel had to come between Cassie and Zack. Cassie was not about to let Zack or anyone else walk all over her.

Adam hit the roof when he heard Zack joking about Cassie. Adam surprised himself and the guys when he blasted Zack and told him to lay off Cassie. He was genuinely surprised by Cassie's tenacity and continued professionalism in the midst of the ER jungle. Except for one incident when a little boy died, she had remained cool, calm, and collected. He could easily understand why she froze. The boy was her son's age. He had no children and the death had saddened him, so he could only imagine what she had been feeling.

One afternoon she was charting at the nurses' station when she felt Adam behind her. His cologne gave him away. He leaned over her to pick up a pen. He didn't touch her, but he didn't have to. Adam could sense she was unnerved by his nearness.

Closing the chart in front of her, Cassie looked up at him in irritation. Straightening, he held up the pen. After writing something down, he leaned over her again to replace the pen. His face was only inches from hers. Jumping to her feet, she moved away from him. Adam smiled in amusement. She picked up the nearest thing to her, a bottle of pills, and threw it at him. He caught the bottle easily and set it back on the table. Giving him one last glare, she stalked away.

She went to the cafeteria for lunch. Cassie was sitting at a table alone, eating lunch, when a smiling brunette sat down across from her.

"Hi. I'm Patricia Blackwell. I work on the fifth floor, in the maternity ward. So you are the beauty all the doctors and respiratory therapists are raving about," she teased.

"I don't know about that, but hello. I'm Cassie Mancini. Nice to meet you," said Cassie, wiping hand on her napkin and holding it out

"I don't hear a Texas twang in your speech, which means you're not a native. Where are you from?"

"Are you dang sure?" Cassie asked, using her best Texas twang.

They both laughed at her poor attempt.

"I'm from here, really. I moved away for a few years. I moved back a month ago," Cassie revealed.

"What brings you back to Dallas?" asked Patricia, taking a sip of her hot tea. "Do you have family here?"

"I was born here. My family is still here as well. TJ, my little boy, and I packed up one day and moved back."

"I did the same thing. I'm from Maryland. I've been here about three years. How old is your little boy?"

"He's four. He'll be five in a couple of months. He loves—" Cassie stopped talking in midsentence when she heard Adam's voice. She turned in the direction of the voice and rolled her eyes in disgust when she saw Adam flirting with the checkout girl in the cafeteria line. When she turned back, Patricia was watching her watch Adam. Her face flushed under the close scrutiny.

"A word of warning. Watch out for Dr. Hart," Patricia advised. "He's as smooth as silk but hazardous to your career here. I'd try to stay as far away from him as I could get if I were you. Let's just say every nurse he gets involved with suspiciously resigns or gets let go from this hospital."

"Have there been many?" Cassie wondered aloud, already knowing the answer to her question but needing to hear it, anyway.

"Only about three since I've been here. Maryanne,

Julia, and Claire." Patricia's eyebrows went up in surprise. "He doesn't discriminate. He seems to like variety. I'm surprised he hasn't hit on you yet. You've been here what? All of five days?" Patricia laughed. "Where are you working right now?"

"ER with Dr. Hart." Cassie grimaced, laying her head on the table. "I'm waiting for an opening on another floor."

"You poor thing. Well, good luck. I've got to run. I'm sure we'll run into each other again sometime."

Cassie threw her napkin on her plate, having lost what was left of her appetite. *Great. Just what I needed confirmed. I'm working with the Don Juan of medicine!*

She was staring down at her tray when a white lab jacket appeared in front of her. Hoping against hope, she slowly looked up. Her eyes locked with Adam's as he set his tray on the table in front of her.

"I don't want to be the cause of gossip on the hospital grapevine just because you sat down at the table with me. I'm new here, and I can't afford to have you ruin my reputation. So please find another table. Better yet," said Cassie, coming to her feet, "you can have this one. I've suddenly lost what was left of my appetite."

She watched his mouth tighten in suppressed anger before it softened into a smirk. "Cassie, I'm heartbroken that you would believe everything you hear. Hospital gossip is notoriously overexaggerated and often untrue."

She was turning to leave when she saw all eyes on them. Everyone was watching her and Adam with avid interest. Cassie knew they were all wond___ if she was his latest plaything, and she

When she looked back at Adam, he was smiling. He was actually enjoying her discomfort.

"I thrive on attention and on rejection. The faster you run, the more intense the hunt," he whispered seductively. "God, you are so sexy when your eyes flash."

Throwing up her hands in exasperation, she stalked away from the table.

"So tell me, Doc," said Shawn, sipping his cola where Adam and Shawn were dining. "How is Cassie working out? How are things with the two of you? Are you playing nice and keeping your hands to yourself?"

Adam frowned as he picked at his spaghetti. He did not want to talk or think about Cassie Randall. She was getting under his skin. There was no denying the attraction between them, but it was more than that. Adam liked her and he respected her. He could easily lose himself in those brown eyes.

Shawn had reminded his friend on an almost daily basis that his sister-in-law was off-limits. The only way Adam could keep his word and keep her at arm's length was to be rude to her. He didn't want her to be attracted to him, and he didn't want to be attracted to her, but he was.

It helped that Adam was so afraid of commitment, he deliberately went out of his way to avoid it. Cassie scared him to death. He felt things for her he had never felt before, and he didn't like it.

"What can I say? She's a great nurse. I am keeping my word to you. I have not laid a single hand on her person since your wedding day. She hates my guts, but it's to be expected."

"Back up a minute," said Shawn, shaking his head. "What do you mean you haven't laid a hand on her since my wedding day? What did you do to her at my wedding?"

"Just a few innocent kisses," Adam said evasively. Turning away from his friend's prying eyes, he thought back to those kisses, and they had been far from innocent.

"Nothing is ever innocent with you, Adam. If Monica had any idea you were into her sister, she would blow a gasket. Peter Randall will run you out of town on a rail if you go near his daughter. Do you have a career death wish? You think Peter was relentless before. He will crucify you if you get involved with his daughter."

"Calm down. There is nothing going on with Cassie and me," Adam insisted. "I think she's incredibly gorgeous and sexy from head to toe, but I can look without touching. I want to take her straight to bed every time I see her, but I can control myself. There is something about her that is driving me crazy."

"Maybe it's the fact that she doesn't want anything to do with you. You simply see her as a challenge. It's the thrill of the hunt. It will pass. Let it pass. Forget about her, Adam. I'm asking you as a friend. Whatever it is you're doing to keep her at arm's length, keep it up. Cassie has been through enough heartache to last her a lifetime. I'd hate to see you break her heart. So tell me, how was the trip you took a few weeks ago to L.A.?"

"Let's just say the vultures are circling. Wade

Kirkland is not even dead yet, and his brother and nephews are dividing up his fortune. He looks bad. I'm not sure how much longer he's going to last. After meeting his family, I can understand why he wants to cut them all out of his will. They are a bunch of money-grubbers. They are not even subtle. One of the nephew's wives threw me out of the house after I informed her I wasn't the chauffeur."

"Wouldn't it be hilarious if he put you in the will?" Shawn laughed.

"Heaven forbid. I don't want any ties to those people."

A week later Adam flew out to California for Wade Kirkland's funeral. Adam had met the man when he was on a business trip to Dallas. Adam had saved his life after an automobile accident, only to discover Wade had an inoperable brain tumor. Once he'd been moved to a room, Adam had gone up to check on him and had heard from the nurses that no one had come to see him. Feeling sorry for the older gentleman, Adam had visited him daily.

When Wade had been released from the hospital, he'd gone back home to California to die. There was nothing else the hospital or doctors could do for him. He'd sent his private plane for Adam on more than one occasion just to play a game of chess.

Adam was in for the shock of his life at the reading of the will. Wade had not only named Adam as executor of his will but had also left him 80 percent of his fortune. He had stipulated in his will that his other heirs would lose their inheritance if they contested the will. Adam didn't sign off on all the paperwork to claim his inheritance. He knew once he signed those papers, his life would change. The Kirklands were pressuring him to sign. Until he signed off on the documents, they would not receive a penny from the estate. Adam knew he was being unfair to them, but he wasn't ready for his life to change.

Chapter 4

Cassie saw a different side to Adam when he was dealing with patients. He was caring, considerate, and the ultimate professional.

Her first child tragedy was almost her undoing. A little boy the same age as her son came into the ER after a car accident. He had been in the front seat of his mother's car, without the seat belt fastened, and had been thrown through the windshield. He was bleeding profusely and barely hanging on to life when he was brought in. Cassie was the attending nurse, and Adam was the doctor. Cassie froze momentarily when he coded. Adam yelled at her to snap out of it or get out of the room. She pushed her maternal feelings aside and helped with the surgery preparations.

Cassie left the room in tears when the child died on the operating table. She stood outside the room, wiping the tears from her eyes.

When Adam came out of the room, she tried to flee. He caught her arm to stop her. "I know that was hard for you because of your son, but if you are going to make it in the ER, you have to toughen up. Go take a break. We'll call you if we need you."

"How do you do it, Dr. Hart?" asked Cassie, facing him. "How do you remain so detached from it all?"

"I'm not as detached as you may think," he admitted. "I've got patients to see."

She watched him walk away.

The few weeks were pure hell. Cassie and Adam were at each other's throat at every turn. They had turned the ER into a battle of the sexes. Everyone in the ER had taken sides.

Cassie and Monica had lunch one day, and she told Monica what was going on. Monica was furious at Adam for putting her sister through the ringer. She offered to talk to Adam for Cassie, but Cassie declined the offer. Adam was her problem, and she was the one who was going to have to deal with him.

Despite everything Adam Hart said and did, she was attracted to him. He would never know it, and she would never admit it to anyone else, but she did have dreams about him. Not dreams of her torturing him to death, but dreams of making love to him, with him. She would always wonder what it would be like. She would just never act on the feelings she had. It was a pointless and hopeless situation. Adam was not the man for her. He proved it to her on a daily basis.

Peter asked her repeatedly what was bothering her, and she refused to tell him or Karen. For some strange reason, she wanted to protect Adam from the Randall wrath.

Cassie had lunch regularly with either Rachel or Patricia. Rachel was the mediator when things got pretty ugly between her and Adam in the ER.

"Cassie, don't take everything Dr. Hart says so personally," said Rachel, sipping her tea during one of their lunches. "He's not a bad guy."

"How can I not? The man takes great pleasure in berating me and ordering me around. Funny I should mention him and pleasure in the same sentence," Cassie said, laying her head on the table.

"I've never seen him like this before. I think he's running scared. He likes you, and he's scared to death. He has this wall built around him, and no one is allowed to enter, but I think you have penetrated the wall. I think you should call his bluff and go out with him. You might be surprised."

"And I might not. I wouldn't trust going to the nearest street corner with the man. He's not my type. I would only be setting myself up for trouble. That's something I don't need."

"She does protest too much." Rachel laughed. "I think he's getting to you. You like him. Despite yourself, you like him."

"If you tell anyone, I will hunt you down and kill you," Cassie joked, lunging for her. Laughing, Rachel dodged her. "Am I losing my mind, Rachel? How can this be normal? I loathe the man, yet I do find him strangely attractive."

"No, you are not losing your mind. It's pure sexual attraction at its best. Or worst, in your case. Your secret is safe with me. I think for the right woman, any man can change. You just need to make him see what an ass he's being. Once you've done that, the rest is a piece of cake."

On Thursday Cassie was more on edge than usual. She kept finding herself watching Adam. Her eyes followed his every movement. She was frustrated with herself as she left the ER and headed to the cafeteria. Her day was just getting better and better. They were shorthanded, and she had about fifteen minutes to eat and get back to the ER.

After getting her tray of baked chicken, salad, creamed corn, and iced tea, she joined Patricia at a table. "I hate to eat and run, but it's hell in there today."

"How goes it on the ER battlefield?" asked Patricia. "I don't see any war wounds or loss of limbs."

"Let me put it this way. Dr. Adam Hart is driving me insane. I can't continue to work under these conditions. No one should have to put up with this."

"I agree. So when are you transferring out of hell?" Patricia smiled sweetly, biting into her apple.

"As soon as I can," Cassie groaned, taking a bite of her chicken. "Enough about me. How are things with you and your husband? Any better?"

"I am ready to put Dave out. I told him last night, if a vibrator could mow the lawn, I'd divorce him," said Patricia seriously. "I guess it was a bit harsh." She then burst out laughing.

Cassie joined in her infectious laughter. "I don't know, Pat. There is still one thing in particular I prefer a man for," Cassie said before taking a sip of her tea.

"Really? And what would that be?" Adam asked, sitting down across from her and waiting for her reply.

Color suffused Cassie's face, and she choked on her iced tea. She hadn't seen or heard Adam approach the table.

Patricia smiled sheepishly as she also waited for Cassie to answer. She looked from Cassie to Adam curiously. There was no denying the sparks.

"Mowing the lawn, of course." Cassie smiled sweetly. She met Patricia's smiling eyes, and they both burst out laughing.

Adam stared at them, not at all amused.

"It's a private joke," Cassie told him, wiping away her tears.

Adam came angrily to his feet. He gave Cassie one last glare before stalking off with his tray.

So he actually has feelings. It may make my task easier, Cassie thought.

The rest of the day Adam avoided her. In fact, when he saw her coming, he went in a different direction. This puzzled her. Something was definitely wrong.

When she questioned Rachel about it, Rachel told her Dr. Peterson had had a meeting with Adam behind closed doors and no one knew what it had been about. Her guess was it had had something to do with the battle of the sexes in the emergency room.

Cassie was on her way back from lunch when Dr. Harrison caught up to her. She looked at him, puzzled, as he walked beside her.

"Ms. Mancini, may I have a word with you?"

She stopped walking.

"Rumor has it you and Dr. Hart are at war. I can help you nail him. I'm told that with your testimony, we could have him brought up on charges of sexual harassment."

"Dr. Harrison, I'm well aware of your feelings for Dr. Hart, and although I may or may not share them, he is a fine physician. I am not going to be responsible for this hospital losing a man with his skilled hands. This hospital needs him."

"And you are willing to let him get away with the hell he's put you through? Don't you want to see him punished? We could cut the smug bastard down to size. He'll be out, and I'll be top dog in the ER."

"I can't help you. If you want Dr. Hart's head on a platter, you'll have to get someone else to serve him up to you. I won't be responsible for ruining a brilliant doctor's career, no matter how much of an ass he is. I have no grounds for sexual harassment. He hasn't done or said anything that I could or would use against him. Now, if we don't get back, Dr. Hart will have both of our heads." Cassie left him standing there.

"Rachel, please ask Dr. Hart to meet me in the break room," said Cassie as she approached the nurses' station. "It's time this war ended."

"Are you armed? Should I frisk you before I go find him? What are you going to do?" Rachel asked curiously.

"If it works, you'll be the first to know," Cassie answered before going into the break room and taking a seat at one of the three tables.

Cassie leaned back in the chair and closed her

eyes. She peered down at her watch and frowned. She had half an hour left in her shift.

"What can I do for you?" Adam asked, sitting down across from her. He was not going to make this easy for her, but she hadn't expected him to.

"I have an early birthday present for you, Dr. Hart," said Cassie. She let out the breath she was holding. "I was approached by a doctor a few minutes ago who asked me to help him get you fired. He seems to think that with my testimony, we could get you out of our hair."

"You are kidding," Adam said in disbelief, coming to his feet. He paced the room and then came back to sit down again. "Who was it?"

"Does it matter? I'm sure he's not the only one who feels that way. I have listened to your belittling comments for weeks. I am not going to put up with it anymore. I have decided to give you one last chance to redeem yourself. I am giving you a chance you haven't given me. You are a fine physician. You care about your patients. There are very few black doctors out there as it is. You are one of the best I have ever worked with, but at the same time you have the worst attitude of them all. I will not be responsible for society losing a fine doctor. I declined the chance to get even. Don't make me regret my decision."

"Why would you do this for me?" he asked, meeting her eyes squarely. His dark eyes held her spellbound.

"I keep asking myself the same question, but I'm hoping you will take a step back and see yourself as I see you. I have listened to you and your cohort day after day talk down to women and be disrespectful to black women in particular. You seem to make a lot of cutting and snide remarks about my Italian ex-husband, but it's okay for you to parade around town with a blond-hair, blue-eyed Barbie doll on your arm. So basically what you are saying is black women should be with black men, unless the man happens to want a white woman. Then it is acceptable."

"I date all women. I'm an equal opportunity dater. Apparently, so are you," he shot back. "Pot, meet kettle."

"Have you ever had an intelligent conversation with a woman that did not include you making a pass or some kind of sexual innuendo? You don't know anything about me," she replied, fuming. "I'm giving you back your career, you sexist pig. I told that doctor that if he wanted your head on a platter, he would have to find someone else to do it. Don't make me regret my decision not to take you down."

"Just out of curiosity, why are you protecting me? It's not loyalty to Shawn, and it's not because you think I'm a brilliant doctor. The truth is you like me." Adam knew by the startled look on her face, he was at least partially right.

"Like you?" she repeated, beyond flustered that he knew how she felt about him. "Is that what your inflated ego is telling you? You are not as hot as you obviously think you are. You are not God's gift to the female gender. I can't stand you." Glaring at him, Cassie came to her feet and left the room.

She went into the bathroom and sloshed cool water on her hot face. After regaining her composure, she left the hospital and went home.

* * *

When she got home, TJ and Mama Rosa met her at the front door. Cassie swung her laughing son up into her arms and spun him around.

"Hi, sweetie," Cassie said, kissing his rosy cheeks. "Are you all packed and ready to spend the weekend with Aunt Monica and Uncle Shawn?"

"Mama Rosa helped me pack." He nodded enthusiastically and pointed to his Ninja Turtles duffel bag by the door.

"Monica called to say she'll be here in half an hour," said Mama Rosa. "TJ, can you go get Mommy one of the cookies we baked today?"

TJ nodded and ran from the room.

"Are you all right, dear?" asked Mama Rosa.

"Not really, but I don't want to talk about Adam Hart any more today. I don't even want to think about the man anymore. He's hopeless. I think I'm all talked out for the day," said Cassie, dropping down on the sofa.

TJ ran into the room and bounded up on the sofa and plopped down next to her. Cassie ruffled his hair. He was so much like his father, it was scary. TJ had the same brown hair and dimples, and unfortunately the same temperament. He took after his mother only in his stubbornness and his eyes. Long dark lashes covered his sparkling brown eyes.

Cassie was looking forward to some quiet time all by herself. Peter and Karen had gone to New Orleans for the weekend, and this was Mama Rosa's bingo night. She would have the whole house to herself for the first time ever. The thought was exhilarating.

After dinner Cassie took a long, relaxing shower. It soothed her tired muscles and eased some of the tension she had felt since her confrontation with Adam. She changed into a royal blue warm-up suit and slipped on a pair of flip-flops. After Monica picked up TJ, she would go rent a couple of movies and spend the night in front of the television with a big bowl of popcorn.

When she made it back downstairs, Monica was sitting next to TJ. He was feeding her a cookie.

"Monica, hi. You look great. How are you feeling?" Cassie asked, hugging her sister.

"Pregnant," said Monica, getting to her feet. "I feel like a beached whale, and I have three more months to go." Monica always looked stunning. It didn't matter what she was wearing; she always made it look good. Today she was dressed in a sailor-style navy blue maternity dress. Her hair was pulled back and tied with a matching navy blue bow. "Sorry to run, but I want to get a jump on the traffic."

"Hey, you," said Cassie, picking up her son. "Give me a hug."

TJ threw his arms around Cassie's neck and planted a kiss on her cheek.

"Now, you be a good boy, okay?" said Cassie.

He nodded.

"I'll pick you up Sunday afternoon, all right?"

He nodded again.

"I love you," Cassie whispered.

"I love you, too, Mommy." He returned her warm hug. Struggling to get down, he went to get his backpack. Putting the backpack in place, he turned to face his aunt. "Let's go, Aunt Monica."

"Thanks again, Monica, for keeping him. He can be a handful. If you need me, call. I owe you one." The sisters embraced again.

"It is our pleasure," said Monica, going out the open door. "We need the practice. Relax and enjoy your evening."

Cassie stood at the door and watched Monica buckle TJ safely into the car seat. After waving until they were out of sight, she went back in the house. Grabbing her purse and keys, she headed for the video store. She rented two movies, a comedy and an action-adventure flick before heading back home.

Cassie's words kept ringing in Adam's ears. *I am giving you a chance you haven't given me. I will not be responsible for society losing a fine doctor. I declined the chance to get even. Don't make me regret my decision.*

He stared long and hard at his reflection. He had never realized how bitter he was or how awful he was being not only to Cassie but to women in general. To him, they had always been a means to an end, and that end to him was sex. It had never bothered him until now. Closing his eyes, he sat down on the sofa.

What have I become? In the process of alienating myself from everyone, I've become something I don't like. Why can't I let myself love or be loved? Why can't I forget about the past? I know in my head the accident wasn't my fault, but my heart refuses to believe it. I don't deserve to be happy. I can't let myself be happy knowing what I've done.

If he were being completely honest with himself, he knew Cassie would have been justified in seeing his head on a platter. She could have jumped on the bandwagon to try and ruin his career. Instead, she had warned him. She had given him a second chance. He desperately needed a new lease on life.

Why would she do this for me after the two months of hell I put her through? Why would she care? I certainly haven't given her any reason to care. I've never given any woman a reason to care. I don't let anyone get too close.

Adam called and canceled his dinner date. He wasn't in the mood to deal with Gia right now. He wanted to be alone. He needed to think.

He took a relaxing shower and fixed himself a sandwich. Sitting in front of the television, he stared off into space. He finished his dinner and turned off the television. Jumping to his feet, Adam grabbed his jacket and left the house. He had to see Cassie. He had to apologize to her, if she would let him. He wouldn't blame her if she slammed the door in his face. He knew he deserved it.

Around eight o'clock Cassie put on her favorite red flannel pajamas. Jogging back downstairs, she popped a bag of microwave popcorn and put one of the two movies she'd rented in the DVD player in the den. She turned on the gas fireplace, lay down on the sofa, and pulled the handmade Mexican blanket over her legs and bare feet.

She hit the START button on the remote control, and the movie began. As if right on cue, the phone rang. She hit the STOP button and got up to answer the phone. She picked it up on the third ring.

"Cassie, hi. It's Karen. I just wanted to let you

know where we are staying and give you the phone number in case you need to reach us."

Cassie picked up the pen by the phone. "Shoot." She jotted down all the information on a pad and laid the pen down. "Got it. I hope you and Dad have a wonderful time."

"Thanks, dear. I'm sure we will. We will see you Monday evening."

Disconnecting the call, Cassie wasn't taking any chances. She carried the cordless phone with her to the den.

Okay, no more interruptions. I've wanted to see this movie for a long time.

She sat down on the sofa and hit the START button again. Lying back on the sofa, she pulled the blanket over her. She sighed in pleasure.

"Peace at last." She smiled as she relaxed against the pillow behind her head. The doorbell chimed, and she closed her eyes. "I don't believe this. I get one night alone, and now no one will leave me alone." Hitting the STOP button again, she grudgingly got to her feet. "What happened to my quiet, peaceful night alone?" she whispered as she walked to the door.

Peering out the peephole, she frowned. Blinking several times, she looked out again to see if she hadn't just imagined Dr. Adam Hart at her door. Maybe it was another one of her fantasies about him. If she stood there long enough, maybe he would go away. No such luck. He rang the bell again.

Am I in heaven or hell? She looked heavenward. *Is this another test? Can't a girl get a day's rest before she faces the fiery dragon again? I'm tired of battling him.*

After counting to ten, she opened the door. She and Adam stared at each other in surprise. He was wearing a pair of black slacks, a black, long-sleeved oxford shirt, and a pair of loafers. His dark eyes met hers and then moved downward.

Cassie couldn't resist a smile. She waved him inside and was touched when he pulled a bouquet of white roses from behind his back. She eyed him and the flowers warily.

"It's a peace offering," said Adam, handing her the flowers. "I hope I'm not disturbing you. You look ready for bed."

"No, you're not disturbing me. Please come in. Have a seat. I'll go put these in water," said Cassie, ushering him into the den. She carried the flowers into the kitchen and leaned against the kitchen sink, smiling. She couldn't believe he was actually in the next room, waiting for her. Her heart did a little flip-flop at the thought. Suddenly her smile was replaced by a frown.

What is he doing here? Why is he being so nice to me? He brought me roses. It has to be another ploy of his. What is he up to now?

When she returned, he was sitting on the sofa, watching television. He looked up when she came into the room. He came to his feet, and she waved at him to sit down.

"Your hair looks nice loose. It's beautiful," he said.

Her hand went automatically to her loose, curly hair. It was hanging down her back in a sandy brown cloud. "Thank you," she responded automatically. "Adam, what are you doing here? Why are you being nice to me all of a sudden? Did you fall out of bed and hit your head or something?"

He smiled at her sense of humor. "Cassie, the reason I came by is to apologize to you. My behavior toward you has been appalling. You were right. You have every reason to hate me and to go after me, but you didn't."

She crossed her arms over her chest and stared at him.

He went on. "I would like to start over, if possible. I'd like to be friends, if it's not too late. Thank you for giving me a second chance. It's more than I deserved for saying some of the things I said to you. Is there any way we can get past this and start over?"

"Adam, have you ever been friends with a woman before?" she asked, frowning.

He shook his head.

"That's what I thought. I have an idea. How would you like to stay and watch a couple of movies with me? To make it easy on you, I'll even go upstairs and put some clothes on." Cassie smiled.

"Must you?" He winked, and they laughed together. "You can't expect me to completely change overnight, right?"

"Adam, I guess that would be too much to hope for. Have a seat, and I'll go change."

Cassie ran upstairs to change. She stared into her closet, at a loss as to what to put on. Settling on a pair of jeans and a sweatshirt, she went back downstairs. She went into the kitchen to get soft drinks for them, then sat down next to him on the sofa and hit START on the remote. Picking up the bowl of popcorn, she offered him some. He took a handful and popped it into his mouth.

They laughed as they watched the first movie and then cheered on the hero in the second one. At the end, they were both applauding the downfall of the villain. Still cheering, Cassie got up and took out the DVD.

"This was fun. I had a good time, but I think I'd better go," said Adam, getting to his feet. "I don't want to overstay my welcome."

"I suppose it is getting late. I had a good time, too," Cassie admitted, following him to the door. "Thank you for the roses. They are beautiful."

"Not as beautiful as you are." His hand rose as if to touch her face and then dropped. He stared at her thoughtfully. "Good night, Cassie."

"Good night, Adam."

He opened the door and then closed it again. She stared at him, puzzled by his hesitation.

"Are you busy tomorrow night?" he asked.

Her eyebrows shot up in surprise.

"There's a new action movie opening, and I was wondering if you would like to go. It doesn't have to be a date. It can be two friends going to dinner and a movie."

"You're serious? Okay, but only if we go dutch."

"Not a chance." He shook his head negatively. "I think I can afford to pay for dinner and a movie for a friend. No strings attached."

"Okay, but I buy the popcorn." She smiled. "What time are you picking me up for this non-date?"

"How does seven o'clock sound? We can grab some dinner first and from there go to the theater, or we can go to Studio Movie Grill," Adam suggested.

"I'm in the mood for some good seafood."

"I know the perfect place. The food is delicious, and the ambience is great, too. I'll see you tomorrow night." He leaned over, and his lips touched her cheek.

Startled by the feel of his lips on her skin, Cassie took an involuntary step back. Her heart was beating wildly as she stared up at him.

Adam wasn't unaffected by the contact, either. He wanted nothing more than to take Cassie in his arms, but he knew he couldn't. He would give the friend thing a try. He wasn't making any promises he could follow through with it, but he would give it a shot.

"I'll see you tomorrow night," he said as he walked out of the house and closed the door.

Cassie smiled at the closed door. It was a start. Maybe he wasn't so bad, after all. Cassie hoped she wasn't making a mistake by going out with him.

Chapter 5

Saturday Cassie went shopping for something to wear. She spent almost the entire day going from mall to mall and still didn't find anything she liked.

What does one wear when two friends go to dinner and a movie? Who am I kidding? Adam and I are not friends and will probably never be friends. He's just making a peace offering. He's trying to be nice. No, there is not a nice bone in his body. Adam wants to get me in bed, and he's using a different tactic to try and get me there. I'm not exactly opposed to the idea. I do find him somewhat attractive. Who am I kidding? I want to jump his bones. I'm nuts. Now I'm talking to myself.

After returning home and emptying her closet, she finally decided on a two-piece black pantsuit. Beneath the jacket she would wear a low-cut red blouse. Around six o'clock she got dressed for her evening out. Leaving her hair loose, she brushed it out and let it hang down her back.

Adam likes it that way. God, what am I doing? I really shouldn't encourage him. He's wrong for me. I shouldn't even be going out with him. Dad and Monica both would have heart failure if they knew about this. In exasperation, she threw the hairbrush on the dresser. Slipping her feet into flat black shoes, she grabbed her purse and left the room. She was halfway down the stairs, when she heard Mama Rosa talking to someone.

Cassie almost lost her footing on the stairs when she saw Adam in the living room. She quickly grabbed the railing and regained her footing.

He looked dashing in a black sports blazer and matching pants. Beneath the blazer he wore a charcoal gray oxford shirt open at the top two buttons. He was laughing at something Mama Rosa was saying while he held the Christmas portrait of Cassie and TJ.

"Hi," said Cassie, coming into the room.

He turned around to face her, still holding the picture. "Hello. You have a handsome little boy," said Adam, placing the photo back over the fireplace. His eyes devoured her. "Wow! You look very nice."

"Thank you, kind sir," Cassie replied. She smiled, biting her lip. "You look quite handsome yourself. Ready?"

"Mrs. Sanchez, it was a pleasure meeting you," said Adam, taking her outstretched hand. "I'm sure I'll see you again."

"Nice meeting you, too, Dr. Hart," said Mama Rosa. "Cassie, I'll see you in the morning. Have a good time."

Adam drove by the theater first to get the tickets in advance so they would not have to wait in a long line. He then drove them to New Orleans Cuisine. He told her it was one of his favorite places to go for Cajun food. They chatted all throughout dinner. Adam was on his best behavior. He had not made a single off-color remark all evening, but then the evening was not over yet.

"I hardly know anything about you. How did you meet Shawn? Tell me about the man behind the legend," she teased.

"Let's see. I was born in St. Louis. I'm an only child. My father was a minister, and my mother was a teacher."

Cassie laughed out loud. She never would have guessed. Adam's father was a minister. It reminded her of the old saying about preachers and teachers having the worst kids.

"I'm sorry for laughing," she said disbelievingly, "but you're telling me your father was a man of the cloth?"

He smiled good-naturedly. "I'll have you know Reverend Louis Hart Jr. was the minister of the biggest Baptist church in St. Louis," he declared. "Now, don't interrupt my story. My father was disappointed I went to medical school. He wanted me to go into the seminary."

Cassie laughed again. Even with her vivid imagination, she could not imagine Adam as a minister. Putting her hand over her mouth to stifle a giggle, she nodded for him to continue.

"I graduated from college in St. Louis, with honors. One day I just packed my bags and moved here. My mother called me and gave me Shawn's name and number. He was the son of a friend of a friend. Since I didn't know anyone here, I called him. We were instant friends. I did my internship and my residency here at County General Hospital.

At the end of my term, I was offered a permanent position there. The rest you know. Now, tell me your life story."

"Mine is not very interesting," she said. "I was raised here. I went to a prestigious drama school my first year in New York. There I met, married, divorced, remarried, and divorced Trent Mancini, who is the father of my child. During the divorce, I was given complete custody of my son. My father was very opposed to my marriage, and we had a parting of the ways for a little while. When I got Monica's invitation to the wedding, I wanted to come home. My father persuaded me to move back." She deliberately downplayed everything to make it sound uninteresting. "Tell me, Adam," she said, changing the subject, "if you had three wishes, what would they be?"

"You just lost me," he said, puzzled. He took a sip of his margarita and sat the glass down.

"It's just a question I like to ask people. If you had three wishes, what would they be? World peace is not an option. Nor is having your own harem," she teased.

He sat back and reflected on the question. Then, sitting up straight, he took another sip of his drink. "First, I would have liked to have said good-bye to my parents. I never had the chance. A year ago on Christmas, they were driving down here from St. Louis to spend Christmas with me. They were killed in an automobile accident by a drunk driver."

Cassie's heart went out to him. She had not meant to make him sad.

He continued. "This is difficult to answer. Let me

think about the other two and get back to you. What would you wish for?"

"First, I probably would have finished college before getting married," Cassie said honestly. "Second, I'd like to get married again. I can't believe I'm actually saying this after Trent, but I would like to have another child, maybe two more. I've always had this dream of having a loving husband, wonderful children, and a nice home. I know this probably sounds silly to you." She laughed nervously.

He caught her hand and gave it a squeeze. "No, it doesn't sound silly. I never really thought about getting married and having a family until Monica and Shawn tied the knot. Now I do sometimes think about it, but I know it's only a pipe dream for me. I am definitely not the marrying kind. I don't think I've ever been faithful to any woman for more than a month. Besides, I think I'd make a lousy father. I don't know the first thing about children. I grew up an only child, so I don't have any nieces or nephews to practice on. I'm not even sure I like children."

At his words, Cassie's heart sank. She already knew all the things he was telling her. It just made them so final when he actually voiced them aloud. Adam Hart was not the man for her, and she knew this for sure now. They were miles apart in their thinking. She supposed she should thank him for being so honest with her up front. He let her know right off, he was not interested in marriage or kids and he wouldn't be faithful. Cassie knew the pain of an unfaithful mate. She wouldn't put herself through that again.

She uneasily pulled her hand from his. "You can practice on TJ anytime you want," she volunteered, smiling weakly. "As a matter of fact, it's what Monica and Shawn are doing this weekend. I wish them luck. He can be a real handful when things don't go his way." She looked down nervously at her watch. "I think we'd better get going if we want to get seats for the movie."

They left the restaurant and went to the theater. Cassie was paying for the bucket of popcorn when she saw Adam do a 180-degree turn. Dropping the change into her purse, she looked up at him.

She followed his line of vision and frowned. The woman Adam and half the men in the theater lobby were leering at was a tall, leggy brunette in a tight red spandex minidress and red high heels. Her large, bouncing breasts were barely concealed by the low-cut, off-the-shoulder dress. She swayed a little more than necessary when she walked.

Cassie was sure that if the woman bent over, her boobs would fall out and the dress would snap up around her neck. The lady in question then had the nerve to roll her eyes and get upset at all the "unwanted" attention she was getting.

Taking the bucket of popcorn from the attendant, Cassie shoved it into Adam's stomach.

"What?" he asked innocently. He caught the bucket and looked down at her wearily. "Now what did I do?"

"Don't try and give me that innocent look. You are being insulting, not only to her but to me as well. Haven't you learned anything about women in the past thirty-four years? How would you feel if

I gawked at every good-looking guy who walked by?" she snapped.

"Since we are just friends, I guess it wouldn't matter," he shot back, smiling at her.

Cassie's face turned red at his accusation.

"Hell, if she didn't want the attention, she shouldn't have left the house wearing that dress. Any woman dressed like that is just asking for trouble," Adam added.

"You know what, Adam? Let's agree to disagree on this one," Cassie hissed, not believing her ears.

"Men are basically dogs, anyway, or at least that's what most women think."

Cassie nodded in agreement.

"So if you dress like a hoochie, then expect to be treated like one," Adam declared, walking into the dark theater and leaving Cassie speechless and fuming in the hallway.

Flabbergasted, she threw her arms in the air and followed him. There was no reasoning with some people, and she knew it. She could accomplish only so much with him in so short a time.

On the drive home, they chatted like two old friends. They didn't talk about anything in particular. They tried to steer clear of hospital talk, but the conversation kept veering back to work.

"Would you like to come in for a while?" asked Cassie as she fumbled to get her house keys out of her purse.

"I'd like that."

He got out of the car and came around to her side. He caught her hand and helped her out of the black Porsche. Hand in hand, they walked to the door. Adam took the keys from her and opened the door. She stepped inside, and he followed her. Adam locked the door behind them, and Cassie jumped at the click of the lock behind her. They walked into the den.

"Please have a seat," said Cassie.

Adam sat next to her on the sofa.

"Would you like something to drink?" asked Cassie, coming nervously to her feet.

His nearness was getting to her. She was in way over her head with Adam. Being friends with him was the furthest thing from her mind. She wanted this man, but she also knew she couldn't have him. She had to put some distance between them and fast before she did something they would both regret.

He pulled her back down on the sofa. Their eyes met and held, and Cassie lowered hers, hoping he would not read the message she was desperately trying to hide. She looked up again, and his head lowered to hers. Lightly his lips touched hers, so lightly that she almost thought she had imagined it.

"Friendship is so overrated," Adam whispered against her lips. With a deep groan, he buried his hands in her thick hair and pulled her face to his. His mouth covered hers in a hungry kiss, which took her breath away. Moaning softly in surrender, Cassie gave in to her feelings. Her lips parted of their own volition under the firm pressure of his, and she returned the heated kiss with all the pent-up passion she had been holding inside. Her arms went around him, and her tongue met his in a fiery duel. His tongue explored the silken recesses of her mouth at his leisure.

Breathlessly, he pulled back and stared down into her flushed face. Her eyes were cloudy with passion as she gazed back at him. Catching the lapels of his blazer, Cassie brought his head back down to hers. Her lips parted under his, and she melted against him.

He returned her heated kiss and pressed her back against the sofa. He unbuttoned her jacket, and his hand covered her silk-covered breast. The wispy lace of her bra was no match for his caressing hand. Her nipple hardened instantly under his masterful touch. As warm lips slid down her throat, Cassie was lost.

Pushing the jacket and blouse from her shoulders, he unsnapped her bra. When his hot mouth covered her breast, she moaned in pleasure and arched into him while holding his head to her. Of their own will, her fingers removed his blazer and unbuttoned his shirt. He tensed when she touched his pert nipples with her fingers. She felt her own nipples turn to pebbles under his gentle touch. Cassie's trembling fingers glided smoothly across his hair-roughened chest, and she was thrilled at his groan of pleasure. His hand slid down her stomach to her thighs. Though she did not even realize it, her legs parted for him. Adam's hand cupped her through the soft material of her pants. A soft moan escaped her parted lips.

"Cassie, we have to stop," Adam whispered as his hand stilled against the apex of her thighs. Removing his hand, he caught her roaming hands. He breathed in deeply the fragrance of Cassie, and it drove him wild. Closing his eyes, he tried to regain what little self-control he had left. He wanted her so badly, he ached, but he knew the time was not right. They had taken too many steps forward to move backward now. He had to slow things down a bit for both their sakes.

She stared up at him through a fog of passion. As reality began to set in, her face turned bright red with embarrassment and she scrambled to pull her clothes together. Coming shakily to her feet, she moved away from him and hugged her arms around herself protectively. Her fingers trembled as she buttoned her blouse.

I'm an idiot. What was I thinking? He probably thinks I'm a sex-starved divorcée. Who am I kidding? I am a sex-starved divorcée.

Cassie felt Adam behind her even before his hands came down on her shoulders. She resisted only for a moment when he tried to turn her around to face him. Raising her chin with his finger, he smiled at her, and to her surprise, he dropped a soft kiss on her parted lips.

"I'm not sorry for what almost happened," he explained, brushing the hair from her face. "I'm sorry I had to stop."

"Why did you stop?" she asked past the catch in her throat. "I wanted you, and you seem to want me. Did I do something wrong?"

"No, sweetheart, you didn't do anything wrong. You did everything right. I like you and I'm attracted to you, but I won't rush you into something you are not ready for."

"Who says I'm not ready?" she asked softly, moving away from him. "Adam, we have been playing this cat-and-mouse game for months."

"And the game is over," he said, moving in front

of her and walking toward the front door. "I care about you, Cassie. This isn't a game anymore. I like being with you. For once in my life I am trying to be a gentleman. I am trying to do right by you. Let me."

His hand caressed her flushed face. He leaned down, and his mouth covered hers in a slow, tender kiss. Cassie swayed into him, and her arms went around him.

"I'd better get going before all my good intentions go flying out the window. Good night, Cassie. Sweet dreams." His lips brushed hers once more, and then he closed the door behind him.

He raised his hand to ring the doorbell but let his hand drop. *Adam, old boy, it's best to leave well enough alone. You are treading on dangerous ground here. Back away from the door and leave.*

Backing away from the door, he went out to his car.

In his car Adam picked up his cell phone and called Donna, a nurse at the hospital with whom Adam had previously been involved with. He knew she wouldn't turn him away, and he was in desperate need of a woman. He had a feeling a cold shower alone would not solve his problem. Just thinking about Cassie's responsive body in his arms made his body react.

"Donna. It's Adam. Are you busy?"

"That depends on what you have in mind, Doctor," she said seductively. "I didn't realize you made house calls. Come on over."

"I'll be there in fifteen minutes or less. Donna, wear something slinky, sexy, and easy to take off."

He disconnected the call and dropped the cell phone on the passenger seat.

Minutes later Donna greeted him in a sexy see-through red negligee. She was not his first choice tonight, but she would do. He had to purge Cassie from his mind.

Donna led him to her bedroom victoriously. She had been trying to get Adam back into her bedroom for the past two months. He was the best lover she had ever had, and she wasn't ready to give him up.

He stared down at the short, dark-skinned woman. Donna was not beautiful like Cassie, but she was extremely sexy and very willing. She had a beautiful body and a healthy sexual appetite to match his.

What would Cassie say if she knew I was here now? She would probably hate me. What am I doing here?

As Donna pulled the straps of her negligee down her shoulders all rational thought left him. She moved toward him. But instead of seeing Donna, he was seeing Cassie. He blinked several times to clear his vision.

"What's wrong?" asked Donna, watching him closely.

Adam turned away from her, still trying to clear his vision.

What am I doing? Less than an hour ago I held Cassie in my arms, and now I'm here with Donna. I'm sabotaging any chance Cassie and I might have. I must have been nuts to come here. Cassie doesn't deserve this, and I don't deserve her.

"This was a mistake," he said softly. "I'm sorry. I

shouldn't have come here. It was wrong." He bolted from the bedroom.

"You are kidding me," Donna said angrily, following him from the room. "What are you trying to pull, Adam? I didn't call you. You called me, remember?"

"I know and I'm sorry. This was a mistake." He made a quick exit, closing the door behind him. He heard something crash against the door as he hurried to his car and drove home.

Cassie was floating on air when she went to pick TJ up on Sunday. She told Monica about the talk she had with Adam, him coming by on Friday, and their date on Saturday night. Monica seemed a bit hesitant to comment on the turn of events. Cassie sensed her sister's quiet disapproval.

Later, when Mama Rosa mentioned Adam and their date to Peter and Karen at dinner, Peter hit the roof. He in no uncertain terms informed his daughter about what a bed-hopping rake Adam Hart was and told her that she would do well to stay as far away from him as she could get.

Cassie proceeded to inform her father that this was her life and she would see anyone she chose. This erupted into a heated argument. Cassie walked out of the dining room, yelling at him, reminding him that it was a little late for him to be playing father now.

The next morning she was gone before anyone got up. When she got to the hospital, the ER was strangely devoid of any male staff. Rachel was with a patient, and Dr. Donnelly was at one of the desks, looking over some X-rays.

Adam stared at the guys, at a loss for words. He had completely forgotten about the damn bet. He and the male staff in the ER had a long-standing bet that Adam could get any new attractive nurse in the ER to go out with him. He watched, open-mouthed, as each guy placed a twenty-dollar bill in the palm of his hand.

There was no way Cassie could ever find out about this, or everything between them the other night would be gone right out the window. She wouldn't understand, and she wouldn't forgive him. After being with Cassie, he couldn't understand it himself. It was time to end the bet once and for all.

"Guys, take your money back," said Adam, trying to give the money back to them. "I didn't take Cassie out as part of any bet."

Holding up their hands, they all refused to take the money back.

"I don't want it, guys." Adam insisted. "If Cassie finds out about this, we are all in deep trouble. As of today, there are no more bets. It's silly. It's juvenile, and it's degrading to women."

"You won it fair and square," said Rafael. "Ted saw you with Cassie at the movies. So tell us, Doc. Exactly how much do we owe you?"

"I barely got a good-night kiss," Adam lied. "Take the money back, and let's forget about the whole thing. Guys, this whole betting thing is history. I don't want to hear any more about it."

They all stared at him in surprise.

Suddenly the door swung open, and they all turned to see Cassie standing there. Adam closed his eyes and died a thousand times when he saw her. He knew it was about to hit the fan.

Cassie was headed to the break room to get a cup of hot chocolate. She'd stopped short at the door when she'd heard Zack's voice, followed by laughter. If she'd had to guess, whatever he had said was crude and in poor taste.

After pushing the door open, she stepped inside. What she saw in the room made her heart stop, and a feeling of dread washed over her. There, in the middle of the room, stood Adam with a stack of money in his hand.

Some of the guys looked embarrassed; others looked pleased. Cassie knew she was not going to like what was to come.

"Damn, I had such high hopes for this one," said Zack, placing a twenty-dollar bill in Adam's palm. "Dr. Hart won the bet again. You cost me twenty dollars by going out with the doc," he added, cruelly watching Cassie for a reaction. "All you had to do was hold out one more day."

Cassie stared at Zack in confusion at first. Then the impact of his words hit her like a physical blow. Adam had bet them he could get a date with her. Color suffused her face as she turned furiously to face Adam. She was not only embarrassed and ashamed, but she was humiliated as well. She walked over to where Adam was standing and stared him straight in the eyes.

He looked at her with a guarded expression. Adam didn't know what she was thinking, and he didn't want to know. All he knew was that he had to explain things to her before the situation got out of hand. He had to make her understand that this was not really his fault. From the look on her face, he knew it was not going to be easy.

"You bet them I would go out with you," Cassie thundered, knocking his hand and sending the money flying into the air. She glared up at him. "Would it have been an added bonus if you had gotten me into bed? Perhaps fifty dollars instead of twenty?" she asked quietly.

"Guys, let's leave them alone," Roger suggested uneasily.

Everyone ignored him and stared from Cassie to Adam, ready to watch the fireworks.

"Go," ordered Adam in a threatening voice. When no one moved, he turned to face Cassie again. "Cassie, let me explain," he pleaded, looking into her furious face.

"Save it, Doctor Feel Good. This says it all," said Cassie, looking around the semi-crowded break room. "You are all pathetic. You need to get a life and stop living your fantasies through Dr. Hart's bed."

"It was a standing bet. I had completely forgotten about it," added Adam, trying to get through to her.

"If you don't want your winnings, I'll take them," said Cassie, picking up the money and stuffing it in her scrub pocket. "I think I've earned it. Although, no amount of money is enough for putting up with you jerks. You are all despicable, but you, Dr. Hart, are the worst of the bunch. What you did was not only cold and calculated but insulting."

"It was just a joke, Cassie," said Roger, coming over to her. "It wasn't meant to hurt you or to embarrass you. Hell, it was made before we got to know you."

"It doesn't make it right! Is that why Zack was so glad to throw it in my face? Not to hurt or embarrass me, surely!" Cassie stormed. "I just hope the next female nurse they put here stays longer than I have. I thought you were different, Roger. I thought you were my friend. Obviously, friendship means very little to you. Or maybe you always stab your friends in the back?"

"Cassie, it wasn't like that," said Roger, looking embarrassed as he shuffled his feet uncomfortably. "We *are* friends."

"No, we're not," she said, sadly shaking her head. "I don't have any friends here. I only see little boys who refuse to grow up."

Cassie took off her badge and threw it in Adam's general direction before turning to leave. Adam caught her arm to halt her exit. He waved for the guys to leave, and they all filed out of the room like tin soldiers.

"Give me a minute, please. Let me explain what happened," Adam pleaded. She tried to squirm away, but he held on to her arm.

"Tell me, Dr. Hart, what was Friday night really about? Did you come by to apologize to me, or was it only a part of the devious plan you had cooked up to win your stupid bet? We saw Ted at the movies, and he acted real weird when he saw us together. Was it part of the bet that someone had to see us together?"

"Cassie." He closed his eyes, and so did she. His crestfallen expression was her answer.

She jerked her arm away from his grasp. "Go to hell." Cassie barely made it out of the room before the tears fell. She ran to the bathroom and closed herself in a stall.

Chapter 6

Cassie dried her tearstained face and was about to come out of the bathroom stall when the door opened and two women came in. She hesitated and waited. She didn't want anyone to know she was crying because of Adam Hart.

"Sharla, I had the most incredible night Saturday night," said Donna, the human barracuda. "Dr. Adam Hart was sensational."

Cassie's heart stopped.

"All the rumors about his sexual prowess are definitely true," Donna revealed. "He called me late Saturday night out of the blue and asked me if he could come over. It was a truly memorable evening. I get warm all over just thinking about it. . . ."

"You're a fool, Donna. He was only using you. Everyone knows Dr. Hart has his eyes set on Cassie Randall."

Cassie pushed the stall door open and left the bathroom. She didn't see Donna's satisfied smile or Sharla's look of pity as she left.

She was halfway to her car when she stopped in

her tracks. Adam's Porsche had her car blocked in, and he was leaning casually against it.

"Move your car, Dr. Hart. I'd like to get home to my son," seethed Cassie, facing him. "I have nothing more to say to you."

"Cassie, we have to talk about this," said Adam, standing up straight. "We can't let things end like this."

"How can there be an ending without a beginning? We have nothing to talk about. You made a fool out of me. You embarrassed me in front of all our colleagues. How do you expect me to be able to face any of them again? Like an idiot, I believed you were sincere, and you were playing a game with me to win a bet. What, pray tell, do you do for an encore?"

"I'm sorry. I never meant to hurt you. What we shared Saturday night was something special. I felt it, and you felt it, too. It was real, Cassie."

"What I felt was lust, Adam," she lied. "Let me spell it out for you. It's been a long time since I've been with someone. What's it been for you? A day? Maybe two? I wanted a man, and you were there."

"You're a lousy liar," he shot back. "Maybe it's been a long time for you, but you didn't want just any man. You wanted me. You were ready to give yourself to me. I know you felt more than lust."

"Maybe I did feel something, but it doesn't come close to the self-loathing I feel now. I was stupid enough to fall for the garbage you fed me. I hope you and the guys had a good laugh about it," said Cassie, moving past him to unlock her car door. She stopped and looked up at him. "Just out of curiosity, why did you stop the other night? You had me right where you wanted me. Why didn't you make love to me? I was available, and I was more than willing. It couldn't have been your conscience, because you don't have one. Maybe you forgot your favorite condoms. No." She laughed bitterly. "That couldn't be it, either. You never leave home without them, do you?"

He pulled her to him and stared down into her flushed, angry face. Cassie tried to pull away, but he held her fast. "No, damn it. I stopped because of you. For once I thought about someone else. I didn't want you to feel guilty and hate yourself in the morning. I knew you were not ready, and I didn't want to take advantage of you in a weak moment. I wanted to make love to you as much as you wanted me to, but I knew it would mean a lot more to you than it would have to me."

"So you were thoughtful enough to offer it to Donna instead?" she sneered, pulling away from him. He released her and took a step back in surprise. "You went from my arms to hers. You really do wonders for a girl's ego and self-esteem. I get you all hot and bothered, and you go running off to another woman to put out the fire. Instead of feeling insulted, I guess I should be relieved," she snarled.

"Are you angry at me for going to Donna or for not making love to you? Whether you believe me or not, I did not sleep with Donna. I went by there, but I couldn't go through with it. Do you want to know why? Because I kept seeing your face, your body, and I couldn't go through with it. She was not the woman I wanted in my arms that night. You were."

"Let me see if I've got this straight," said Cassie, unlocking the car and throwing her purse inside. "You deliberately went over to Donna's, but you couldn't have sex with her, because you were thinking about me. So does that mean you were thinking about her when you were with me?"

"I did not sleep with her," he shot back. "Damn me for the thought but not the act. I didn't make love to her."

"No, you had sex with her. I was kidding myself to believe someone like you could change. The only difference between you and a prostitute is they take money for their favors and you don't. Oh, I forgot! So do you!" She got furiously into her car, slammed the door shut in his face, and waited for him to move his car.

When she got home, Peter was waiting for her. She tried to slip past him and go up to her room, but he came to his feet and turned to face her.

"Cassie, I'm sorry about last night. You were right. You are an adult, and I shouldn't interfere in your personal life. I just don't want to see you get hurt again. Adam Hart is poison. I was only trying to save you from heartache."

"I'm sorry, too. I know you are only trying to help Dad, but it is my life. You can't live my life for me. You can't prevent me from being hurt if it's inevitable. Thank you for caring, but please don't try to interfere in my love life again. It's off-limits even to you. Just for the record, I won't be going out with Adam again. Where's TJ?" she asked, changing the subject.

"He went with Karen on some errands. She wants

to show him off to all her friends." Peter frowned. "Honey, are you all right? You seem upset."

"I'm fine. I'm going up to take a nap. Have TJ wake me when they get back," she said tiredly. She went upstairs to her room. Once there she collapsed on the bed and replayed the day's events in her mind.

The following day Cassie almost called in sick but changed her mind. She would prove to them she was stronger than they gave her credit for. She would go in there, and she would hold her head high like nothing had ever happened, even if it killed her.

She went into the break room to put her sack lunch in her locker. She opened the locker door and out popped five small helium-filled balloons with streamers and chocolate attached to them.

"What in the world?" A shadow fell across her. She looked up and closed the locker door. "Did you do this?"

"I wish I had thought of it," said Roger, leaning against the locker next to hers.

She made no response as she turned to walk away.

"Cassie, I'm really sorry about yesterday."

She stopped and turned around to face him. "Are you sorry you placed the bet," she asked, meeting his eyes, "or sorry I found out about it?"

"Both," he said sincerely. "I like you. I think you are a great nurse, and I would like for us to be friends. I'm not like the rest of those guys. I don't believe women are sex objects or playthings. I think you know me better than that." Smiling, he held out his hand. "I'm Roger Harris." She caught his outstretched hand. "For what it's worth, Dr. Hart does like you. We've all seen it."

She followed his gaze and turned to see Adam coming her way. Roger made a hasty exit. In the small room there was no way to slip past Adam without nearing him. He stopped directly in front of her.

"Did you like my peace offering?" he asked without preamble.

"I don't want anything from you. I have nothing to say to you. Leave me alone," responded Cassie, trying to slip past him. She grabbed the balloon streamers and held them out to him. "Take them. I don't want them."

Adam unwrapped a piece of chocolate. Her eyes moved to the morsel as he brought it to his mouth. His eyes closed in delight as he bit into it. "This is delicious. You should try one," he said, blocking her exit.

"Fine. I'll keep the candy, but I don't want you." She took the candy from the balloons and tied them to his wrist.

"Cute, Cassie, but they clash with my outfit." He stopped her hasty exit. "Please give me a few minutes to explain."

Her frosty gaze met his.

"I'm sorry about what happened yesterday. The stupid bet was a game all the guys played way before you came along. It wasn't personal. I ended it, Cassie. All future bets are off. Whether you believe me or not, I had forgotten about the bet when I asked you out Saturday night. When I took you in my arms, a bet was the farthest thing from my mind."

"Really? And what were you thinking when you took Donna in your arms?" she asked, folding her arms over her chest.

"I was thinking it should have been you. I made a mistake. I shouldn't have used her to try and forget you. Cassie, I swear to you, nothing happened with her. I have a confession to make." Adam crossed his fingers behind his back. "I gave Shawn my word I would not make a play for you. He reminded me of my promise a few weeks ago."

"I don't believe this. Does anyone believe I am an adult and I can take care of myself? This is the reason you have been harassing me? To keep me from being attracted to you? You really do give yourself a lot of credit, Doctor."

"Basically," he said and smiled. "I never realized how cruel I was being until you made me see me through your eyes. You saved me from myself, Cassie."

At this point she didn't know what to think anymore. Could it have all been an act? She didn't think so. So if he had promised Shawn to stay away from her, then he hadn't asked her out to win a stupid bet with a bunch of morons.

"Have you ever lost a bet?" she asked curiously, folding her arms across her chest again. A smile tugged at the corners of her mouth.

"No," he answered truthfully. "I want to be with you. Not only am I attracted to you, but I like you as a person. I know I've done some lousy things in the past, but I can change. Give me one more chance to prove to you I am a likable person and to show you I can be a decent human being."

Cassie stared at him, not knowing what to say. This was not the confrontation she had expected. Her anger slowly started to dissipate. Could she trust him not to hurt her again? Would she be willing to give him another chance? Common sense said no, but her heart wasn't listening to her head.

"This is your last chance, Adam. If you screw up, don't ever come near me again. If it turns out to be a disaster, you have to promise me, you will help me transfer out of here. There will not be any more chances, and I won't be able to work with you anymore."

Looking around the empty room, he leaned in and brushed his lips across hers. Her eyes fluttered closed, and heat washed over her at the contact.

"I'll pick you up at seven," he said, walking away.

What am I? A glutton for punishment? I should probably walk away before it's too late. Maybe it's already too late, Cassie thought.

After work she went out and bought a new outfit with the money Adam had won from the bet. She bought a royal blue minidress that stopped just above her knees. She would wear it tonight as a symbol to remind her of what a louse he could be.

Adam arrived at the Randall house promptly at 6:45 P.M. He knew he was about fifteen minutes early, but better early than late.

He got out of the black Porsche and stretched his six-foot-plus frame. He was dressed in black slacks, a black turtleneck, and a black sports jacket.

He popped a mint into his mouth before ringing the doorbell.

"Hello, Dr. Hart. Please come in," greeted Mama Rosa, warmly leading Adam to the den. "Cassie is not quite ready."

"Hello, Mrs. Sanchez. It's nice to see you again," Adam said, returning her warm smile. "I'm a few minutes early. I can just wait here for her."

"Can I get you something cold to drink while you wait?" she asked as Adam took a seat on the sofa. "I'll go tell Cassie you're here."

"No, I'm fine." He picked up the remote control and turned on the television.

Mama Rosa was turning to leave the room when Peter came in.

"I saw a car outside," said Peter. "Do we have company?" He came up short when he saw Adam. His look went from warm and friendly to angry. "What are you doing here?"

"I came to see your daughter," replied Adam, coming to his feet. He knew he shouldn't goad Peter, but he couldn't resist. "Cassie and I have a date."

"Get out of my home. You are not taking my daughter anywhere. You will date her over my dead body."

Neither of them saw Mama Rosa quickly leave the room.

"Whatever it takes," Adam shot back. "My relationship with your daughter is none of your business."

"You don't have a relationship with my daughter," Peter returned, fuming. "I will not let you use her, the way you've used seventy-five percent of the nurses at the hospital."

"Peter, you give me way too much credit. And here I thought it was only twenty-five percent. My numbers must be off."

Cassie was almost ready when she heard the brief knock on the door before Mama Rosa entered. Cassie could tell by her expression something was wrong.

"Mr. Peter is home early, and Dr. Hart is also early. They are downstairs together, in the den. You'd better hurry."

Cassie slipped into her shoes and flew down the stairs. By the time she made it to the bottom of the stairs and before she could reach her destination, she heard the escalating voices. Taking a deep breath, she went into the den.

Her father and Adam both stared at her with accusing eyes. Her father was angry that she had told him she was seeing Adam again, and Adam was furious that she'd failed to warn him about the opposition and hostility he would face by coming there to pick her up.

"Adam, hi. I'm ready when you are," she announced. "Good night, Dad." Cassie tentatively pulled Adam to the front door. When she closed the door behind them, she let out a sigh of relief.

She knew she would have to face her father some other time. Given his reaction, Cassie figured he would probably wait up for her.

They went to dinner at a fancy Chinese restaurant that had recently opened in North Dallas. From there they went to Have Hart to hear a band and do some dancing. True to his word, Adam was a perfect gentleman. They laughed and talked about everything from work to politics.

When he dropped her back home, he saw her safely inside. He caught her hand and drew her to him. Instead of watching the descent of his mouth, she tiptoed to meet it. His mouth touched hers in a gentle caress. Her arms went around him, and her lips parted under the gentle pressure of his. After several passionate kisses, Adam extricated himself from Cassie's arms and left.

Smiling to herself, Cassie twirled happily around the living room. She came to an abrupt stop when she saw Karen sitting on the sofa. Gathering her composure, she walked over to the sofa and sat down next to her.

"I'm a little surprised you waited up for me, Karen," said Cassie, eyeing her stepmother. "I thought it was Dad's style, not yours."

"He's just worried about you, Cassie. Your father doesn't want to see you get hurt." She held up her hand to silence her stepdaughter. "Hear me out. Peter has been on the hospital board a long time. For years he has heard of Adam's exploits. Last year he even recommended to the board that it not renew Adam's contract. So it does rankle him a little that you are seeing a man he despises. The feeling is quite mutual between the two of them, and I would hate to see you get caught in the middle."

"I really appreciate your concern, but this is my decision and this is my life. I'm sorry Dad hates Adam and doesn't approve of him, but I happen to like him. I like him a lot."

"Then move cautiously and carefully," Karen said quietly. "Don't rush into anything with Adam. You have all the time in the world." Cassie watched Karen leave the room and let out a deep sigh. Was it going to be this way each time she went out on or came back from a date with Adam? Maybe it was time she started looking for her own place.

Leaving the room, she went to check on TJ. He was sound asleep, hugging the stuffed teddy bear to his chest that Monica had given him. Cassie showered and went to bed.

The following week at work was a breeze. Adam had a completely different attitude toward her, and so did some of the other guys. She wasn't sure what he had said to them, but whatever it was, it worked. There were no off-color remarks directed at her or any of the other nurses. The sexual revolution was over. Adam surprised her on two separate occasions. First, he ate lunch with her and Patricia. A few days later he had lunch with her and Rachel.

Rachel was amazed at the change in Adam's personality. She demanded details. Cassie gave her the abbreviated version of the past few weeks. When she finished, Rachel was smiling her "I told you so" smile.

On Friday Adam caught up with Cassie as she was backing out of the parking lot. She stopped when she saw him waving to her. She rolled down the window as he walked up to her car.

"I'm glad I caught you. Things were so hectic in there, I didn't get a chance to talk to you before you left. Do you have any plans for tomorrow?"

"Actually I do. I have a date with my son." She smiled. "We are going to an arts and crafts store to buy T-shirts and paint. We are designing our very own T-shirts. You are more than welcome to come along." Realizing what she was saying, she almost kicked herself. "Forget I said that. I know you are not into kids or family-oriented activities and that sort of stuff."

"I'd love to come along," said Adam, surprising them both. "I'd like to meet TJ. Do I get to paint my very own shirt?" he teased.

"It's a requirement. You're serious about this? You want to spend the day with me and my son?"

"Yes, Cassie, I want to spend the day with you and your son." He leaned inside the window and dropped a soft kiss on her lips. "How about I pick you two up about eleven? We can go to lunch and then go pick up the shirts and paint."

"How about you meet us at my house and I will drive us there? I don't think the three of us will fit into your Porsche," she teased. "I know I'm not getting in the trunk."

"You have a point. Do I have to come inside? Can't I drive up, honk three times, and you two run out of the house?"

"And miss the look of loathing on Dad's face? Not a chance. I've got to run. I'll see you tomorrow."

When Cassie arrived home, she told TJ that Adam was joining them on their outing tomorrow, and he seemed a little apprehensive. She assured him that Adam was a nice man and that he and Mommy were friends. TJ was not convinced and remained skeptical.

* * *

On Saturday Adam was getting ready to leave when the doorbell rang. Looking down at his watch, he picked up his car keys. He didn't have time for a long visit. He was due to pick up Cassie and TJ in about forty-five minutes in his recently purchased Jeep.

He opened the door and took a step back as Shawn barreled into the house. No need to ask why he was ticked off. Adam already knew the answer. Shawn knew about him and Cassie.

"You gave me your word, Adam. I leave town for a week, and you can't keep your hands to yourself. What happened to your rule about not dating women with children? Cassie has a child. Remember him?" said Shawn, glaring at his best friend.

"Shawn, you are my best friend, not my father. I never should have given you my word in the first place. I know you may find this hard to believe, but I like Cassie."

"Adam, you have liked every woman you've loved and left. Why her? She's not even your type," Shawn shot back.

"This is none of your business. Maybe my type has changed. Maybe, just maybe, she's exactly what I've been looking for."

"Which means what exactly? Adam, Cassie doesn't need someone who refuses to accept love and refuses to give it in return. Until you face your fears and get some help, you are going to end up hurting her and yourself. Go get counseling. She doesn't deserve this."

"I don't have a problem," Adam said vehemently. "You have the problem, Shawn. I accepted the fact I caused my parents' death. You just can't accept it.

I don't know what I feel for Cassie, but until I do know, I am going to keep seeing her. I am not going to let her go until I am ready."

"You selfish bastard," hissed Shawn. "You don't want a relationship. You want a new bed partner, but you are willing to string her along and let her think you want more. What happens to her and TJ after you are through playing with their emotions? You are going to break her heart, and you don't give a damn. For once in your life, think about someone else. Think about what this is going to do to Cassie when you walk away from her."

"Who says I have to walk away from her?" Adam shouted. "Maybe, just maybe, I will not walk away this time."

"Whenever you get cold feet, you run. You do this every time. When this blows up in your face," said Shawn angrily, "and it will, don't say I didn't warn you." Shawn turned on his heels and stormed out of the house.

Adam stared after his friend. He dangled the car keys from his finger, not sure what he should do. He wanted to be with Cassie, but he couldn't make any promises as to how long he would stay around. He wanted to follow his head, but he couldn't. Instead, he closed the door behind him and decided for once to follow his heart and see where it led him.

Cassie and TJ were waiting in the den, watching television, when Adam arrived. They were laughing and singing along with the Disney theme song when he entered the room. At the end of the song, he applauded.

"Bravo. Bravo. Encore. Encore," Adam said and whistled. He looked very handsome and comfortable in black jeans, sneakers, and a black polo shirt.

Cassie frowned slightly. She was beginning to notice a trend in his wardrobe, a basic black trend. She stood up and took a bow. TJ followed her lead. Taking his hand in hers, she walked over to Adam.

"TJ, this is Dr. Adam Hart. He's a friend of Mommy's. He's also Uncle Shawn's best friend, who was at the wedding. Adam, this handsome and talented young man is my son, TJ."

Smiling, Adam dropped down to one knee and held out his hand to the small boy. Hesitantly, TJ took the outstretched hand.

"Hi, TJ. It's nice to finally meet you. Your mom has told me a lot about you. I hope we can be friends."

"Hi," responded TJ shyly, studying Adam closely.

Cassie smiled and let out the breath she was holding when her son relaxed and smiled for the first time.

The three of them had a good day together. Lunch went smoothly, and from there they went to the arts and crafts store. They each picked out a T-shirt and paints and glitters to decorate with.

When they got back to the house, Mama Rosa had already draped the game room in old sheets to protect the furniture and the floor. She had also left them a pitcher of lemonade and a tray of homemade cookies.

Much to Cassie's amazement, TJ and Adam became instant friends. Even more surprising was the fact that Adam seemed to be genuinely enjoying himself. He was a natural with kids. He and TJ laughed and chatted easily with each other.

When Adam was leaving, TJ made him promise to come back again. Cassie watched in surprise as they embraced warmly. Her hand in his, she walked Adam to the front door. He brushed her lips lightly with his. Not satisfied, Cassie pulled his head back down to hers for a soul-shattering, heart-stopping kiss. When she finally pulled away, they were both breathless.

"I'm glad you came today," said Cassie, staring up into his eyes. "You've definitely got TJ's stamp of approval."

"I'm glad I came as well," agreed Adam, caressing her cheek. "TJ is a wonderful little boy. You're lucky to have him, and he's lucky to have you. I'll talk to you later. I want to be off the premises before dear old dad comes home. He might have me arrested for trespassing." Adam laughed, then gave her a quick kiss.

Chapter 7

The following Saturday Cassie and TJ had a picnic in the park. Later that afternoon, after dropping off TJ, Cassie went to Adam's house.

Looking around the beautifully decorated den, Cassie sat down on the plush charcoal gray leather sofa. The room was large but cozy. The black fireplace was flush with the wall. In one corner was a large LCD television.

They sat lounging on the sofa in Adam's den after eating the wonderful meal Adam had prepared for them. She moaned as he planted kisses on her neck and down her throat.

Adam invited her to a hospital-related formal dinner. Cassie was hesitant at first, until he reminded her that at some point they would have to take their relationship public. He then surprised her with a ball gown. He went into the bedroom and came out with a clothes bag. He proceeded to lay the bag across her lap. Cassie frowned, puzzled.

Coming to her feet, she unzipped the bag. Cassie was speechless as she took the gown out of the bag.

She stared at the beautiful gown in awe. It was a strapless black sequined gown. The split on the side stopped at midthigh. Cassie was positive it was something she could never afford to buy for herself on her salary.

Adam talked her into keeping the gown and wearing it to the dinner. Cassie had some reservations about it, but she relented.

Cassie left about an hour later. Adam walked her to her car and kissed her. She pulled out of the drive, and he went back inside. *I look forward to an interesting evening,* he thought.

Adam stared in appreciation as Cassie sailed down the staircase. He gave a whistle of appreciation at the vision before him. Cassie smiled brightly when she reached the bottom step.

"You look incredible," said Adam, catching her hand and twirling her around slowly. "I knew that gown was made for you." He kissed her cheek.

"Thank you, sir. You look very handsome tonight." She gave him the once-over, still smiling. Adam was wearing a black tuxedo with a matching bow tie and cummerbund. Underneath, he wore a white shirt. Black leather dress shoes encased his feet. They were still gazing at each other when Mama Rosa came into the room.

"You two look so lovely," she said, clapping her hands. "Go stand by the fireplace and wait for me. I need to get my camera."

They waited patiently for Mama Rosa to get her camera. After several shots, they were able to leave.

When Cassie and Adam walked into the banquet

hall, all heads turned their way. Everyone seemed surprised to see Adam.

"I must be seeing things," said Dr. Seabrink, the chief of staff, as he greeted them. "Dr. Hart, you decided to grace us with you presence tonight. And who is this vision on your arm?"

"I thought it was time to make an appearance, and this lovely woman is Cassandra Mancini," said Adam, shaking his hand.

"You look familiar. Have I seen you somewhere before?" Dr. Seabrink asked, taking Cassie's hand in his.

Cassie opened her mouth to speak, but no words came out as her eyes locked with those of her father. She turned accusing eyes to Adam.

"Dr. Seabrink, can you excuse us for a moment?" She pulled Adam out of earshot and whirled on him. "You knew my father would be here, didn't you?" she asked through gritted teeth. "Why didn't you at least warn me he would be here?"

"Yes, I knew he would be here," Adam said, catching her elbow and steering her away from the exit door. "If I had told you they would be here, would you have come? No, you wouldn't."

"You don't know that for sure," she snapped, jerking her elbow from his grasp. "Is there anything else I should know?" She spotted her uncle Jared and aunt Victoria. "Just great. I can't seem to go anywhere in this town without running into a member of the Randall clan."

"Don't look now, but your father is charging this way on his white horse. Daddy to the rescue. Pops does not look too pleased, either."

"I wonder why," she responded sarcastically and

turned, steeling herself for the confrontation she knew was about to take place.

"Cassie, you look beautiful," said Karen, eyeing her dress with appreciation and smiling. "Hello, Dr. Hart. Nice to see you again."

"Thank you. So do you," Cassie said to her step-mother. Karen was always picture-perfect. Tonight she wore a blue designer gown.

"Hello," said Adam, smiling back at Karen. "You are captivating as always, Mrs. Randall." His eyes moved to a silent Peter.

"Peter, doesn't Cassie look lovely?" asked Karen, slipping her hand in his. She shot him a warning look, which was not lost on Adam or Cassie.

"Yes, she looks very appetizing. You have great taste, Dr. Hart. This obviously is something Cassie would not have picked out for herself. Good thing she has you to dress her. Do you have a collection in your closet you choose from depending on the height and size of the woman?" asked Peter, glaring at him.

Cassie was mortified by her father's response. She knew he didn't approve of her relationship with Adam, but she hadn't expected this kind of reaction.

Adam's arm slid proprietarily around Cassie's waist, and he kissed her cheek. "How did you guess?"

Peter made a move toward Adam.

"Peter," said Jared, coming from out of nowhere. "Let's go outside for some fresh air. Dr. Hart, Cassie."

Cassie breathed a sigh of relief as she watched

them leave. She turned to face her stepmother and aunt.

"Come on, Cassie. Let's mingle," said Adam, kissing her cheek again and steering her away from Karen and Victoria.

"I guess your mission was accomplished," Cassie snapped as she took a champagne flute from the waiter. "You ruined my father's evening and put me at odds with him."

"Are we going to spar all night?" He leaned down, and his mouth touched hers lightly. "Have I told you how lovely you look tonight? Your eyes sparkle like diamonds when you are upset."

"Flattery will get you nowhere." She emptied her flute and placed it on a passing tray. Picking up another one, she took a sip.

"I wouldn't drink too much of that on an empty stomach." Without waiting for a reply, he took the flute out of her hand and placed it back on the tray. He picked up a bottle of water and handed it to her. "If you're that thirsty, try this. I'll be right back. Don't move a muscle." He kissed her cheek before leaving.

"We need to talk," said Peter, catching Cassie's arm and leading her out of the banquet hall. Once they were out of hearing range of the partygoers, he exploded. "Have you completely lost your mind? Adam Hart is poison. I'd be ashamed to be seen with him, too."

"Stop right there," said Cassie angrily. "Yes, I am seeing Adam. I am not ashamed of him or my relationship with him."

"I was stating facts. Ask him how many nurses he has gone through in the past two years. He's a user, Cassie. He's only after one thing. Once he gets that, he's gone on to the next innocent victim. You deserve better than him. If you were smart, you would run the other way. I don't want to see him break your heart."

"Dad, this is my life, and I will live it my way, not yours. If I choose to date Adam or Jack the Ripper, it's my choice. I happen to like Adam. If you don't, that's your problem."

"Cassandra, you are setting yourself up for a bad fall!"

Cassie had heard enough. She turned to walk away.

"We are not finished," said Peter.

"Yes, we are," she said quietly. "You can bad-mouth Adam, but it won't change the way I feel about him. I'm going back inside to find my date." Taking a deep breath, she went back inside. She scanned the room until she found Adam.

He was talking to Dr. Neeley when he saw her coming his way. Adam stared at her as she walked toward him. He held out his hand, and she took it. Pulling her to his side, he slipped his arm around her small waist.

"Dr. Neeley, have you met Cassandra Randall? She is such an asset to the ER team. She sure whipped us all into shape."

"No, but I've seen her around the hospital," replied Dr. Neeley. "It's nice to meet you, Cassandra. Now I can put a name with the face. This is my wife, Suzanne."

Cassie felt an instant dislike for the petite brunette. Maybe it had something to do with the indecent way she was leering at Adam.

"So you are a nurse?" said Suzanne, her voice sugary sweet. "How quaint. I suppose it is a great career plan if you want to snare a doctor. I guess it works."

Cassie bristled, and she felt Adam's arm tighten around her waist.

"Easy," he whispered for her ears only. "Excuse us." He whisked her away before she could open her mouth. Adam put his finger to her lips. "Just let it go. She's an empty-headed twit. Let it go, Cassie." He brought her hand to his lips. "Come on. Let's go find our table."

As they made their way through the banquet hall, Adam told her who the various people were. Some she recognized; others she didn't. He knew almost everyone. He told her that after dinner there would be a short presentation and then dancing.

Adam and Cassie found their table and sat down. Cassie almost spilled her water when she looked up to see her father glaring at her with disapproving eyes. She watched him pull a chair out for his wife and then take the seat across from her. Her discomfort became worse when her uncle Jared sat down next to her.

"Isn't this nice and cozy?" Peter asked, glaring at Adam. "I wonder who had a hand in these seating arrangements. You haven't attended one of these functions in years, and magically, tonight you are seated at my table."

"Just luck, I suppose. Peter, I'm touched that you think I have this much pull," Adam returned, smiling.

Cassie turned accusing eyes on Adam, and he just shrugged.

"Is there a problem with the seating?" Dr. Gray asked, watching the exchange between Peter and Adam curiously.

"No problem at all," Jared said quickly, looking from Peter to Adam. "Everything looks wonderful, doesn't it, guys?"

Neither man commented as they stared at each other.

The next hour was the most uncomfortable hour Cassie had ever spent. Jared, Karen, and Dr. Gray tried to keep the conversation going, while Peter's eyes shot daggers at Adam the entire time. Adam didn't pass up a chance to caress Cassie, and her father looked on with anger.

Cassie barely tasted her food. She was almost afraid to excuse herself from the table for fear there would be bloodshed in her absence. "Excuse me," she finally said, pushing away from the table. All the men came to their feet. "I'll be right back." She had to get some air.

Cassie took refuge in the bathroom and stared at her reflection in the mirror. She almost didn't recognize herself. After washing her hands, she retouched her lipstick and left the bathroom. She found Karen waiting for her in the foyer.

"How do we keep this evening from turning into an even bigger fiasco?" Cassie asked, sitting down next to Karen on the sofa.

"Leave your father to me. After the presentation, there will be dancing. I love to dance. Don't you?" She smiled. "Honey, you knew this wouldn't be easy. The animosity between your father and Adam was there long before you came back to town. Just give it some time. Miracles can happen if you believe. Come on. Let's go back inside."

The presentation was about the new wing the hospital was adding. All the new doctors at the hospital were all asked to stand. At the end of the presentation, they introduced all the hospital board members. Finally, the floor was turned over to the DJ. He opened up with a ballad.

Cassie watched couples file out to the dance floor. Adam stood and held out his hand to her. She caught it, and he led her to the dance floor.

"You outshine every woman in this room," he said in a seductive voice.

She shivered as his lips touched her temple. "I guess it would be foolish to ask if you are responsible for our seating arrangements," she stated, looking up at him.

"Ask me no questions. I'll tell you no lies." Leaning down, his lips touched hers, and he twirled her around the dance floor.

"You've definitely made it a memorable evening."

His arms tightened momentarily around her waist. "The night is still young, sunshine," he whispered as his lips touched the side of her neck.

Cassie shivered in anticipation of the promise his words implied.

After dancing to several faster tunes, they went back to their table. To Cassie's delight, Peter and Karen were nowhere in sight.

"Stay put. I'll be right back," Adam told her. He returned minutes later with a small plate of different desserts. "Try this one." He held a piece of fudge to her lips. Cassie took a small bite and closed her eyes. It was wonderful. The fudge melted in her mouth. "The look on your face could get you in trouble if you're not careful," he teased.

"It's delicious. Try it," she said, licking her lips.

Adam leaned over and his mouth touched hers. His tongue traced her lips. Cassie trembled with pleasure.

"You're right. It is delicious," he said.

Cassie took the rest of the fudge and fed it to him. After the last bite, he took her hand and licked the crumbs away. Cassie shivered at the erotic feel of his tongue on her palm.

"Let's get out of here," said Adam, pulling her to her feet.

Her heart was pounding madly as Adam helped her into his car. She nervously toyed with her hands as they lay in her lap. He turned on the radio and covered her fidgeting hands with his. Cassie was nervous beyond words. Trent was the only man she had ever been with. She was torn between telling Adam and keeping the secret.

When he pulled into the garage at his house, Cassie closed her eyes. She hesitated only briefly when he opened her car door and held out his hand to her. Placing her hand in his, she let him assist her. She quietly followed him into the house. He showed her into the living room.

"Make yourself comfortable, sweetheart. I'll be right back," Adam said before disappearing into the kitchen.

Relax. How can I relax? I'm terrified. Coming to her feet, she curiously studied the paintings on the walls.

"I bought this one in New Orleans," said Adam,

sipping a glass of wine. He held one out to her, and she took it.

She followed him down the hall, through double doors, and into the master bedroom. He took the still half-full wineglass out of her hand. She watched him place both wineglasses on the nightstand.

His head lowered, and their lips met. Cassie deepened the kiss by parting her lips. She pressed her body closer to his. Strong, sure hands molded her body to his. Cassie protested briefly when his mouth left hers, until warm lips moved down her neck to her bare shoulders. His mouth moved back up to cover hers in a hungry kiss. Returning his kiss, she pushed his jacket from his shoulders and let it slip to the floor. With nimble fingers, she removed his bow tie and cummerbund, then unbuttoned his shirt and pulled it from the waist of his tuxedo pants. The shirt joined his jacket on the floor.

He unzipped her gown and took a step back. He caught the top of her gown and slowly peeled it away from her body. Adam sucked in his breath when her bare breasts sprang free of the gown. His hungry eyes devoured her as he slid the clinging gown down her shapely body. Cassie moaned as warm hands glided upward and then covered her breasts. Her nipples hardened under his palms. His gaze shifted from her flushed face to the vision standing before him, clad only in a pair of black bikini briefs and a pair of sheer black panty hose. With deliberation, he took the pins out of her thick hair and watched it fall down her back and chest in a sandy brown cloud. Cassie unzipped his pants and pushed them past his hips to pool at his feet. The remainder of their clothing followed suit.

When their naked bodies touched for the first time, they both moaned in pleasure. Her nipples bore holes in his chest as Adam leaned her backward onto the black satin sheets. Her mouth eagerly met his as she held on to him for dear life.

"You are so beautiful," he whispered in a husky voice. "I have dreamed about this moment. Reality is even better than the dream." He rolled on his side so he could look at her body. One finger traced her nipple, and it grew taut. Slowly, his hand slid down her flat stomach to the apex of her thighs. Her legs parted eagerly for his caress.

The ringing telephone brought them out of their passionate state. They both froze, and it took them a minute to realize what the intrusive noise was. Adam's head dropped to her breast, and Cassie held her breath, hoping the phone would stop ringing. The machine picked up the call.

"Hi. You guessed it. I'm busy and can't take your call right now. I'll get back to you as soon as I can. Leave a message after the beep."

"Adam, it's Karen Randall. If you're there, please pick up. I really need to speak with Cassie."

A feeling of dread stole over Cassie as Adam reached over and picked up the telephone. He handed it to Cassie with a quick kiss.

"Karen, what's wrong?" Cassie asked, sitting up and pulling the sheet up to cover her breasts. "Is something wrong with TJ?"

"He's running a fever. I checked it about twenty minutes ago, and it was one hundred and two. I gave him something for the fever, and it isn't working. His temperature is now one hundred and three point five."

Cassie jumped out of bed and began pulling on her clothes. She quickly told Adam about TJ's fever.

"First, fill the bathtub with lukewarm water. Let him sit in the water until it cools. I'll be there as soon as I can," Cassie said. Adam zipped her gown and took the phone from her.

"Karen, what are all his symptoms?" he asked, pulling on his pants. He grabbed his shirt and put it on as well.

"Chills, fever, and a stomachache. He keeps saying his tummy hurts. Dr. Hart, he seems to be in a great deal of pain," replied Karen.

"Forget everything Cassie said. We will meet you at the emergency room in about fifteen minutes," Adam said.

Cassie's eyes met his briefly before he left the room. She had to run to catch him.

Once in the car, he dialed the emergency room to find out which doctors were covering the ER. He asked to be patched through to Dr. Reynolds. "Doug, it's Adam. Peter Randall is on his way there with his grandson. Have the OR prepped and ready for a possible appendectomy."

They beat Peter and Karen there by only a few minutes. Cassie was a nervous wreck while TJ was being examined. When it was confirmed it was his appendix, TJ was rushed in for surgery. Adam went in to observe, which left Cassie alone in the waiting room with Peter and Karen.

"He's going to be fine, Cassie," said Karen,

hugging her. "You have to be strong for your son. He's going to be okay."

"I can't lose him," Cassie cried, dropping down in a chair. "I can't. He's my little boy. He has to be okay."

Karen moved away, and Peter took the chair beside Cassie. He pulled his daughter into his arms and held her while she cried.

Cassie was on pins and needles while she waited. When Adam came through the door of the waiting room hours later, she shot out of her seat and into his arms.

"He's okay, sweetheart," assured Adam, holding her in his arms. He pulled back from her and framed her face in his hands. His mouth touched hers lightly. "They will come out and get you in a few minutes so you can see him. He's being moved to recovery."

The rest of the night was a blur for her. She got to see TJ briefly before he was admitted and taken upstairs to a private room. He slept through the night.

While sitting at TJ's bedside, Cassie fell asleep in Adam's arms. He refused to leave her side. Eventually they let out the foldout couch, and Adam phoned housekeeping and had them bring up pillows, sheets, and a blanket. He also had one of the nurses bring them both scrubs to change into.

Cassie was sound asleep when Adam eased himself from the bed at dawn. He checked on TJ and went down to the cafeteria for breakfast.

Cassie woke with a start when TJ called out to her. Her eyes flew to her son. He was watching her. She got out of bed and quickly went to him.

"Hi, sweetie. How are you feeling?" she asked, leaning over him and planting a kiss on his forehead.

"I hurt, Mommy. What's wrong?" His head moved, and he saw the IV attached to his small arm. "What's this?"

"Don't mess with it, sweetie. I know you hurt. If Mommy could take away your pain, I would in a heartbeat. The pain will go away soon. I promise."

"Adam just left. He told me not to wake you," said TJ.

Cassie smiled at his thoughtfulness.

"I hurt, Mommy."

"I know, sweetie. Try and relax." She pushed the button for the nurse. "My son needs pain meds. Can you bring him something?"

A few minutes later the door opened, and Cassie turned, expecting to see the nurse with something for TJ's pain. She smiled when Adam came in.

He carried a coffee and a bag. He handed her both. "I hope coffee and a bagel will do. It's strawberry, and there's also strawberry cream cheese."

"Sounds wonderful," said Cassie, taking the bag. "Thank you for staying with me last night and for breakfast."

"You're welcome. I looked over TJ's chart. He's doing great. He'll probably be released tomorrow."

As Adam predicted, TJ was released the following day.

A week later everything was back to normal. At least Cassie thought it was until Peter suggested she invite Adam to join them for dinner. She was shocked, suspicious, and very reluctant to invite Adam to dine with her father.

Monica convinced her to accept the peace offering Peter was extending. She and Shawn would come to the dinner to make the evening more bearable for Adam.

That evening Peter was surprised to see Monica and Shawn, but he didn't let on that he wasn't expecting them. Karen, of course, was glad to see them.

They had drinks in the den while waiting for the housekeeper to finish preparing dinner. Once dinner was served, they all went to the formal dining room.

"So, Adam, how are you and TJ getting along?" asked Karen, trying to ease the tension. "I hear the two of you are good friends."

"He's a terrific little boy. Today we spent the day together, just the two of us. We went to the zoo. We had a great time," Adam replied.

"TJ is crazy about Adam," said Cassie, squeezing his hand.

Smiling, he squeezed back and then brought her hand to his mouth for a kiss.

"That's great," said Monica. "I'm glad the two of you are getting along so well. I'm a little surprised. I didn't think you liked . . . ouch," said Monica, glaring at her husband.

They all knew what Monica was about to say. Again, silence fell around the table. Cassie smiled at Adam, and he returned the smile.

"Adam, tell me," said Peter, setting down his fork, "does Cassie remind you of Monica?"

"They are like night and day, but they are sisters."

Adam looked curiously at Peter. He didn't know where the conversation was headed, but he knew he wouldn't like it.

"Is that the attraction?" asked Peter coldly. "You couldn't have Monica, so you went after the next best thing?"

There was a simultaneous gasp from Cassie, Karen, and Monica. They all stared at Peter, aghast that he would say such a thing.

"What? I don't know what you are getting at, Peter, but you are way off base," said Adam angrily, throwing down his fork. Adam had to fight to control his emotions.

Cassie came slowly to her feet. Monica threw her napkin on the table and came to her feet as well.

"I can't believe you said that," seethed Cassie. "I knew you didn't like Adam, but I didn't realize how much until now. How can you be so cruel? If this is your idea of what fatherly love is about, count me out."

Shawn stood up. "As usual, thank you for an interesting evening, Peter. Don't expect a return engagement anytime soon," he stated. "Let's go, Monica, before I say something to your father I will live to regret." Without a backward glance, Shawn left the room.

"I can't believe you did this, Dad. You purposely hurt Cassie and Shawn in your vendetta against Adam," Monica charged. "Shawn is my husband, and if he chooses not to come back here, neither will I." Monica stalked from the room.

"I was trying to make a point," Peter said in his own defense, glaring at Adam. He got to his feet and faced Cassie.

"And you made it," said Cassie angrily. "You don't care who you hurt as long as you get your way. If I choose to date Adam or anyone else, it is none of your business. If I can't see him and live here, then maybe I should find someplace else to stay."

"He is nothing but trouble! He is only using you! One would think after the first loser you picked, you would be more cautious!" Peter shouted, glaring at Cassie and then at Adam.

Cassie flinched as if he had struck her. She could not believe he had thrown Trent up in her face, and especially in front of Adam.

"If I choose to be with Adam, it is my choice! Not yours!" Cassie shouted back. "I have had it with you! You can take your fatherly concern and shove it!"

"You may find this hard to believe, Peter, but I care about your daughter," said Adam, trying to keep his calm. He was determined he would not blow up at Peter. He was not going to make an already explosive situation worse.

"Spare me, Doctor. I know all about you and your caring reputation. Get out of my home, and don't come back," Peter thundered.

"Cassie, this is hopeless. For your sake, I tried, but I don't stay where I'm not welcome. Don't worry, Peter. I will not grace your door again. You've made your point. This is your home and I'll respect that, but if Cassie wants to see me at my house, you can't do a damn thing about it." Adam turned to Cassie, who was furious. She had had such high hopes for the evening. She had actually believed he and Peter could sit down to dinner without any fireworks. "Cassie, I'll call you later."

Silent tears slid down Cassie's cheeks as she watched Adam leave the room. She turned accusing eyes back to her father and then looked at Karen, who had been quiet during the whole fiasco.

Karen was staring blankly at her husband. Her thoughts were unreadable. She slowly got to her feet and left the room. Cassie had never seen her stepmother look so lost or hurt. Cassie followed her out of the room.

Chapter 8

It took Cassie only a few minutes to make a decision. She ran upstairs to tell Mama Rosa she was going out and she wasn't sure if she would be back before morning. Shoving a gown, a toothbrush, and other necessary essentials into an overnight bag, she left the house and drove to Adam's place.

Standing nervously outside of Adam's house, she sat her overnight bag down and rang the doorbell. She shifted from one foot to the other and chewed absently on her nails.

When the door opened, she almost forgot to breathe. Adam was standing there in a paisley print silk robe and matching pajama bottoms. His chest was bare, and dark hairs peeped out of the loosely tied robe. His eyebrows rose in question when she picked up her bag and stepped inside. Closing the door, he turned around to face her.

"What took you so long?" he asked. "I hope you are not here as an act of defiance or rebellion, but because you want to be with me."

"I want you, Adam. Make no mistake about it," said Cassie, setting down her bag and moving closer to him. "I don't care what my father or anyone has to say. I want to be with you."

Pulling his head down to hers, his mouth covered hers hungrily. Her purse and keys were forgotten as he swung her up in his arms and carried her upstairs to his bedroom. Setting her on her feet by the bed, he unbuttoned her blouse slowly. It fell, unheeded, to the floor.

"I've dreamed about this moment for months," Adam whispered against her neck. "I've seen you naked a thousand times in my dreams. I can't believe you're really here."

"I'm here. This is no dream, Doctor. I've wanted you from the first moment I saw you," confessed Cassie, pushing the robe from his shoulders and nibbling at his hard flesh.

His hands cupped her breasts tenderly, and her nipples hardened instantly. He unsnapped the black lace bra and let it drop to the floor. Cassie trembled when his tongue flicked her nipple. She moaned and trembled against him when he took her breast into his mouth and suckled it. Her hands pulled his head closer as he applied the same care to the other breast.

Raising his head, he gazed down into her passion-glazed eyes as he unzipped her skirt and slid it down her hips. Without breaking eye contact, she stepped out of it and kicked it aside. Next came her shoes, panty hose, and panties in rapid succession. She stood before him gloriously naked.

With shaky hands, she caught the drawstring of his pajamas and loosened it. With very little assistance they slipped to the floor, and he kicked them aside.

Cassie's breath caught in her throat as she stared at his naked body with hungry eyes. She had imagined him like this in her dreams. Her heartbeat accelerated at the sight of Adam standing before her in all his naked glory.

Her hands trembled as they touched his bare chest. Her eyes followed her hands as they moved down his chest to the flat, hard planes of his stomach. She followed the dark hairline down to his strong, muscular thighs. Tentatively, she caressed his proud, erect organ, and her caresses grew bolder at his moans of pleasure.

Kneeling down in front of him, she took him into her mouth. Adam surged against her and gasped aloud. Catching her arm, he gently pulled her back to her feet. Cassie stared at him in question and surprise.

"I am already about to explode," he confessed breathlessly. "I don't think I could take much more. I want you so much, Cass."

"Then take me," she whispered, boldly wrapping her arms around him and meeting his mouth in a hungry kiss.

Adam broke off the kiss and pulled open the nightstand drawer. She lay back on the bed and watched him put the condom on. When he pulled her back into his arms, she melted against him and her lips parted eagerly beneath his. His mouth left hers to nibble at her earlobe and neck. Moving downward, his tongue flicked over her nipple, causing it to harden instantly under his touch. Cassie moaned aloud when he took her breast into his mouth. She arched her body suggestively against him.

Wandering hands moved from her breasts down between her parted thighs. She surged against him as one finger slid inside her wet sheath. She bit her lip to keep from crying out as wave after wave of pleasure washed over her.

"Cass, love, I'm sorry, but I can't wait," said Adam, covering her body with his. He rested his forehead against hers.

"You don't have to," whispered Cassie, guiding him home.

Her breath left her when he slipped inside. She bent her knees to allow him a deeper penetration. Their bodies clung and then retreated in the age-old magic of love. They both cried out their passion as they soared together. Sated, they drifted back to the peaceful shore.

"Are you alive?" he asked, rolling on his side, pulling her with him. He kissed the top of her head as she snuggled against him.

"Hmm, barely," she purred, stretching and then resting her head on his chest. "Let's do it again."

"God, give me strength," he said and laughed, kissing her parted lips. "At least give me a few minutes to recover, and we most definitely will do it again and again and again. And while I'm waiting for my body to catch up to yours, I see no reason why I can't give you pleasure." He smiled wickedly as he slid down her body. His goatee tickled her stomach, and his tongue circled her navel and then darted inside.

At the first touch of his lips on the core of her being, Cassie's body quivered uncontrollably. His tongue circled and then thrust inside of her. She lurched and would have gone through the ceiling had he not been holding her. Tremors shook her body with each thrust. His mouth did all sorts of wonderful, crazy things to her body. She squirmed and whimpered under the tender assault of his tongue, until the world began to crumble around her. She caught his head between her hands and held on for dear life when she exploded into a million pieces.

Her body was still convulsing when she heard in the distance the ringing of a telephone. Seconds later he thrust into her welcoming body. She screamed out in pleasure and met him thrust for thrust. She was on fire, and only Adam could extinguish it.

He rolled over onto his back, pulling Cassie on top of him. She rode him until she was completely exhausted, and he took it from there. He lifted her and eased her back down until she thought she would die from sheer pleasure and exhaustion.

Adam suckled her tender breast in his mouth. His hand moved down to where their bodies were connected, and his fingers rubbed against her and played with her until her body caught fire again. Cassie threw her head back and closed her eyes at the sensations he was creating. Slowly, he began to move beneath her.

"Ooh! Don't stop. Don't ever stop," she whispered breathlessly as Adam picked up the pace. Cassie found her second wind—or was it her third?—as she moved with him. She smiled in satisfaction when Adam finally stiffened against her and then collapsed beneath her. His breathing was now shallow and loud. They were both soaking with perspiration and exhausted.

"You are incredible," he said in a breathless voice. "Reality is even better than the fantasy. I didn't know you had it in you, Cassie."

"It still is," she said and smiled coyly. She started to rise from the bed, but he stopped her.

Catching her face between his hands, he kissed her lightly. "Thank you," said the serious face below her.

She frowned at him with eyebrows raised in question.

"For showing me the difference between making love and just having sex. It's never been like this before," he explained.

Fifteen minutes later Cassie was almost finished with her shower when the shower door opened and Adam stepped inside. The cool air made her nipples stand up, and Adam smiled wickedly, closing the door behind him. Taking the soap from her slippery hands, he rubbed it between his hands to work up a lather. With sure hands, he spread the soapy film on her now throbbing breasts. Cassie arched toward him suggestively. His hands then wandered down between her legs, and Cassie closed her eyes in pleasure. He brought her to the peak and then stepped back, before sending her over the edge again.

Adam placed the soap in her trembling hands. She lathered the hair on his chest and worked her way down. Smiling, she felt him surge against her caressing fingers. Stepping back from her, he took the soap and placed it on the ledge. He carried her back to bed, and they made love again.

An hour later Adam lay there watching Cassie in his arms. God, she was beautiful and passionate. She was made for lovemaking. His hand covered her breasts, and she moaned softly but didn't open her eyes. Her hair covered the pillow like a sandy brown cloud. When his hand moved down her stomach, he had to stop himself from venturing farther. Removing his hand, he eased out of bed.

What am I doing? I'm acting like some lovesick teenager. Oh, God. I think I'm falling in love with her. I've never been in love before. Now what am I going to do?

Cassie woke to the heady aroma of bacon. She sat up in bed, pulling the sheet up to cover her nakedness. The door opened, and Adam strode into the room, carrying a tray of food. He was clad in a pair of red boxer shorts.

"Your breakfast, madam." He sat the tray across her lap. Leaning over, he planted a soft kiss on her lips.

She eyed him warily. "I didn't think you could cook," she said, adjusting the sheet around her.

He pulled the sheet down to expose her breasts. "Please don't cover the merchandise. I love looking at you. You earned breakfast, lunch, and dinner in bed, sweetheart. I'm quite the catch. I'm a good-looking, single doctor who can cook in bed and out." He winked at her. She returned his warm smile as he slipped into bed beside her. "Eat up. You're going to need your strength as you discover my other many hidden talents."

That night marked a turning point in their relationship. Adam changed right before her eyes. He began to include TJ more and more in their plans. Cassie was floored when he talked her into registering TJ for soccer. She was very reluctant until Adam agreed to help out by taking him to practices. Cassie was shocked when Adam signed on as the assistant coach of the soccer team and bought the uniforms for the team.

TJ was excited about playing and about Adam being one of the coaches. Shawn, Monica, Peter, and Karen all showed up for the first game. TJ's team, The Outlaws, had some really good players. Cassie didn't know until Adam told her that there were no scores or winners and losers at their age.

After the game Adam took them out to eat. Shawn and Monica joined them, while Peter and Karen declined the invitation.

Cassie and Adam decided to keep their relationship as private as they could.

Adam was strictly professional at the hospital. The laughing, smiling, carefree man from their time alone was gone. Back was the arrogant, pushy doctor who barked out instructions in the ER and watched everyone jump at his command.

"I guess he didn't get lucky last night," Zack joked one afternoon, slapping Roger playfully on the back.

Cassie winced at the untruth of his statement. *If you only knew how lucky, Zack!* she thought.

That same afternoon, when she returned from lunch, Adam handed her a piece of paper and walked away without saying a word. Puzzled, she watched his retreating back until he was out of sight. Cassie stared at the paper with a mixture of happiness and sadness. This was what she had been praying for months ago. She was being transferred as of tomorrow to the maternity ward.

Was this Adam's way of saying it was over? Was he pushing her away after finally getting her in bed? Cassie didn't know how to react. Doubts about their relationship set in.

On impulse, she called a florist and ordered a dozen white roses to be sent to Adam. The card simply read *Just because.*

Cassie was having lunch in the cafeteria when Rachel came in, smiling. She sat down across from Cassie and opened her carton of milk.

"Okay, Randall. What gives?" she asked, smiling. "What happened with you and Dr. Hart? Did you send the roses or not?"

"What roses?" Cassie responded coyly. "So how did Adam react when he got them?" she asked, bubbling over with laughter.

"I knew it. Let's just say his feet haven't touched the ground yet. He's been in a bad mood all day. He misses you. Speak of the devil and he appears. Don't look now, but your handsome prince is coming our way."

"Hi," they chorused, and then both laughed.

Cassie didn't have time to panic before Adam took the seat next to her. Her eyes met his and neither of them heard or saw Rachel leave the table.

"Thank you for the roses," he said and smiled. "It was a nice touch. No one has ever sent me flowers before."

"I'm glad," she responded. "Why didn't you tell me about the transfer?"

"Because I needed you to look surprised. Working together is not a good idea. It's better this way.

Now I can't be accused of giving you preferential treatment." His hand covered hers. "Did you think the transfer was my way of saying good-bye?"

Cassie flushed under his direct gaze. That was exactly what she thought. She knew Adam had commitment issues.

"Cassie, Dr. Hart," Roger said, smiling at them. "Is it safe to sit down? I'm not getting in the middle of a war zone, am I?"

After a brief hesitation, Adam waved for him to take a seat. They would get to finish their conversation later. The three of them ate lunch together.

That weekend, Adam invited Cassie and TJ to spend the entire weekend with him. Cassie was hesitant at first, but she wanted TJ to get used to Adam.

Adam and Cassie were lying back on the sofa, exhausted after the tiring day they had. They had gone to the new children's museum and then to the amusement park. TJ had fallen asleep right after his bath.

Adam's arms tightened around her when she tried to sit up. He dropped a kiss on her forehead. *I could get used to this,* she thought.

"Cassie, why don't you and TJ move in with me?" he asked out of the blue. "I want us to be together."

She stared at him, speechless. She had to be hearing things. Adam Hart had just asked her to move in with him. "You are kidding, right?" she asked, sitting up. Her eyes met his, and she saw the seriousness in his expression.

"No. I'm not kidding. I enjoy being with you.

When you are not here," he said softly, "I miss you. I would love for you and TJ to move in with me."

Smiling, she caressed his hair-roughened cheek. "That's the nicest thing you have ever said to me. Adam, if I had only myself to consider, I might jump at the chance, but I have more than me to think about. I have a small child to consider. It's not the message or the image I want to convey to him. I may have had a failed marriage, but I do believe in the sanctity of marriage. I know you are not ready to take that step, and neither am I. I enjoy being with you also, and TJ adores you."

"What about you, Cass? Do you adore me?" he teased. "Somehow I knew you would say no to cohabitation, but I had to give it the old college try. I've never asked anyone that before," he admitted, kissing her hand.

"I know." She smiled at him. "It's why I feel honored that you chose me. Thank you for asking me."

"First, you adore me, and now I honor you," said Adam suggestively, swinging her legs onto the sofa and easing her into a reclining position. "I adore you, too. I adore your eyes." He kissed each eyelid. "And your cheeks." His mouth touched each cheek in a light caress. "Your mouth is oh so kissable. Your lips are like soft petals." His tongue traced the outline of her lips. His mouth nibbled both earlobes before gliding down the column of her throat. "Then there's your beautiful body." His eyes moved over her body in a heated caress. "Are you ready to show your adoration yet?"

"Real smooth, Doc." Laughing, she pulled his head down to hers, and her lips parted under his eagerly. "I'd be happy to," she whispered, nibbling at his lower lip. Catching the bottom of his shirt, she pulled it up and over his head. She ran her fingers through the coarse hairs on his chest, and Adam moaned when she nipped one flat nipple. Her tongue circled first one and then the other. "How's this?"

"No! Don't hurt my mommy!" screamed TJ, running into the room. He stared from Cassie to Adam in confusion.

They came to a sitting position as TJ hurled himself at Adam. Adam held his struggling body firmly and sat him down on the sofa between himself and Cassie.

"TJ," said Cassie calmly, catching him by the arms. "It's all right, sweetheart." She pulled her trembling son into her arms and held him to her. Her mind flashed back to another time and place, and she paled at the memory. TJ must have thought Adam was hurting her. "Honey, I'm all right." It took her several minutes to finally calm him down. He glared accusingly up at Adam.

"You tried to hurt Mommy. I thought you liked us. You are just like him." TJ began to cry.

Cassie caught his small face between her hands and kissed away his tears. "No, honey, he's not. It's not what you think. Adam was not trying to hurt me. We were kissing. That's all."

"TJ, I would never hurt you or your mom," intoned Adam, holding out his hand to the frightened little boy. TJ looked up at Adam with questioning eyes.

"I swear. Scouts honor. We were only kissing. Sometimes when two adults like each other, they kiss," said Adam.

TJ looked at his mother for confirmation.

"That's right, honey. Adam and I are dating. We really like each other. Do you understand what I'm trying to say?"

"Adam is your boyfriend?" TJ said softly. He looked up at Cassie and then at Adam with big, wide brown eyes.

Cassie was speechless. Leave it to a four-year-old to make them both squirm with such an innocent question. She was hesitant to answer. She didn't really know how to answer his question. Was Adam her boyfriend?

"Yes," said Adam after a brief hesitation. "I'm your mom's boyfriend, and she's my girlfriend." He winked at Cassie.

TJ seemed satisfied with that answer. "Can I see you kiss Adam, Mom?"

Smiling, she looked up at Adam. He leaned over and brushed his lips across hers.

"You kiss him, Mommy."

Adam leaned down, and she kissed him lightly. A giggling TJ jumped onto Adam's lap and hugged him. Cassie and Adam joined in the infectious laughter, and Adam hugged them both.

"I love you, Adam," said TJ.

"I love you, too." He said the words to TJ, but his eyes never left Cassie's face. He wasn't ready to confess it out loud, but he knew he loved her. He loved both of them.

Cassie didn't need to say the words. Adam could see it in her eyes. She was in love with him.

On Sunday, as she stared in Adam's closet, Cassie realized there were so many variations of the color black. She forced Adam to go shopping. She told him that she was tired of dating Count Dracula and that it was time for him to put some color in his wardrobe. Adam protested all the way to the department store.

Cassie picked out several shirts for him in colors she liked: aqua, purple, sky blue, ocean blue, white, olive, and mauve. Adam drew the line at pink and quickly vetoed the shirt she held in front of him.

TJ sat quietly in the chair by the dressing room as Adam modeled the shirts for Cassie. When he started fidgeting, Adam called an end to the shopping trip. After they made their purchases, they took TJ to see a movie.

By Thursday night, Cassie was missing Adam. She paced back and forth in her room. She wanted to see Adam. She wanted to be with Adam. Adam had told her he was spending a quiet night at home.

Running downstairs to the hall closet, she grabbed her coat. Making sure no one was around, she ran back up the stairs and quietly closed her bedroom door behind her.

Cassie opened her bureau, took out a dark purple sheer lace teddy, matching stockings, and garters, and laid them on her bed. She took a quick shower and went back to her bed and sat down. She applied lotion and perfume to her body before slipping into the teddy and stockings. Brushing her hair back from her face, she added a touch of blush and lipstick. Giving her appearance one last look in the mirror, she pulled on her coat and belted it.

Knocking softly on Mama Rosa's door, she told her she was going out for a little while. Mama Rosa didn't bother to ask where she was going. She already knew the answer.

"Okay, guys, read 'em and weep," said Shawn, laying down a royal flush. "I win again. Show me the money," he bragged, raking in the chips.

"Guys, I think he's cheating," complained Adam, getting to his feet. "Anyone else want another beer while I'm up?"

"Ever know a lawyer that didn't cheat?" said Derek, Shawn's younger brother, taking a sip of his beer. He looked at his almost empty beer bottle. "I could use another one."

"I think we should search him," said Jeremy, backing away from the table and heading toward the bathroom.

They played several more hands, and Shawn won most of them. When the doorbell rang, nobody moved. They all stared at Shawn.

"Maybe if he gets up, it will break his run of luck," said Roger. "Let's take a vote. All hands for Shawn answering the door."

They all raised their hands.

"Fine," said Shawn, pushing his chair back. "I'll get the door, and then I'm going to kick you guys' butts."

Cassie was smiling when she rang the doorbell. *Come on, Adam, before I catch a chill.* She unbelted her coat and unbuttoned it. When she finally heard the door being unlocked, she opened her coat and let it slip from her shoulders.

To her horror, her brother-in-law opened the door. Cassie let out a squeal before she pulled the coat back on and belted it. Her face was bright red as Shawn stared at her in surprise. He tried unsuccessfully not to laugh.

Closing her eyes in embarrassment, she turned to run away. Shawn caught her arm and pulled her into the house. Lowering her head, Cassie refused to meet his eyes. She wasn't sure how she would be able to face him again.

"You are definitely Monica's sister," Shawn noted and laughed until he cried. "You both have such wonderful timing."

Cassie bristled and hid her face.

"Calm down. Monica pulled a similar stunt with me in Atlanta last year. She more or less had the same results as you did. You'll have to ask her about it some time. Stay put and I'll go get Adam for you."

So much for surprises. So much for spontaneity. I just flashed my brother-in-law. At least I gave him a good show.

She sat down on the sofa and chewed on her fingernail. Putting her head down on her knees, she closed her eyes.

"Cassie," said Adam, coming into the room. "What are you doing here? This is our poker night. There are five guys in the den, waiting for me to lose some more money to them."

"Making a fool out of myself," she responded, coming to her feet. "Did Shawn tell you what happened?"

"No," said Adam, pulling her into his arms. "He

said you were here. What's up?" he asked, kissing her soundly.

"Adam, who would you rather play with?" she asked, opening her coat. "Them or me? Take your time in answering."

Adam's eyes almost fell out when he saw what she was barely wearing. His eyes caressed every inch of her scantily clad body. The sheer purple teddy hugged every inch of her and left nothing to the imagination.

"Give me three minutes to get everybody out of here," he whispered against her mouth. "Wait for me upstairs, in the bedroom." His mouth devoured hers before he gently pushed her toward the staircase.

Smiling, Cassie walked up the stairs. She was halfway up when she dropped the coat on the stairway and continued on her way up. She heard Adam's moan and his whistle before she reached the top. Turning around to face him, she pushed both thin straps off her smooth shoulders but caught the front of the teddy before anything could be exposed. Blowing him a kiss, she disappeared inside his bedroom.

Adam felt his body react to the beautiful seductress on the stairway. *Poker be damned!* He rushed back into the den.

"Okay, that's it for tonight, guys. Everybody out," said Adam breathlessly, rushing everyone out of the room. "Something has come up that requires my immediate attention."

They all complained and grumbled as they left. Shawn was still laughing when he left. He told Adam that Cassie looked dynamite in purple.

It took Adam only a minute to figure out what had happened. Cassie had been expecting him to open the door and not Shawn. No wonder she was embarrassed.

Laughing, Adam took the stairs two at a time. She was definitely worth keeping around. At this point in time Adam couldn't imagine what his life would be like without her. He didn't want to imagine his life without her. She had come to mean too much to him.

Chapter 9

Adam was getting ready for his date with Cassie when the doorbell chimed. He looked down at the thin gold watch on his wrist. If it was Cassie, she was very early.

He opened the door and wished he hadn't. Peter Randall stared back at him. Opening the glass door, he stepped back to let Cassie's father enter the house.

"What are you doing here, Peter, or can I guess?" said Adam, moving toward the living room. "I would offer you a seat, but my guess is you won't be here that long."

"You're right," agreed Peter, following Adam. "It won't take that long. And yes, this is about Cassie. Let her go before this goes any further. She's getting too attached to you, and so is TJ."

"Getting attached to me," Adam repeated. "What does that mean? I care about Cassie and TJ."

"Then let them go," Peter insisted. "Cassie went through hell with that Mancini family. She deserves to be happy."

"She is happy," argued Adam. "She's happy with me."

"For how long? Until you get tired of her and find a replacement? If you care anything about Cassie and TJ, end it now, before she falls in love with you. She is looking for happily ever after and the white picket fence. What are you looking for? She wants marriage and a family. Is that even a possibility with you? TJ needs a father. Are you up for the job?"

Adam remained silent. Peter was asking a lot of tough questions he couldn't answer. He was stating the facts, which Adam was well aware of. The only problem with what Peter was saying was it was already too late. Adam believed Cassie was already in love with him. He was in love with her as well, but this was all so new to him. He hadn't even told Cassie how he felt. He couldn't bring himself to say the words *I love you* aloud.

Maybe Peter was right. Maybe Cassie and TJ did deserve better. Adam wasn't sure he was ready for love, marriage, and a family. TJ was a great kid, but was he ready to be a father? He wasn't even sure he was committed to being a boyfriend. He and Cassie were dating, exclusively, but he wasn't sure if he was ready to take the next step in their relationship.

"Get out," said Adam quietly.

"You know I'm right. You and Cassie are on a collision course with disaster. Do the right thing and let her go."

Cassie arrived at Adam's around 7:00 P.M. for their date. They were going to see a production of the Dallas Black Dance Theatre after dinner.

Using her key, she unlocked the door and went inside. She came up short when she found Adam lying on the sofa in the den, with his eyes closed. He was not even dressed for their date yet. Instead, he was wearing warm-up pants and a T-shirt.

"Adam, is something wrong?" asked Cassie, peering down at him.

His eyes flickered open, and he sat up. "I must have lost track of time," he said quietly. Rubbing the back of his neck, he came slowly to his feet. "What time is it, anyway?"

"Seven o'clock. If you're too tired, we don't have to go out. We can stay here instead. We could order a pizza and watch television. Or I could go out and rent a couple of movies."

"No," he said distractedly. "Cassie, there's something I have to tell you. I don't know how to say this, so I will just get to the point. I don't think we should see each other anymore." He went over to the bar. "I think it's for the best, before one of us gets serious, and we both know neither one of us is ready."

She watched him fix a drink and remain over by the bar. When his words finally sunk in, she stared at him in hurt confusion. Things had been going so well between them. So well, in fact, she had been afraid it wouldn't last. A week ago he had asked her to move in with him. Now he wanted to break up. She could sense there was more to his decision than he was letting on. The Adam she had gotten to know would not give her the brush-off, the way he was doing now. Not after the closeness they had shared. It had taken her months, but she had finally broken down all the walls he had built around him. She had gotten to know the real Adam Hart, and she had fallen in love with him.

"Fine," said Cassie. "Have it your way."

She walked out the front door, slamming it behind her. She was confused, and she was furious! *I am not going to let you push me away! Not now! We belong together. You just don't realize it yet!* Taking a deep breath and counting to ten, she opened the door and went back inside. There she found Adam sitting on the sofa in the den, with his head in his hands.

"Now, do you want to tell me the real reason you're pushing me away? I don't buy the garbage you just spouted at me, Adam. I know how happy you are with me. You care so much, it scares you to death."

Adam came to his feet, facing her. "There have been so many women. I barely remember names or faces. You could easily become one of them. You *are* one of them," he stated cruelly. "I can't do this anymore, Cassie. I can't be the man you want me to be. You deserve so much more than I can give you. I'm not ready for a relationship. I'm not a commitment kind of guy. I'm a liar and a cheat. I lied to you about everything. Shawn did not warn me to stay away from you. It was all a game to me."

Her heart fell as she stared at him. Gone was the man she had come to know and love. The monster she had first met had replaced him. The mask was off, and she was seeing him for who he truly was. "I don't believe you. You're lying."

"Am I? Can you be sure? Is that the kind of man you want? Don't you think you deserve more? You deserve all the love and happiness someone has to offer, but I'm not the one. I'm not ready to settle down, and I may never be ready to say 'I do.' The idea of marriage and family makes me break out in a cold sweat. I like being a bachelor. I like dating and sleeping with other women. This is not what I want. You are not what I want, and I am not what you need." He left the den and walked over to the door. Cassie followed him. Opening the door, he stared at her tearstained face. He reached out to touch her face but then let his hand drop to his side. "Good-bye, Cassie," said Adam, closing the door behind her.

In a fit of rage, Adam threw the liquor container he'd been holding at the closed door. He returned to the den. Dropping down on the sofa, he cried. He cried for the loss of Cassie and, for the first time, for the loss of his parents.

"I almost believed this was for real! I almost believed I could be happy or that I deserved to find happiness," he muttered.

Outside the door, Cassie fell to her knees and cried. She jumped when she heard something crash against the door from the inside. Cassie didn't know if she was crying for Adam or for herself.

After getting a grip on her emotions, she dialed Monica's number. Monica told her to come right over. Monica met Cassie at the front door. She took one look at her sister's tearstained face and pulled her into the house. Putting an arm around her shoulder, she led her over to the sofa.

"What's wrong?" asked Monica anxiously. "Did something happen with Adam? What did he do this time?"

"It's over," said Cassie, wiping at her tears. "He dumped me. I slept with him. He got what he wanted, and now it's bye-bye, Cassie, and on to the next unsuspecting victim." She lost control of her emotions and burst into tears in her sister's arms. Monica held her until the tears finally stopped.

"Honey, I don't know what's going on with Adam, but I know he loves you. I have never seen Adam as happy as he is with you. He truly adores you, and it scares the hell out of him. He's just running scared. Give him some time."

"I can't do it anymore. I'm done. We are done. Can I hang out here until everyone at home goes to bed? I know I look awful, and I don't want to have to tell Dad he was right, again. Maybe, I should let him pick my next boyfriend." She sniffed, wiping her eyes. "One more thing. Did Shawn warn Adam to stay away from me when I first came to town?"

"I'm sorry to say he did and so did I. Shawn knows Adam better than anyone, and he wanted to spare you any unnecessary heartache. I know he had no right to do it, but he wanted to protect both of you. He was furious with Adam for going back on his word and asking you out."

Shawn found Adam in his dark house, lying on the sofa in the den with a bottle of Bacardi 151 lying on his chest. Shawn turned on two lamps, and Adam squinted and then cursed as the bright light flooded the room.

"No need to ask what you're doing here," said Adam, opening the half-empty bottle and tilting it to his lips. Before he could take a sip, Shawn grabbed the bottle and screwed the top on it. "Give it back, Shawn. I need it right now. What I don't need is a lecture or speech from you."

"No, you don't. What you need is to have your head examined. What you don't need to hear me say is 'I told you so.' I knew this was going to happen. You get cold feet and you run for cover. You need her."

"Wrong," said Adam, coming slowly to his feet. "I don't need anyone. Remember? I'm the loner. I'm the guy most unlikely to fall in love and get married. I'm the guy parents warn their daughters about. I'm the guy who killed his parents," he said in an anguished voice. "I love her, Shawn. I bet you never thought you would hear those words come from my mouth. I love Cassie Randall with all my heart, but I am not worthy of her. She deserves so much more than I can give her. You said yourself I would only end up hurting her. You were right. Peter was right. Hell, everyone was right."

"You are the one who is wrong, my friend. You did not kill your parents, and you don't want to lose Cassie. You are just misguided. Both of you deserve some happiness, and I think if you let her go, it will be the biggest mistake of your life. She loves you, Adam. Despite everything you have said, done, and tried to do to dissuade her, she still loves you. Don't close the door on your relationship. Let yourself be happy."

"Cassie and I are finished. I am through trying to be someone I'm not. I'm not Mr. Happy Family Man who wants a wife, two children, and maybe a dog. That's your life, not mine. I like my life just the way it is. No strings. No commitments. No worries and no hassles."

"And no love," Shawn shot back. "I'm asking you for the last time to go get some help. You need counseling, Adam. You need professional help to deal with your parents' deaths. It's been a year now, and you are no closer to forgiving yourself than you were when it happened. Their deaths were an accident. You were not driving the car that hit them. You are not responsible. How many times do I have to tell you for you to believe it?"

"I will never believe it, because it was my fault. If I had not volunteered to work and had flown to St. Louis, the way I did every year, they would still be alive." Rubbing the moisture from his eyes, Adam paced the room like a caged animal. "You know, I don't even remember ever telling my father I loved him. I don't even remember the last time I told my mother I loved her. I never even got a chance to say good-bye to them."

"Then fly up to St. Louis and say good-bye. Go to the cemetery and say good-bye. Tell them you love them, and then let it go once and for all. They knew you loved them. They loved you, Adam. They were so proud of you. Proud of what you had become. Your father referred to you as his son, the doctor. I know the two of you didn't get along well, but he loved you. They both did. Your parents would not want you to spend the rest of your life blaming yourself for something you had no control over. They would want you to forgive yourself and get on with your life, and they would have loved Cassie. She's perfect for you. She brings out the best in you."

"I know you don't agree with what I'm doing, but I think it's for the best. I don't want to hurt her any more than I already have."

"Whose best, Adam? Not yours and certainly not Cassie's. You have taken too many steps forward to move backward now. Don't let it end like this. Tell her you love her."

"It's too late," said Adam sadly. "There's no going back for us."

Cassie decided to move out of her father's house and find an apartment. Monica was quick to offer her old house as an alternative place to stay. Monica's former home in Garland was on the market, with no takers.

They came to an agreement on rent, and Cassie jumped at the chance to have her own place. Peter was upset at first but quickly got used to the idea, and finally they made peace. He and Karen helped Cassie, TJ, and Mama Rosa get moved in. Karen helped her wallpaper TJ's room and the kitchen.

When they finished, Cassie was pleased with the end results. It felt like home. TJ loved his room and the house and wanted to know if they could live there forever.

Fixing up the house took up all of Cassie's spare time, so she didn't have a whole lot of time to dwell on Adam. She spent as much time as possible with her son and her family.

Two weeks after moving into the house, Cassie went to dinner at Shawn and Monica's. Dinner at the Bennetts' consisted of take-out Chinese and whatever dessert Monica had a craving for. This turned out to be peach cobbler à la mode.

Cassie had no idea her sister and brother-in-law were trying to play matchmaker, and so she was surprised that Adam was there when she arrived. Cassie was ready to turn and leave, but Monica talked her into staying.

For most of the evening, they played Trivial Pursuit and then Pictionary. Adam and Cassie won both games.

"And the reigning champions once again," said Adam in his best announcer voice, "are Adam and Cassie." Laughing, he held up his hand, and Cassie gave him a high five.

"That's what I get for playing with my husband," Monica quipped, struggling to get to her feet. Standing up, Shawn held out his arm for her, and she pulled herself up. She winced and then doubled over in pain. "Gee. I swear this little girl is going to be one heck of a soccer player. I'll be right back."

They all laughed. This was the fourth time in the past half hour she had to go to the bathroom. Cassie smiled as her sister waddled out of the room. She remembered those days only too well.

Monica's scream sent them all running to the bedroom. They found her doubled over leaning against the bed.

"I'm right here, sweetheart," Shawn reassured, kneeling down beside her. "Adam, what's wrong with her?"

"Put her on the bed so I can examine her," ordered Adam, unbuttoning his sleeves and pushing them up to his elbows.

Cassie pulled back the comforter. Just as Shawn was about to lay Monica on the bed, her water broke. Cassie rushed into the bathroom to get towels. She laid them on the bed, and Shawn put Monica on top of them.

Shawn and Cassie stood quietly by while Adam did the examination. When he finished, Cassie's eyes flew to his stern face. Something was wrong, and they all sensed it.

"Adam, what's wrong?" cried Monica. "Something is wrong with my baby. Tell me what's wrong."

"The baby is in a breach position. We don't have time to wait for an ambulance, since your water broke," Adam explained. "Shawn, put Monica in your car, and Cassie and I will follow you to the hospital."

From his car phone, Adam called to alert the ER team they were on their way. He then gave the phone to Cassie. She called Peter and Karen to let them know what was happening.

When they arrived at the hospital, Cassie and Adam jumped out of his car and ran inside.

"I'm going in the delivery room to assist," said Adam, heading for the scrub room. "Are you coming?"

"Yes," said Cassie breathlessly, running to keep up with him. She almost bypassed Peter and the rest of the gang in the lobby. "I'm going into the operating room with Monica. I'll let you know something as soon as I can."

Ten minutes later, amid tears of joy, Hope Rene Bennett was born. She weighed in at eight pounds and two ounces and was twenty inches in length. Dark, straight hair covered her tiny head.

Cassie's and Adam's eyes met briefly as they stared at the tiny miracle in Shawn's arms.

Touching her baby's hand, Monica looked straight at Adam. "See what you are missing out on, Adam? You and Cassie could have everything Shawn and I have if you would give yourself a chance."

Cassie's tearful eyes met Adam's. Then without a backward glance, she walked out of the operating room.

Adam left the operating room shortly after Cassie. Monica's words were echoing in his head. He went down to his office and sat down at his desk.

How I wish I could have those things! I'm sorry, Cassie, but I can't change who I am and what I am. You have to forget me.

Leaning back in the chair, he closed his eyes and tried not to think about a future without Cassie. He didn't want to imagine how lonely he would be in the years to come or how he would regret not having children. Deep in his heart, he wanted kids, three, maybe four, but he knew it was only a dream for him. He would never have any. If he couldn't have Cassie, then he never wanted to marry.

I do love you, Cassie. Please, God, help me to do the right thing for once. I don't want to hurt her anymore or to hurt TJ. I have to let you both go for all our sakes.

Slipping away from the crowd in the recovery room, Cassie took the elevator down to Adam's office. Quietly she opened the door and went inside. What she found stopped her cold.

Adam was leaning back in his chair with his eyes closed. Silent tears ran down his copper cheeks. Hesitating only for a moment, Cassie went to him. She kneeled down beside his chair.

"Adam," she said softly as her hand touched his leg.

His eyes popped open, and he jumped to his feet, knocking his chair to the floor in the process. He gave her an accusatory glare before backing away from her. Turning his back on her, he walked over to the window and looked out. "What are you doing here?" he asked in a strained voice. Embarrassed, he quickly wiped the moisture from his eyes.

"I came to make sure you were all right." She took a step toward him and then stopped. "I saw the look on your face when you looked at Hope. I saw the longing, Adam. I know somewhere deep inside you, you want to feel what Shawn was feeling in there. You want a family, but you are too afraid to admit it. I saw it in your eyes when you looked at me. We could have what they have, Adam. You need me, and worst of all, you love me. I know it, and you know it. Loving me scares you!"

Adam stared at her, and his gaze softened. "Disappointing you scares me more. I do love you," he admitted softly.

Cassie's heart soared, and tears of joy came to her eyes. This was the first time he had actually said the words. His next words drove a knife straight into her heart.

"I love you more than I have ever loved anyone in my life, but it changes nothing. I don't know the first thing about relationships, love, or commitment. Just talking about it makes me weak in the knees. I am not the father figure you want for TJ, I am not ready to get married, and I am not ready to be a father. Cassie, I don't know if I will ever be ready for those things. More importantly, I don't know if I want those things. Those are the things you want. I like my life the way it is. I don't want the responsibility of a wife and a family. I don't want to depend on anyone, and I don't want anyone dependent on me. I like being alone."

"You want all those things and more. You are just too much of a coward to reach out and take them. I feel sorry for you, Adam. You are an emotional cripple. I have to admit you are right about one thing. I don't need you in my life. I need someone I can count on. And yes, someone I can depend on."

"Don't feel sorry for me. Be glad I am man enough to know my limitations and shortcomings. Be glad I am honest enough to know I am not what you need. Be thankful I do love you enough to walk away. One day you will thank me for this, Cassie. You will look back on this day and say 'Thank you, Adam, for sparing me all the heartache you could have cost me and my son.'"

"Maybe you're right," said Cassie, totally exhausted and frustrated beyond words. "Maybe it is time to get off this roller-coaster romance we have. It's time I stopped thinking about what I want and think about what my son needs. He needs stability. I need stability, and we both know you are anything but stable. I am through beating my head against a brick wall. You win, Adam, and you lose. You lose because you will never let yourself know what it feels like to be loved and to be happy. Good-bye, Adam. Have a nice life." Giving him one last look, she walked out the door.

* * *

The following weekend Peter and Karen looked after TJ. They wanted Cassie to go out and mingle, but she had her own plans.

I can't give up on you, Adam! Not without a fight! We belong together! I just need to convince you of that fact!

Cassie stared at her reflection in the floor-length mirror. She pushed her long sandy brown hair over her shoulder. She looked like a goddess in the deep blue thigh-high nightgown. It clung to every curve of her body like a second skin. On impulse, she grabbed the hairbrush and brushed her hair back. Picking up a hair clip, she pinned her hair on top of her head. Slipping on a short, matching blue paisley robe, she tied the sash at her waist. She dabbed her favorite perfume behind her ears, between her breasts, and along her collarbone.

Cassie had never seduced a man in her life, but tonight she was willing to try anything to make Adam realize that they belonged together. She couldn't let him walk out of her life without a fight. So what if just this once she didn't fight fair. She was going to meet him on his level. She pulled back the sheets on her bed. After dabbing the sheets with perfume, she turned down the lamp and left the room.

She went downstairs to wait for Adam. She was pacing the floor nervously, chewing on her fingernails, when the doorbell rang. Taking a deep, steadying breath, she opened the door.

Adam stared at her in shocked disbelief. His eyes roamed over her figure appreciatively before coming back up to rest on her flushed face.

Cassie was the perfect seductress standing there in her shimmering short blue robe and her bare feet, her toenails painted red. "Hi. Come in," said Cassie nervously, stepping back to allow him to enter. Her heartbeat quickened at the heated look in his piercing brown eyes. "Have a seat," she suggested softly, following him into the living room. She followed his footsteps in determination.

Wetting her dry lips, she looked up at him and moved in for the kill. Taking the clip out of her hair, she gave it a shake and it tumbled over her shoulders. With trembling hands, she untied the robe and let it fall from her shoulders.

She watched the expression in Adam's eyes go from surprise to understanding, darkening with passion. His eyes slid suggestively down her scantily clad body in a scorching caress.

Closing his eyes, he walked over to the sofa and sat down. He knew he should leave, but he couldn't. Curiosity made him stay. He couldn't wait to see what her next move would be. "Cassie, don't do this," he begged in a weak voice. His eyes continued to caress her body. "I can't fight you this way."

"Then don't fight me," she whispered. "Let me show you how much I love you. Give in to your feelings." Following him, she kneeled down on the sofa beside him and put her arms around his neck. Her lips brushed his lightly at first. She deepened the kiss and pulled back when he responded to her.

Adam knew he was fighting a losing battle. He also knew he should have left when he had the chance. It was too late now. He couldn't walk away from her. Nor could he deny his feelings for her.

"Cass," he whispered in a breathless voice. He caught her head between his hands and stared intently into her passion-glazed eyes. He saw all the love and hope he didn't want to see staring back at him.

Pushing him gently back against the sofa cushion, she covered his body with hers. True enough, she felt the evidence of his mounting desire pressing into her stomach. Her mouth covered his hungrily, and the fight was over. She had won. Correction, they both had won.

Swinging her up into strong, capable arms, he carried her into the dimly lit bedroom. They shed their clothes in record time. Cassie pushed Adam onto the bed, on his back. Her quivering body slid over his as her hot mouth and hands caressed him lovingly. Her mouth left a fiery path the entire length of his body. Her mouth and hands brought him to the brink several times, but she would back off before he reached total fulfillment. He was powerless and helpless under her tender assault of his body. He trembled beneath her with need.

When he reached for the condom he had placed on the nightstand, Cassie took it out of his hand and put it on for him. Bare flesh against flesh, he rolled over on top of her and slid smoothly into her hot, moist sheath. She welcomed him and bit her lip to keep from screaming out at the sheer pleasure of his deep, penetrating thrust. She met him wildly, thrust for thrust, until they both collapsed on the bed in a trembling heap.

Tired and spent, Cassie closed her eyes and held Adam close to her. When she opened them, he was staring down at her with a weird look on his face.

Withdrawing from her, he got slowly to his feet. Picking up his clothes, he glared down at her. He was trembling with rage. Adam had been beaten at his own game, and he didn't like it. He was angrier with himself than with her. He should have left when he knew which way the wind was blowing.

Cassie felt a chill go down her spine at the way he was watching her. For some reason, her plan had backfired. She might have seduced him into her bed, but now he despised her for it.

"It's over, Cassie. I don't want to see you anymore! It was great sex, but that's all it was! Let me go. I'm not worth what you are putting yourself through. It's time to say good-bye."

As tears spilled down her cheeks, Cassie shoved him away from her and jumped up from the bed. Running into the bathroom, she slammed the door shut behind her. She opened the shower door and stepped inside. Turning on the tap, she stood under the running water.

Cassie had given it her best shot, and it had blown up in her face. Adam would never know what seducing him had cost her emotionally. She had never been the dominant one before in bed. Even after years of marriage to Trent, she had never really felt totally comfortable with him in bed. Cassie had always waited for him to make the first move. His rejection had shot her self-confidence to hell.

Cassie cried herself to sleep that night, but the next day she pasted on a smile when she went to pick up her son. She zoomed in and out of her parents' house before they could quiz her about how she had spent her night.

Chapter 10

She took TJ for a picnic in the park. She was at a loss when TJ asked her to call Adam to join them. Cassie reminded him, she and Adam were no longer dating.

The next morning Cassie and Karen were putting the finishing touches on the decorations for TJ's birthday party. When Cassie went back inside to get the other spool of tape, she heard the doorbell ring. She wrapped the balloons around her wrist and went to answer the door. It was probably Peter with the cake. It was too early for any of the guests to arrive.

Not bothering to look, she opened the door. She stared in surprise at Adam. He was dressed casually in black walking shorts, a black T-shirt, and sandals.

"Adam, what are you doing here?" Cassie asked, pushing a lock of hair behind her ear. She folded her hands together in front of her.

He held up the package he was holding, and she stepped back to let him enter. He stared down at her in appreciation. She was wearing a red two-piece short set and sandals.

Adam entered the house, looking around at the party decorations. He made his way to the living room, leaned over, and set the box down on the coffee table.

"It's a birthday present for TJ. I wanted to drop it by before the party started. I won't keep you from getting things ready. Tell TJ I said happy birthday."

"Why don't you tell him yourself?" Karen suggested, coming into the room. "He's been asking about you. I think he'd like to see you. Why don't you stay at least until he gets here? Then, if you want, you can leave before everyone else arrives."

"I don't think it's a good idea. I don't want to make anyone uncomfortable," he hedged, looking at Cassie.

"Adam, if you don't want to stay, then leave, but don't let the door hit you on your way out," seethed Cassie, stalking out of the room.

She was trying unsuccessfully to tape the HAPPY BIRTHDAY sign to the wooden fence when a slight breeze blew the sign down for the third time. The breeze also carried with it the fragrance of familiar cologne.

"Need some help?" asked an amused voice behind her.

She refused to acknowledge him. Grabbing the sign, she tried for the fourth time to tape it down, but to no avail. She slapped it against his chest, turned on her sandals, and marched into the house. She returned minutes later with a box of thumbtacks. Placing the box in Adam's open palm, she stood back and watched him tack the sign to the fence.

"That's what I call teamwork," Adam declared.

Cassie faced him squarely with her hands on her hips. Biting back a retort, she left him standing by the fence.

Later that day there were a few tense moments between Adam and Peter at first, but they kept their distance from each other. Cassie was surprised that Peter didn't even ask what Adam was doing there. He simply ignored him.

"Adam! Adam!" TJ squealed, running to his favorite person.

Smiling, Adam kneeled down and swung him up in his arms. TJ gave him a big hug, which Adam returned wholeheartedly.

"You came. I knew he would, Mom," said TJ excitedly, looking from Cassie to Adam. "Are you two friends again?"

Cassie and Adam both looked embarrassed and at a loss for words. Neither knew how to answer his question.

"I'd love to stay," Adam said, looking at Cassie, "if it's all right with your mom."

Cassie nodded her consent. "TJ, go on up and get changed. Adam will be here when you get back. You wouldn't want to miss your own party."

Silence reigned supreme in the room as Cassie, Peter, and Adam watched TJ leave with Karen. When the doorbell rang, Cassie was happy for the distraction, and she went to answer it.

"Monica, hi. Come in," said Cassie, hugging her sister. "I need your help to keep Peter and Adam as far away from each other as possible."

"Adam is here?" Monica asked in surprise. "How did he even know about the party?" She paused. "Shawn must have told him." Monica followed Cassie into the living room. "Hello, Adam. Are you lost? Looking for directions? I'd be happy to give you some." She smiled sweetly.

"Charming as ever, aren't you?" Adam stated sarcastically, walking away. He was not going to let Monica or any other member of the Randall clan get under his skin today. He'd stay a while longer and then leave.

Cassie's gaze followed Adam out to the patio. "Monica, it's okay," said Cassie, smiling sadly at her sister. "I am not going to let anything ruin this party. TJ wants him to stay."

A short while later, Cassie grabbed Shawn as he passed by and had him point the camera in Adam and TJ's direction. Adam threw back his head and laughed at something TJ said, and then he hugged him. At the moment she envied her child. She remembered when Adam used to laugh with her and hold her.

"I can't get over the change in Adam," Karen said, watching Cassie watch TJ and Adam. "He's like a completely different person. You know, I can almost imagine him bouncing a baby on his knee."

"I can't imagine him bouncing anything on his knee weighing less than one hundred pounds," said Monica sarcastically.

Cassie made no comment. She knew Karen was right. Adam had changed. He was now a caring and giving man. It had happened so gradually she'd barely noticed it. She watched Adam and TJ play with the game Adam had bought for him.

"Cassie. We have to talk," Peter said urgently, ushering her into the house. "We have a major problem."

"Dad, if this is another 'Adam Hart is scum' lecture, save it. I've heard it all before. I don't need a refresher course. I don't agree with you, but this isn't my fight anymore. Adam and I are not dating. He's here because TJ wants him to be here. Your wife asked him to stay for the party."

"I'm glad to hear it, but this is not about Adam. We have more pressing problems than him. The Mancinis just left the house about five minutes ago."

Cassie sat down slowly. She knew this moment was inevitable once Trent received the official court documents informing him of her whereabouts.

"Do they know where I live?" she asked, fighting a losing battle with her emotions.

"No. Mrs. Whitaker told them you were out of town for the weekend. She said Trent's father did all the talking. She also said they were both furious when they left. So what are you going to do now? I think you and TJ should move back into the house for a few days."

"No, it's time for me to stop running. I have to face Trent." She closed her eyes. "TJ has been so happy since moving here. Trent is going to destroy that." Cassie came slowly to her feet. "Can you keep the party going for me? I need to go upstairs for a few minutes. I don't want TJ to see me upset. I'll be down in a few minutes."

"Do you want me to send Karen or Monica up?"

She shook her head. She just needed a few minutes

alone. She hugged her father and then went up the stairs to her bedroom. She dropped down on the bed and lay across it.

She wasn't sure how long she was in that position when a knock on the door startled her. Wiping at her tearstained eyes with the back of her hands, she rolled over on the bed to see who was at the door.

When Cassie saw the unwelcome visitor, she rolled onto her stomach and faced the wall. Adam came around the bed and kneeled down in front of her.

"What's wrong?" he asked.

Cassie ignored him and continued to stare at the wall.

"Cassie, talk to me," said Adam, touching her hand.

She jerked away from his hand as if fire had touched her skin and then turned her head away from him. She was not in the right frame of mind to deal with him right now. TJ was her first priority.

She stared at him, not saying a word. She was so tempted to pour out her heart to him and tell him everything, but she resisted the urge. What good would it do now? All she wanted him to do was take her in his arms and tell her everything would be all right, but she knew it was never going to happen. Everything was not all right. At the present time nothing was right in her life. She didn't want his concern or his pity. She couldn't deal with both Adam and Trent. She just wanted him to leave her alone with her misery.

Finally she spoke. "You are my problem. You come here and play with my son like nothing has happened, and all I can do is watch. You have made it perfectly clear to me that whatever it was we had is over and you don't want me in your life. I've accepted that. I'm trying to get on with my life. Let me. We're not friends, Adam. We never were. I don't confide my problems to you or lean on you to fight my battles for me. Just go!"

He stared down into her misty eyes with a hurt look on his handsome face. "Fine. Consider me gone." Slowly, he got to his feet and left the room.

Cassie stood and went into the bathroom. She felt bad about the things she had said to him, but she was in pain, too. She was in love with a man who didn't want to be in her life, but he refused to stay out of it. She washed her face with cold water and then went downstairs to rejoin the party.

The party broke up about five o'clock. Cassie and Mama Rosa cleaned up the party remains in record time and then headed home. They had a light dinner, and TJ went to bed without any prompting. He was so exhausted, he fell asleep immediately.

Cassie and Mama Rosa were watching a movie when Cassie's mind began to drift. She couldn't forget the look of pain on Adam's face at her cruel words earlier. She knew it was wrong of her to lash out at him because she was angry at Trent, and she regretted hurting him.

An hour later Cassie stood outside Adam's front door, chewing on her fingernails. Nervously, she knocked on the door. When the door swung open, she wiped her hands on her walking shorts. Adam stared at her in surprise.

"I know I should have called first, but I wanted to apologize to you for what I said earlier. Can I come in?" Cassie asked, pushing her way inside.

She came up short when she saw a woman in a bathrobe reclining on the sofa. The lady in question came to her feet, smiling. She was a few inches taller than Cassie, dark skinned, thin, and very attractive.

Cassie's heart constricted as she stared at Adam and then at the woman. She felt stupid for coming over to apologize when obviously nothing could hurt him. *He probably called her up on the way home from the party. What am I thinking? He more than likely had a date already lined up.*

She was backing out the open front door when Adam caught her arm to stop her. Her eyes couldn't meet his. She didn't want him to see the pain in her eyes.

"I'm sorry for barging in. I didn't realize you had company. Good night," she said in a strained voice. She had to get out of there before she turned into a blubbering idiot and really embarrassed herself. She tried to pull out of Adam's grasp, but he refused to let go of her. She jerked her arm from his grasp. "I hope the two of you have a wonderful night," Cassie said, slamming the door shut behind her.

Adam sat down on the sofa and stared at the closed door in silence. The woman sat down next to him, saying nothing. Catching his hand, she gave it a squeeze and then laid her head on his shoulder. His arms went around her in silent communication.

"It's obvious she's in love with you. Why didn't you

tell her who I am? You know what she's thinking about us," said the woman.

"It doesn't matter," Adam sighed sadly. "It's better this way. I'd much rather lose her now than later. Cassie is out of my life."

"But not out of your heart," the woman ventured, hugging him. "I think you're making a mistake, big brother."

"Gloria, I don't deserve her. She's too good for me. I've done so many things wrong and hurt so many women," said Adam, closing his eyes.

"And you recognize it. You deserve all the love and happiness this world has to offer. Cassie is the woman your parents would have wanted for you. I want her for you. Adam, don't let the best thing in your life slip away without a fight."

Cassie was looking over a chart at the nurses' station, when Rachel nudged her. She looked up and then stared in stunned silence as Trent walked toward them. Cassie wrote *ex-husband* on a piece of paper and slid it over to Rachel. She watched Rachel's mouth drop open in surprise.

Unwilling to let him make a scene in front of everyone, she told Rachel to show him to the break room and went there to wait for him. She rubbed at the chill bumps forming on her arms and paced back and forth. When the door opened, she braced herself and took a deep breath. She knew this would not be a pleasant confrontation, but it was inevitable.

"You made a fool out of me. You knew what I was coming over to ask you. How dare you take my son and disappear?" he shouted, kicking the door shut behind him. His dark hair was disheveled, and his face was mottled with rage.

"Trent, lower your voice. This is a hospital," she hissed back. "No. You made a fool out of yourself by telling the press that you and I were getting back together. Being married to you twice was enough for me. As for our son, I have every right to take my son anywhere I choose. You keep forgetting I have complete custody of him. I did exactly what I was supposed to do. I let the court know I was leaving. It's not my fault they apparently lost the paperwork."

"I'll just bet they lost it. You had a moral responsibility to let me know you were leaving with my child."

"You have the nerve to talk to me about morals. You! The man who had numerous affairs while we were married and had pictures taken of his indiscretions. Pictures were not enough for you, but you had to video your little sexcapades as well. How sick is that? You dare preach to me about my moral responsibility?"

"I love you, Cassie. I have always loved you. I want us to try again. We are a family. I want my family back."

"What you want is to win that election, but you will have to do it on your own merit, not because you are playing respectable husband and father."

"You are coming with me right now," Trent said, grabbing her arm. "You and my son are flying back to New York with me today. Father is waiting for us at the hotel."

"Take your hands off me," Cassie hissed, jerking

away from his grip. "I am not going anywhere with you, and your father can go straight to hell as far as I'm concerned. If you don't leave, I will call security and have you thrown out," she stormed, picking up the phone. Trent grabbed the phone and hung it up. He caught her arm to keep her from moving away from him. "I am not crazy enough to marry you a third time," seethed Cassie, jerking away.

Trent pulled her struggling body into his arms. "You and TJ are coming home with me if I have to tie you up and gag you. I am through playing games with you. You are not going to cost me this election. You are my wife, and you are coming with me! I love you, Cassie. I will always love you!"

"I don't love you, Trent. You are crazy if you think I would go anywhere with you. Take your hands off me." Cassie tried to squirm out of his painful grasp.

Adam was making rounds when he received an overhead stat page. He picked up the phone in a patient's room and called the front desk.

"Dr. Hart, it's Rachel. I think you should get down to the maternity ward right away. Cassie and her ex-husband are in the break room, having a shouting match."

"I'm on my way," said Adam, slamming down the phone and running out the door. The little he did know about Trent Mancini he didn't like.

He heard the raised voices the minute he rounded the corner of the nurses' station. Rachel was standing by the break-room door.

"I haven't called security yet," she informed Adam. "But he is starting to scare me. Should I go ahead and call them?"

"No. I'll handle it," said Adam, walking past her. "Just keep everyone out until he's gone."

When Adam pushed the door to the break room open, he could see the anger in Cassie's eyes as she struggled in the man's grasp. "You have about five seconds to get your hands off of her," he said, his voice deadly calm, from the doorway.

Cassie sighed in relief and then visibly relaxed against Trent when she heard the familiar voice. Slowly, Trent released her, and they both turned to face a furious Adam.

"This is none of your business, mister. This is between me and my wife," said Trent, glaring at Adam.

"Ex-wife, "Adam corrected, moving farther into the room. "Are you okay?" he asked, looking at Cassie.

She nodded and rubbed her sore, bruised wrists.

"Either you leave quietly, or I will call security and have you thrown out," Adam growled.

"Oh, I see. She's gone black now. That's a big change for you, Cassie. So tell me, is it true what they say about black men?" Trent sneered, glaring at Cassie and then at Adam.

In the blink of an eye, Adam had him pinned to the wall by his lapels. Trent tried to shove Adam, but he didn't budge. "Stay away from Cassie. Don't call her or come near her again, or you will have to deal with me."

Trent tried again to loosen Adam's grip. "You are making a big mistake, Dr. Hart," said Trent, reading the name badge. "You obviously have no idea who you are dealing with. Maybe Cassie should fill you in. I am not a man to be messed with."

"Then that makes us even," Adam said, shoving him away. "I repeat, Mancini, you can either leave or be thrown out. There are no other options. I won't wait for security to do it. I'll do it myself."

"You've just made the biggest mistake of your life. Cassie will marry me again," Trent vowed, "and there won't be anything you can do to stop it." Trent's eyes locked on Cassie. "I'll be in touch," he snarled and stormed out of the room.

Trent was gone for now, but she knew he would come back. He would not give up easily. He wanted her back, and she knew he would stop at nothing to get what he wanted. He'd won her back once before and she'd remarried him, but what he didn't know was that Cassie was now older and much wiser. She was also very much in love with Dr. Adam Hart, and there was nothing Trent could do to change that fact.

"Thank you," Cassie said, staring up at Adam. "How did you know I needed you?"

"Rachel paged me." He brushed the hair from her cheek. "Are you sure you're okay? You seem a little shaken."

"I'm fine. Thanks again. Can you give me a few minutes alone, please?"

"Sure." Adam turned to walk away but then stopped and turned back to her. "If you need me, Cassie, don't hesitate to call."

Cassie fought back the tears as she watched him leave. She wanted nothing more than for him to take her in his arms, but she knew that wasn't going to happen. It was over between them.

* * *

A few days later Rachel called to invite Cassie to a surprise birthday party for a mutual friend at the hospital. After giving it some thought, she decided to go.

Needing a change, she made an appointment with a hairdresser Monica recommended and went in for a complete makeover. Shelly, the hairstylist, had the perfect cut for her. Cassie watched her long tresses fall to the floor with apprehension. When she was allowed to look into the mirror, she was impressed. Her sandy brown hair stopped just above her shoulders. With the long tresses gone, her hair had a fuller, bouncier look. The style was perfect for her small, heart-shaped face.

She dressed in a royal blue pantsuit. Brushing her hair out, she found that it bounced back into place easily. Adding eyeliner, a touch of blue eye shadow, and red lipstick, she smiled at her reflection.

She was on her way out the door when the phone rang. She debated answering it for a few seconds. Cassie grabbed the phone on the third ring. "Hello."

"Hello, beautiful."

"What do you want, Trent? I'm on my way out."

"Then I will make this short and sweet. Tell your boyfriend, he won't know what hit him. He's about to have more trouble than he can handle."

"He's not a threat to you, Trent. Adam and I are no longer together. If you go after Adam, I will make sure your election is over before it begins."

"Do your worst, Cassie, and I will do mine. I'm officially out of the race."

"What do you want, Trent?"

"What I've always wanted. Your unconditional surrender. You have two weeks to decide if you want to be the reason Adam Hart loses everything. In three weeks we get married, or I bury him. If you don't believe me, just watch the headline news."

Cassie slammed down the telephone. She quickly picked it up again and dialed Adam's cell phone. "Adam, it's me. I need to see you."

"Your place or mine," he said in a teasing voice.

"Get your head out of your bedroom," she snapped. "I'll be there in half an hour." She disconnected the call and phoned Rachel to let her know that she couldn't make it to the party, as she headed out the garage door.

Cassie was on pins and needles as she drove to Adam's house. She had to warn him that Trent was coming after him.

Adam called and canceled his date. Cassie was coming over, and he didn't know what to think or expect from her. When the doorbell rang, he opened the front door to let her in.

She stepped inside the house with some reservations. She hadn't been back to Adam's house since the night she found him there with another woman. Folding her arms in front of her, she turned to face him. "I'm here to warn you about Trent. I don't know what he's going to do, but I know he's coming after you."

"Thanks for the warning, but you could have

saved yourself a trip. Better men than your ex-husband have come after me. Let him come."

"Adam, please take this seriously. He doesn't make idle threats."

"Consider me warned. Was that it, or did you come because you missed me?" His hand moved to touch her face.

Cassie caught his hand before it made contact with her skin. "Like a bad rash," she said and smiled, releasing his hand.

"I see the razor-sharp tongue is back. Your eyes tell a different story. They are the key to your soul."

"Listen to me, you arrogant, egotistical jerk! This is not a game. This is your life, Adam. Trent is furious at you, and he's coming after you. He's not someone you want to tangle with. He could be dangerous."

"You said all that without taking a breath. I'm impressed," Adam teased. "I can also be dangerous. If he comes after me, I'll be ready for him."

Cassie's eyes narrowed on him, and she turned to leave. He was not taking her warning seriously. She had wasted her time in coming.

"Leaving so soon?" He stepped in front of the door and blocked her exit with his body. "Have you had dinner yet?"

Looking up at him in surprise, she folded her arms across her chest. "Let me see if I have this straight. You don't want a relationship with me. You don't want to sleep with me, but you're inviting me to have dinner with you."

His eyebrows rose suggestively, and he smiled. "I never said I didn't want to sleep with you."

"Get out of the way, Adam," she snapped, trying

to shove him aside. "I'm leaving. Why not call up Donna? I'm sure she would be happy to accompany you both places."

"You have to eat. I have to eat. Let's eat together. It's just a friendly dinner. You can call it a non-date."

"Why do I suddenly have a feeling of déjà vu? Could it be because I've heard this line before from you?"

"I'm serious, Cassie. I don't want to be your enemy. I know us being friends would be a stretch, but I'd like to try." He saw the indecision on her beautiful face. "It would be much easier on both of us if your eyes were not shooting daggers at me all the time."

A smile touched her lips. "So you noticed that. Okay, Adam, for TJ I'm willing to give it a try. Dinner is dutch, and it's not negotiable. If I let you pay for dinner, you might expect something in return."

"I wouldn't expect anything, but I wouldn't turn away anything you wanted to give me, either," he said and winked.

They went to one of Cassie's favorite seafood restaurants. Over dinner and drinks, they talked about everything under the sun except for their past relationship. They kept the conversation light.

When they arrived back at Adam's house, he walked her to her car. Cassie was a bit startled when he leaned over and kissed her cheek. She quickly pulled away and unlocked her car door.

Adam stood staring after her car as she drove away. It took all his willpower to not go after her.

When his lips had touched her skin, he'd felt her tremble at the contact. He'd wanted to take her in his arms and never let her go. He stood there until her car was out of sight. Out of sight, but never out of his mind or his heart.

Chapter 11

A week later Adam was walking to his car when a woman approached him. She stopped in front of him. Smiling, she handed him an envelope. "Dr. Adam Hart, you've just been served. Have a nice day."

"What?" Adam stared at the envelope in his hand. Opening it, he scanned the documents. Stuffing them back inside the envelope, he marched into the hospital. He went to the human resources department. Dr. Adam Hart and County General Hospital were being sued for sexual harassment by Donna Martin and Tara Winters, a former hospital nurse.

HR immediately called in Randall and Associates as the hospital's lawyers. Adam was glad just this once to have Peter Randall on his side. Despite the way he felt about him personally, he knew Peter was one of the best lawyers in the state.

After the meeting with HR, Adam went home, with strict instructions not to contact the two women named in the suit, Donna Martin and Tara

Winters. Adam was the first to admit that things had ended badly with both women and that it was his fault, but sexual harassment had played no part in it. Both nurses had gone after him because he was a doctor. He knew Donna was furious because he'd ended things with her by telling her he was with Cassie.

He sat at his computer and searched for private detectives. Calling one up, he hired him to find out who was paying the legal fees for the two women behind the lawsuit. He also requested a complete dossier on Trent Mancini. Adam was sure all of this would lead back to Cassie's ex-husband, but he wanted confirmation before he made his next move.

Cassie was floored when Monica told her about the lawsuit. Why would Donna sue Adam for sexual harassment? Everyone knew she was after him. This made no sense. It took all of five minutes for the truth to dawn on her. This was Trent's doing. He had warned her he was going after Adam.

She was mortified when she received a subpoena for a deposition. Cassie phoned her father immediately. He told her she had to appear in court and to tell the truth. Because she had been involved with Adam at one time, he suspected they would want her statement about how the relationship had started. Her father asked her if there was anything damaging she could say against Adam under oath. Reluctantly, Cassie told him about the bet. Her father tried to hold his emotions in check as he told her to downplay it as much as she could if the subject came up. He warned her not to volunteer any information and to answer only the questions they asked of her.

When she walked outside her house the morning of the deposition, reporters were camped out on her lawn. Suspecting as much, her father had come to whisk her away and told the press they had no comment.

Her deposition went from bad to worse as they questioned her about the night Adam left her and went to Donna. They brought up the bet, and Cassie downplayed it as much as she could without perjuring herself.

Trent had turned the lawsuit into a media circus. Reporters were all over the hospital. The story was on the news each night. She learned from the news, Adam was on a leave of absence. The media was referring to him as Dr. Heart, Dr. Feel Good, and the Love Doctor.

Cassie tried to call him, but he wasn't answering his cell phone or his home phone. She phoned Monica and was told that Adam was staying with them for a few days to hide out from the press.

Three days after Cassie's deposition Adam told Shawn they were flying to Los Angeles. He booked a flight, and Shawn met him at the airport.

Once on board the plane, Adam leaned back in his first-class seat and closed his eyes. He made a lot of decisions on his way to L.A. After the lawsuit was settled, he was going to ask Cassie to marry him. He didn't want to waste any more time away from the woman he loved. He was on the verge of getting everything he could possibly want, and he wanted to share it with Cassie.

When the plane landed, the rental car was waiting for them at the airport. Adam logged the address of their destination on the GPS system, and they drove to the high-rise office building in downtown L.A.

"You realize once you sign those papers, life as you know it will never be same," said Shawn as they took the elevator up to the thirty-fifth floor.

"Life as I know it changed the day Cassie walked into my life. There's no turning back now. I'm claiming my inheritance, and then I'm asking Cassie to marry me."

An hour later Adam Hart walked out of the high-rise building, worth millions of dollars. He was now president and CEO of Kirkland International, one of the leaders in electronic equipment. It seemed ironic to him because he was just getting the hang of working his BlackBerry and he rarely used his laptop.

Back in Dallas, Adam had his lawyer and best friend draw up a new will leaving equal shares of his vast fortune to Cassie, Gloria, and Shawn. Adam knew Shawn's dream was to open his own law firm. To facilitate that dream, Adam wrote his best friend a check for five million dollars and then hired him to oversee his financial affairs.

He called Gloria to see how she was doing. Gloria was the result of an affair between Adam's father and the church organist. Gloria's mother had left town shortly after discovering she was pregnant with Gloria. Gloria found Adam a year later and told him the story. A DNA test confirmed she was his sister. Gradually, Adam and Gloria formed a bond.

As usual, she was working overtime to help take care of her mother and brother. Adam asked for her bank account number and bank routing number so he could wire her a little cash to help her out. He smiled as he hung up the phone. His little sister was in for quite a surprise when she saw her bank balance.

Next on his agenda was the downfall of Trent Mancini. He called his broker and instructed him to buy up all the shares of Mancini Industries available. Adam wanted controlling interest in Trent's company so he could boot him out. What better revenge than to give the company as a wedding gift to Cassie.

Cassie was running late at work and called Monica to pick TJ up from day care. Around six o'clock Monica called Cassie to tell her she'd drop him off later. He was helping her get dinner ready.

Cassie knew she had the power to end the nightmare for Adam. All she had to do was marry Trent and it would all be over. So much damage had already been done. She wasn't sure if the lawsuit had been dropped, and if Adam's career would recover from it.

When she got home from work, she picked up the phone and hung it up again. She sat down on the sofa and picked up the phone again. She chewed on her fingernail as she dialed Trent's number with her other hand. When he answered, she almost hung up. She cleared her throat before speaking. "It's me. You win."

"I'll catch the next flight out. I knew you would come to your senses before I went after your father next."

"You go after my father and I will come after you." She slammed down the phone. *I truly hate him! I don't know if I can do this. Can I marry a man I despise to save the man I love?*

Cassie knew she wasn't going to like what Trent had to say when she let him in the house. She stared at Trent, speechless.

Trent smiled at her. "It's simple, Cassie. You marry me, and I make the lawsuit against your boyfriend go away. You refuse, and when I'm finished with him, he won't be able to remove a hangnail."

Her cell phone rang. Cassie looked down at it and saw Adam's name. She didn't pick it up. Trent hit the speaker button on the phone to force her to answer it.

"Hello. Cassie, I'm dropping TJ off for Monica," said Adam.

Cassie didn't respond.

"Cassie, are you there?" Adam asked.

"Yes. That's fine. Thank you," she said distractedly and then disconnected the call.

"His timing couldn't be better. When your boyfriend brings back my son, you are going to put on the performance of your life for him. You are going to be ecstatic about our engagement and upcoming

marriage. For Dr. Hart and your family, you are
going to be the happy, loving fiancée."

"I'm not that good an actress," snapped Cassie.
"No one is going to believe I've had a change of
heart, no pun intended. They know I despise you."

"Your boyfriend's livelihood depends on your
performance. I think we need practice," said
Trent, pulling Cassie into his arms. His mouth covered hers in a punishing kiss. Cassie stood motionless. She refused to part her lips for the intrusion
of his tongue. When he released her, she took a
step back from him and wiped her mouth with the
back of her hand. "You'd better get used to this,
Cassie. Once you're back in my bed, you'll never
leave again."

The doorbell rang, and Cassie stood frozen. She
didn't want to open the door. She didn't want to
see the look on Adam's or TJ's face at the news of
her engagement.

"I'll get it for you, sweetheart," said Trent, walking over to the door. Without looking out, he
opened the door.

Cassie watched TJ and Adam both recoil at
seeing Trent.

"Hi, buddy." Trent picked up a stiff TJ and
hugged him. "Dr. Hart, you're here just in time to
help us celebrate." He set TJ on his feet and he
went to his mother.

Adam looked from Trent to Cassie. He stepped
past Trent and into the house. He noticed Cassie
wouldn't look him in the eye. Something was
wrong. He could feel it. "What celebration would
that be?"

Trent walked over to Cassie and slipped his arm

around her waist and kissed her cheek. "Cassie and I are getting married next weekend."

Adam's eyes flew to Cassie's flushed face. He felt like he had been sucker punched. Cassie was marrying Trent. It couldn't be true. "Cassie?"

"No!" cried TJ. "I want Adam to be my daddy. Mom, you can't marry *him*. You love Adam, and he loves you."

Cassie wanted the floor to open up and swallow her. Feeling the color seep into her cheeks once again, she closed her eyes and counted to ten. When she opened her eyes, there were three sets of eyes staring at her waiting for her answer.

"TJ, Adam is only a friend. He's not going to be your daddy," said Cassie, kneeling down to him. "Your dad and I are getting back together. We are moving back to New York with him."

"I'm not going," TJ said stubbornly, moving to stand by Adam. "I'm staying here with Adam." He looked up at Trent hatefully. "Mommy kisses Adam. We had a sleepover at Adam's, and they were kissing on the couch. I bet she doesn't kiss you. She likes Adam better, and so do I."

"Trenton Jackson Mancini," Cassie gasped, staring at her son. There was nothing she could do to comfort him. If she had any other choice, she wouldn't be marrying Trent, but he had left her no choice.

"I hate him. I want Adam to be my daddy," TJ said, bursting into tears and hugging Adam's legs.

Adam did the most natural thing in the world to him. He picked up TJ and hugged him. Carrying him over to the sofa, he sat down with TJ on his lap.

Wiping an errant tear from her cheek, Cassie followed them over to the sofa. She sat down beside them. "TJ, come here," she said softly. With some hesitation, TJ went to his mother. Cassie hugged him to her. "TJ, you know Adam and I aren't dating anymore. I know this is probably confusing for you. I love you, and I love your dad," she said past the catch in her voice. "We are going to be a family again. Honey, it's what's best for everyone."

Adam stared at Cassie. She still refused to look at him. He saw the tears streaming down her cheeks. He didn't believe a word she'd just said. Something was definitely wrong. He couldn't and wouldn't confront her in front of TJ, but she couldn't avoid him forever.

"TJ," said Adam, placing his hand on the boy's back, "your mom only wants what's best for you. Look at me." TJ stopped sniffling and looked at Adam. "Your mom loves you more than anything. She would be lost without you. She's doing what she thinks is best. You have to accept and respect that."

"You are no longer needed here, Dr. Hart. I can take care of my family," stated Trent, glaring at Adam.

Adam stood facing Trent. He resisted the urge to drop-kick the other man. "I'll leave when Cassie tells me to leave."

"Adam, please," said Cassie, still not meeting his eyes. "I think it's best if you go."

Trent pulled TJ from Cassie's arms, and the boy reached out to Adam. "TJ, say good-bye to Dr. Hart. You won't be seeing him again after tonight."

Adam was furious as he took TJ from his father. This was the jerk Cassie was remarrying. Adam could see Trent had no concern whatsoever over his son's anguish.

"I love you, Adam," TJ cried, hugging him. "It's not fair. I don't want you to leave us."

"I love you, too. Take care of yourself and your mom." Adam set him on his feet and walked out the front door.

Cassie quickly wiped her tears away. "Let's go get you ready for bed," she said, catching TJ's hand and leading him up the stairs to his room. She got him dressed for bed and tucked him in.

When she went back downstairs, Trent was sitting on the sofa, talking softly on his cell phone. Cassie shook her head in disgust. She could tell from his body language and the tone of his voice, he was talking to a woman. Some things never changed. She took the phone from him and disconnected the call.

"Next weekend does not work for me as a wedding date," she snapped. "It's too soon. There is too much I have to do to get ready."

"You will do what I tell you to do if you know what's good for your boyfriend." Trent took the cell phone from her. "That was an important call."

"Aren't they all? What was her name? Did you happen to tell her you're getting married, or does she care?"

"That was business, Cassie," he lied. "Even if it wasn't, my extracurricular activities are none of your business."

"You're right, it's none of my business, as long as you aren't planning on sharing my bed," she snapped. "I don't share. You know that already. In fact you should have learned that from the first and second time around. Does this mean I'm free to have affairs also?"

Cassie and Trent argued for the next hour about his affairs, Adam, and the upcoming nuptials. In the end, she could do little to stop him from getting his own way. After all, he held the upper hand. She was glad when Trent left the house to go to his hotel room. She told him in no uncertain terms that he was not welcome in her home or her bed. She was drained from dealing with him as she took a nice, long, relaxing shower.

Cassie walked out of the bathroom with a towel wrapped around her. She stifled a scream when she spotted a figure standing by her bedroom window. Adam.

"Why did you come back? How did you get in?" she asked, moving closer to the bed.

"I saw Trent's car leave." He moved toward her with the grace of a predatory animal. He stopped in front of her. His hand came up and caressed her face. "Don't marry him, Cassie," Adam said softly. "He's not the man for you. I am."

Cassie stared at him, not sure she had heard him correctly. She didn't want to read more into his words than what he actually meant.

He leaned down, and his mouth touched hers in a gentle kiss. Cassie stepped closer to him, and his arms went around her. He nibbled at her lips and teased her with his tongue until her lips parted. Adam was in no rush as his tongue explored the honeyed recess of her mouth. Their gentle kiss turned hungry and passionate as he buried his hands in her thick hair.

A soft moan escaped her as her tongue teased his. She held him close, never wanting to let him go. Adam opened the towel and let it slide from her body. He took a step back from her, and his dark gaze caressed every inch of her body.

Cassie unbuttoned his shirt and pushed it from his shoulders. She backed him into the bed and gently pushed him onto its downy softness. She had one night with the man she loved, and she knew she had to make it last forever.

They made slow, passionate love to each other the first time. The second time their desperation was in each touch and in each caress.

Around dawn the next morning Cassie stared at Adam as he slept. Her heart was breaking at what she was about to do. She had to end it and get him out of her life. Hot tears wet her cheeks as she slipped from Adam's arms and from the bed. She took a quick shower and slipped a nightshirt on. Going back into the bedroom, she sat on the side of the bed.

"Adam, wake up," said Cassie, shaking him. "You have to go." He sat up slowly, and Cassie got up from the bed. "I'm not sorry about what happened, but you have to leave. That was good-bye. I wanted to say it in a way you could comprehend," she lied uneasily.

"What?" Adam stared at her in disbelief as he got to his feet. He didn't want to believe what she was saying. "Are you saying last night meant nothing to you?" he asked, furiously turning her around to face him. He was filled with anger and hurt at her words. "I don't believe that. You are lying. Why are you doing this, Cassie? You don't love him. You love me. We made love."

Her misty eyes met his flashing brown ones, and she looked away guiltily. She didn't want him to be able to tell she was lying. "It was just sex, Adam," she stated casually. "I wanted to make love to you one last time before we said good-bye forever. Loving them and leaving them is your specialty. Why should last night be any different for you?" Her heart was breaking with each lie she told. "How does it feel having the tables turned, Adam? Think about all the women you have done the same thing to, and imagine how they must have felt." She took a deep breath to calm her nerves before she continued with her hurtful words. "I thought I was in love with you, but I was wrong. I love Trent. I always have, and I always will."

His face went from disbelief, to pain, to fury in the blink of an eye. He advanced on her and stopped directly in front of her.

"You are still in love with Trent?" he hissed through clenched teeth. "So what was this? One last romp in bed before you married the man you love? What was I, Cassie? A poor substitute, second best? It sure says a lot about you. You are engaged to the man you love, but you had sex with me. I guess I was wrong. Maybe you and Trent deserve each other, after all." She watched as he hastily pulled on his clothes. "Have a nice life," he yelled as he left the room. Cassie followed him down the stairs.

Giving her one last glare, he stormed out of the house. Adam's heart was breaking into tiny pieces as he slammed the door behind him. With shaking hands, he took the velvet box out of his pocket and opened it. A huge marquis diamond winked back at him. Slamming the box shut, he placed it in his pocket and got into his car.

Trent returned the next day, around lunchtime. He brought with him a man, who, he informed Cassie, was her new bodyguard. No one was to come in or go out of the house without checking with Trent first. There were to be no exceptions.

Cassie was livid and threw a fit. Trent had the bodyguard wait outside while he and Cassie argued. He told Cassie he'd come back last night and seen Adam's car. He also told her he hoped she'd enjoyed her last night in her boyfriend's arms, because he would not get past the front door again.

Cassie was still fuming hours later, when Monica came by. As she approached the front door, Monica heard the bodyguard on the phone with Trent, and she was furious when she stormed into the house.

"Cassie, what is going on?" Monica asked, facing her. "Why is there a bodyguard at the front door?"

"Have a seat," said Cassie, trying to find the right words to tell her sister the truth. "Trent and I are back together. We're getting married on Saturday."

"What! You are marrying Trent? Why on earth would you marry that man a third time? Are you insane? Cassie, he treats you like you are his possession."

"I love him," Cassie lied, turning away from

Monica's questioning eyes. "Trent, TJ, and I are going to be a family."

Monica walked around in front of Cassie. "You've tried that twice already. Look me straight in the eye, and tell me you love that man."

Cassie turned away.

"You love Adam. Cassie, why are you doing this?"

"I told you. I love Trent. We are giving our marriage another try."

"That's bull. You don't love him. Something else is going on here, and it has nothing to do with love. Is he threatening you? Are you afraid of him? Honey, you can tell me."

"Monica, please stop," begged Cassie. She hated lying to her sister, and she wasn't very good at hiding her feelings. "There is nothing to tell. I'm doing what's best for everyone. Trent and I are getting married on Saturday. I would like for you to stand up for me."

"I can't do that. Cassie, this is wrong." Monica caught her hand and led her to the sofa. "Think about what you are doing. Don't marry Trent on the rebound. I know you love Adam and he loves you."

"Adam and I were a mistake. We were doomed from the start. I don't love him, Monica. I thought I did, but I love Trent. I've always loved Trent. Monica, I know you don't agree with my choice in men, but I need you there with me on Saturday. Please be there for me."

"Fine." Monica threw her hands in the air. "I'll do whatever you need me to do. I don't agree with it, but you are my sister and I love you. Honey, I only want what's best for you, and I don't think that's Trent. So what are you going to tell Dad?"

"I'm not," said Cassie, getting to her feet. "I'll tell him after the wedding. I know that's not fair to him, but I don't want to fight with him about this."

"I'll tell him."

Cassie turned to face Monica.

"You can't marry Trent without the family being there. Dad will want to be there," said Monica.

"I doubt that. He hates Trent even more than he does Adam. He probably won't even show up."

"He'll be there," said Monica, hugging her sister. "We will all be there for you. What are families for?"

Monica stayed until Trent showed up. That was her cue to leave. Trent and Monica had never got along, and they were not about to connect at this late stage of the game.

Chapter 12

At the hospital Adam went over the file with avid interest. Trent Mancini had been a busy boy in his quest to ruin Adam's life and career. The tables were about to be turned. Adam now had the money and the power to destroy Trent with a simple phone call, but he didn't want to do it that way. He wanted to catch him by surprise. Adam also wanted him to go through the hell he had put him through tenfold.

He called Shawn and Monica and told them to meet him at his house. They needed to know the reason for Cassie's about-face.

Adam drove home, parked next to Shawn, and got out of the car. He unlocked the front door, and they followed him inside. Adam quickly disabled the alarm system and steered Shawn and Monica into the living room.

"My private detective discovered something real interesting. Trent is the one footing the attorney's bill for the lawsuit. I think he's using the lawsuit against me to blackmail Cassie into marrying him," said Adam as Shawn and Monica stared at him in surprise.

"Are you sure about this?" asked Monica. "I know it sure would explain a lot of things. I know my sister, and she's not in love with him. She loves you, and you love her. You have to stop her from marrying him. You have to do something. I tried talking her out of it, but her mind is made up."

"And what do you propose I do? Kidnap her?" asked Adam. "He has a security guard at her house. He's making sure I don't come near Cassie before the wedding."

"Tell me about it. I have to be cleared to see my own sister, who is living in *my* house. Let's hit him when he's the most comfortable and vulnerable, at the church on their wedding day," replied Monica.

"That's not a bad idea," stated Shawn. "We know the church. There are numerous entrances and exits. Monica and I can help you kidnap Cassie. Also, you have a perfect hideaway cabin in the woods. You could take Cassie there. You two need some alone time. We can take care of TJ for a couple of weeks."

"You're serious?" asked Adam in disbelief. "You want me to kidnap Cassie at her wedding?"

They both nodded in agreement.

"This is insane. This could blow up in all our faces, but I'm willing to do what I have to do to stop that wedding. Have a seat. I'll go get a pad and pen," said Adam, leaving the room. He returned shortly and sat down. "If we are going to do this, we have to come up with a fool-proof plan. No one else can know about this, especially your father. He may not want her to remarry Mancini, but he doesn't want her with me, either."

An hour later they were all satisfied with their plan. The trio had covered every escape route and every possible scenario that could go wrong. They each had a job to do to make sure the plan went off without a hitch.

Adam had his own plans for Trent Mancini, other than spoiling his wedding. The man had tried to ruin him, and now it was his turn to feel the pain. Trent was about to lose everything.

Two days before the wedding, Cassie was watching the news when she heard that the lawsuit against Adam and the hospital had been settled. An out-of-court settlement had been reached with the two women in question. There were no details on the settlement, other than that the women had been awarded an unspecified amount.

Trent had kept his word, and now she had to keep hers. She had to marry him. There was no backing out now.

On the morning of the wedding Cassie stared at her reflection in the full-length mirror. Her shoulder-length hair was pinned atop her head by two white flowered hair clips. Her makeup was picture-perfect. Her soft brown eyes held no happiness for this day. This was her wedding day, and she felt like she was walking to the executioner's block. She was marrying a man she didn't love to protect the man she did love.

She wore an exquisite white designer gown of silk, satin, and pearls. Her bare shoulders shimmered with a light coating of body glitter. The bodice was snug, and the gown had a fitted waist. It flared at her hips, and the train was at least four feet long. Trent had bought the gown because he didn't like the black dress she'd chosen. Her life was no longer her own. Trent was in control again.

Can I really go through with this? This is not how I imagined things would turn out. Can I stand before God and promise to love and honor Trent when, in fact, I hate him? If I do this, it's forever. He'll never let me go this time.

Her family had tried unsuccessfully to talk her out of marrying Trent. They knew she was in love with Adam. Cassie had tried to convince Monica that she was marrying Trent because she loved him. Cassie knew her sister didn't believe her.

Peter Randall had read his daughter the riot act. He could not believe Cassie would marry Trent again. He had called her on her so-called love for Trent. He'd used his best interrogation tactics to break her down, but Cassie wouldn't budge. It didn't take a genius to figure out she had made a deal with Trent to save Adam. This had infuriated her father even more. He'd told her Adam was a grown man and he didn't need her to protect him.

Cassie and Peter had both said a lot of things to each other that neither could take back. He'd walked out of her house and vowed not to go to her farce of a wedding.

Cassie had no idea, but Monica had talked to their father and he was sitting out in the pews with the rest of the guests. He couldn't bring himself to walk her down the aisle, but he was there.

From his hiding place in an alcove, Adam stared

at the beautiful vision before him. Cassie looked
like the princess he always knew she was in her expensive wedding gown. He knew she would make a
beautiful bride. She could have and should have
been his bride. Maybe if he hadn't gotten cold feet
and messed things up with her, she would be his
bride. She still could be his wife. It wasn't too late.
Once he carried her out of here, they would have
their chance.

His heart ached as he watched her from where
he stood, she didn't even know he was there. *She
told me she was in love with Trent. So, why doesn't she
look happy? She's not happy, because she doesn't love him
and she doesn't want to marry him. Time to make a
move. I have only one shot to pull this off while Monica
has everyone out of the room. So far, everything is going
according to the plan. Shawn is keeping Trent occupied
in the groom's room. TJ is with Karen and Peter. Time to
get the show on the road.*

He pulled the ski mask over his head and moved
silently toward Cassie. Adam was directly behind
her now. He was getting ready to reach out and
touch her when she spoke.

"I can't do this," Cassie whispered to the empty
room. "I can't go through with this charade. I can't
marry a man I don't love. I have to stop the wedding." She snatched the veil from her head and
turned to flee. She came up short when she saw a
masked man all in black blocking her path. Cassie
opened her mouth to scream, but no sound came
out as he anticipated her reaction. His hand covered her mouth to muffle her scream. Cassie struggled in his arms, which left Adam little choice but
to wrestle her to the floor. He was careful not to

hurt her, and he took the brunt of the fall. Quickly reversing their positions, he trapped her on the floor. He had the upper hand when the air was knocked from her. Before she could catch her breath and continue her struggle, he taped her mouth shut. The struggle resumed immediately as she fought to free her body from his. What seemed like minutes was actually only a few seconds before he stilled her movements. Holding her in place, he taped her hands together in front of her. He slipped the engagement ring from her finger and dropped it into his pocket.

Cassie squirmed and kicked, but he was stronger. He held her legs, taped them together, and rolled her into a blanket. Adam was a bit winded himself as he watched the rise and fall of Cassie's chest. She put up more of a struggle than he thought her petite package could, but he knew fear gave people an extra adrenaline boost. He hefted her up and threw her over his shoulder.

Cassie was terrified as she squirmed and bucked, making him stumble. He swiftly regained his footing. Pain shot through her as he gave her bottom a hard whack. Her sharp intake of breath caused her body to stiffen momentarily. Her breathing was harsh as she struggled and then resumed her kicking. She had no idea what he was doing when he stopped so suddenly, but he caught her as she almost fell.

As planned, Adam dropped two notes on the bureau; one was for her parents, and the other one was for Trent. He laid the ring on top of Trent's note.

The door opened, and Adam put his hand to his

lips as Shawn entered the room. Shawn waved for Adam to follow him.

Adam carried his package as he followed Shawn out the back entrance. Luck was with them, as they made it to his Jeep undetected. Shawn dropped the keys in Adam's open palm and opened the door for Adam to put Cassie in the SUV. Adam deposited Cassie on the floor of his SUV. He quickly closed the door.

"Good luck," whispered Shawn, touching his knuckles to Adam's. "You're going to need it."

"Thanks." Adam eased into the driver's seat with a satisfied smile on his face. He waved to his friend. His smile disappeared when Cassie started kicking the door.

He pulled out of the church alley and onto the main street. Their plan had gone off without a hitch. He picked up his cell phone and dialed a number.

"I have Cassie," he whispered into the phone. "Consider the wedding canceled. You can go out and make the announcement. Try not to smile too much when you tell Trent she's flown the coop. I'll be in touch."

"Adam Hart, I love you. Take good care of my sister," said Monica. "If you hurt her again, you will have me to answer to. I don't need to tell you how furious Cassie is going to be with both of us."

"I can handle Cassie. Just make sure your father doesn't try to track her down. If all else fails, tell him she's with me. That should make his day," Adam said and laughed. "We will be out of contact for the next two weeks. If you need me, leave a message on my cell phone. I'll check it daily, although

I'm not sure what kind of reception I'll have at the lake cabin. Thanks, Monica. I'll talk to you soon." He ended the call and tossed the cell phone on the passenger seat. He turned on the radio and then popped the top on his Coke and took a long drink and set the can back in the cup holder as he eased onto 635, heading south. He took the 175 exit and headed toward East Texas. They had a three-hour drive ahead of them. Adam wanted to get to the cabin before nightfall. He would wait until they were out of the city limits to unwrap his beautiful hostage from the blanket. He wasn't taking any unnecessary chances with her. Cassie was way too resourceful for her own good.

Cassie was terrified at the thought of what this madman might do with her. She squirmed and tried to wiggle out of the blanket confining her. Her breathing was labored through the blanket. Tears of frustration ran down her cheeks as her efforts went unrewarded. She collapsed on the floor, tired and spent.

What is he going to do with me? Where is he taking me? Visions of being raped and murdered kept popping into her head. This made her renew her struggle for freedom. *I don't want to die like this. I have to fight to stay alive. It wasn't supposed to end like this. I'll never see my family again. TJ, I love you, sweetheart. I'll never see Adam again. Adam, please save me! Where did that come from? It must be the fear. Why else would I visualize Adam charging to the rescue?*

When the vehicle came to a sudden stop, she rolled between the seats. She let out a grunt of pain as her head hit something. She cursed her abductor in her mind a thousand times. Panic gripped her as she heard the passenger door open. She pulled her legs to her chest and waited for her moment to strike. When she felt his hands on her legs, she kicked out with all her might. She smiled in satisfaction at the painful curse she heard him utter as he flew out of the vehicle and landed on the ground with a thud.

I won't make this easy for him. I will fight him every step of the way. As long as I live and breathe, I will fight to survive.

Adam groaned as he lifted himself off the ground and dusted off his jeans. He should have been prepared for her quick thinking. Cassie was a fighter.

He cautiously leaned into the Jeep again. This time he was ready for her. She tried the same stunt, and he grabbed her legs. Holding her still, he closed the door and put the ski mask on. The windows of his vehicle were not tinted. They were black. No one could see inside.

"If you hold still a minute, I'll unwrap you, you little hellcat," he said in a muffled voice.

Cassie stilled and waited for him to comply. When she was free of the blanket, she launched herself at him. Her head butted his mouth, and he fell back against the door in pain. He cursed as he spit out blood. He felt his lips begin to swell.

"Try that again and I will put you over my knee. I'm not going to hurt you," he whispered, disguising his voice. He lifted her onto the backseat and strapped her in.

Cassie kicked him, and he went sailing out the door. He caught his balance before he fell, but he lost all patience with her. Adam unsnapped her seat belt and twisted her around so her bottom was in the air. He gave her two hard whacks on her backside.

Cassie tried to scream out in pain and mortification, but the only sound that came out was a muffled grunt because of the tape. When he sat her back down, she winced in pain. Her bottom was stinging. He strapped her into her seat again.

She watched him through leery, confused eyes. There was something familiar about him. Something she couldn't put her finger on. He picked up a bottle of water and showed it to her. She nodded. Cassie would have agreed to almost anything to get the tape off her mouth.

He eased the tape off her mouth and poured, and she was forced to drink or drown. Adam watched a droplet of water run down the corner of her mouth to her throat. The droplet disappeared into the bodice of her gown. His eyes darkened as he wished he could be that droplet of water. He almost groaned aloud at the mere thought of it.

Cassie shivered at the look in his eyes. She knew that look, and it scared her to death. He wanted her. There was no denying it. "I've had enough," she said nervously, turning her face away from him. "I have a son. My little boy needs me. Please don't kill me. What do you want with me? Where are you taking me?"

"Away," he said in a gruff voice. "Far away. You need some quiet time to gather your thoughts. Call it a well-deserved vacation." He didn't want to talk to her more than necessary. Adam was silent as he took a blindfold out of his pocket.

"What are you doing with that?" she asked, shrinking back against the seat in fear. "Are you going to strangle me?"

"Never," he whispered in her ear. Adam covered her eyes and tied the blindfold in place. He hopped down and closed the SUV's door behind him. He eased into the driver's seat and started the Jeep.

Adam turned off the main road onto a dirt road. He was glad there was a little daylight left; otherwise they would be in pitch darkness. There were no streetlights out in the country.

He drove about ten miles before reaching their destination. He pulled up to the gate and got out of the SUV. Unlocking the gate, he opened it. He drove through the gate and locked it behind him. He pulled up in front of the cabin and killed the engine, then took the keys out of the ignition and got out of the vehicle.

This place brought back fond memories for him. The two-bedroom, one-bathroom cabin was his retreat away from the big city. This would be the perfect hideout for them. They would have time to talk and work out their problems.

Unlocking the door, he went inside the cozy log cabin. He turned on the lights and walked over to the fireplace. Squatting down, he broke one of the fire-starter logs in half and struck a match to it. As it started to blaze, he added a couple of logs to the flames.

A few days ago he had driven down and made sure the cabin was clean and well stocked with the necessities. Monica had also gone shopping for Cassie, and he had the clothes in her room.

It was definitely a remote hideaway. The furniture

was Early American. The fireplace was cobblestone. The floors were all hardwood, well maintained and sparkling. He could see his own reflection in the floor. A large rug covered most of the floor in the living room. The kitchen was rather small. A dinner table and four chairs sat to the left of the kitchen. Both bedrooms were good-size rooms with queen beds, and they shared the Jack-and-Jill bathroom.

He went back outside to get Cassie before she froze. He shivered at the cold and rubbed his arms. The long-sleeved black turtleneck did little to block out the cold air. The howling of the wind was ominous. The temperature had dropped by several degrees since he'd left the city.

I guess I should have listened to the weather forecast. It looks like we may be in for some bad weather. I'm prepared for almost every situation.

He walked back to the SUV and opened the door. Adam unsnapped Cassie's seat belt and quickly jumped back. She kicked out at him, and this time he was prepared as he caught her feet.

"Nice try. Haven't you learned your lesson by now?" He scooped her up into his arms and carried her inside, where he dropped her unceremoniously onto the sofa.

Cassie sat motionless on the sofa. She was too afraid to move. She was trembling with cold and fear. Her teeth began to chatter. She jumped when a blanket was wrapped around her shoulders.

She knew the door was open, because she could feel a draft, but she had no idea what her captor was doing. Then, she heard him fiddling with the SUV. *What is he doing?*

Adam had gone back outside and popped the hood on the Jeep. He unplugged the battery and removed it from the SUV and closed the hood. Adam carried the battery inside and put it in the closet in his bedroom. Even if she found it, he was positive she wouldn't know how to put it back in the SUV and reconnect it.

He checked his cell phone. NO SERVICE flashed on the small screen. Turning it off, he put it in a dresser drawer. "We won't need this anytime soon," he said, closing the drawer. *I've put her through enough hell for one day. I'd better go untie her and face the wrath of Cassie.*

The minute he untied Cassie, she would probably slug him for putting her through this. After that she would make a mad dash for the Jeep. He had to stay at least two steps ahead of her.

When he returned to the living room, she was still sitting on the sofa, where he'd left her. He watched the rapid rise and fall of her chest, which told him she was terrified. He dropped the car keys on the end table and silently walked over to her. He took a pocketknife out of his back pocket. Holding up her hands, he cut the tape binding her wrists together. He also cut the tape that bound her legs.

Cassie was frozen with fear as he removed the remainder of the tape from her hands. She quickly scooted away from the heat of his body. A sense of dread filled her as she waited for his next move.

Chapter 13

"You can remove the blindfold, Cass," said a familiar voice. "You were never in any danger." Warm, gentle hands stroked her face.

Her heart skipped a beat. She knew that voice. She knew the smell of his cologne. There was only one person who called her Cass.

With shaking hands, she untied the knot holding the blindfold in place. Slowly opening her eyes, she glared at him. "You imbecile!" she shouted, launching herself at the man smiling at her. Her small fists pounded on his chest, until he captured her hands in his.

Adam grinned as he let her pin him to the sofa. He couldn't think of any place he'd rather be right now as her heaving breasts pressed into his chest. His arms went around her, and he stared up into her flashing eyes. With her struggle renewed, Adam dodged a well-aimed knee just in the nick of time.

"Careful," he admonished. "You may damage something we might need later."

"Are you insane?" she shrieked, enunciating each word as she tried to break free from his grip. Her hands itched to slug him. She wanted to knock the smirk off his handsome face. "You scared ten years off my life, you jerk! You kidnapped me from my wedding. You also spanked me! What do you have to say for yourself, you lunatic?"

"This," Adam said, pulling her head down to his. Her eyes were round as saucers as they settled on his mouth moving closer to hers. She was torn between kissing him and killing him. She wanted to resist, but her head was not listening to her heart. Against her will, her mouth met his in a hungry kiss. Their week apart melted away as he held her and his mouth ravaged hers. She was lost as she melted against him and returned his heated kiss. His tongue plundered and ravaged her mouth, and she let him. She gave as well as she got, returning his ardent kiss with a passion of her own. His mouth left hers and captured her lips again and again.

Cassie couldn't have resisted him if her life depended on it. Three hours ago she was set to marry another man, and now she was with the man she loved.

Sanity slowly returned, and Cassie broke off the kiss. Pushing away from him, she scrambled to her feet. She grabbed the car keys from the table and made a mad dash for the door. She threw open the front door and ran out, expecting Adam to be in hot pursuit. Shivering in the cold, she quickly unlocked the Jeep and hopped inside. Locking all the doors, she put the key in the ignition and turned it. Nothing happened. She tried again, with the same results. *That explains what he was doing outside earlier. He knew I would try to leave.*

When she returned to the cabin, Adam was still reclining on the sofa, where she'd left him. He turned his head in her direction when she came in and closed the door. He patted the space beside him on the sofa. Shaking her head in disbelief, she walked over to the sofa and looked down at him.

"I don't know what kind of game you're playing, but you can count me out. I don't know why I'm here, but I'm not staying here with you. Take me back and I might forget about this. You ruined my wedding. In case you've forgotten, kidnapping is a federal offense."

"You call it kidnapping. I call it a rescue mission. I rescued you from yourself. What happened to 'I can't do this. I can't marry a man I don't love. I have to stop the wedding'?" he asked, mimicking her.

"You were spying on me!" she bellowed in outrage. Cassie picked up a pillow off the sofa and hit him in the face with it. "How long were you there? It doesn't matter. You must have totally misunderstood me."

"No, I didn't misunderstand." He tossed the pillow aside and got to his feet. Adam caught her arm before she could move away. He turned her around to face him. "You came to your senses, and you were getting ready to run out on your intended. You were going to leave him standing at the altar."

"I was not!" she lied, blushing and trying to squirm out of his grasp. From the expression on his face, she knew there was no use lying to him. He had seen and heard everything as she got ready to flee from the church. "Even if I was running out on Trent, it doesn't excuse what you did. Why did you bring me here?"

He released her and took a step back. "You looked like you could use a vacation," he replied sarcastically. "I hear planning a wedding is stressful business." He let out a grunt as her fist connected with his abdomen. He hadn't seen it coming and hadn't had time to brace himself for the blow.

"You are so not funny," she hissed through clinched teeth. "I want to go home. I am not staying here with you."

"You should be thanking me for saving you from making the biggest mistake of your life, again. You married that loser twice already."

"The biggest mistake of my life is you!" Her words hit their mark, and she felt a small measure of satisfaction at the look of pain in Adam's eyes.

"Okay. You were about to make the second biggest mistake of your life. Honey, why don't you go change clothes? Dinner won't be a formal affair."

Cassie shot him a murderous glare.

"The room to the right is yours," he said, pointing. "You should find everything you need."

As his words sank in, she became even more livid. She let out an exasperated scream before stomping from the room. Furious, she slammed the bedroom door shut with such force, it shook the whole cabin.

Doubting him, Cassie opened drawer after drawer and fumbled through the clothes, shaking her head. They were all her size, but not things she would buy for herself. Her wardrobe consisted of a pair of sneakers, several pairs of shorts, tank tops, halter tops, thong panties, socks, a pair of jeans, two T-shirts, one pair of sweats, and four negligees. There wasn't a single bra in the drawer. On the dresser was a plastic zipper pouch that held deodorant, a razor, lotion, a bottle of expensive perfume, toothpaste, and a toothbrush.

He couldn't have pulled this off alone. I bet he had help, and I bet I know who helped him. Monica!

Cassie reached behind her to undo her gown. Reality was cold and brutal when it hit her. The gown was fastened at the top with a row of tiny hooks. There was no possible way she could remove it without Adam's help. Cassie dropped down on the bed in exasperation and let out a squeal of frustration. She'd rather sleep in the gown than ask him for help.

An hour later Adam knocked on her door before stepping inside the room. He found her sitting on the bed Indian style, still wearing the gown. With arms folded across her chest, she glared up at him.

"You look beautiful in that gown, but I would think you would be more comfortable in something a little less formal."

Cassie was smiling when she came to her feet. She closed the distance between them in a flash. "Then take it off me," she whispered seductively, presenting him with her back. "Undress me, Adam." She didn't miss the pleased look on his face at her suggestion. She smiled at his sharp intake of breath.

Adam undid the tiny hooks above the zipper

and then slid the zipper down her back. His warm hands were splayed on her bared shoulders as he parted the material of the gown. She shivered when she felt his lips trail a path down her neck to her bare shoulder. His hands parted the gown further, and he tried to push the material from her arms.

Cassie ducked under his arms and moved away from him. "Dream on. I think I can take it from here."

His eyes twinkled with merriment as he watched her hold the gown in place. "Are you sure? I watched you put it on. So it's only fair I get to watch you take it off. Do it slowly so I can really enjoy it. Hey, I undid it for you."

"I'm not an exhibitionist like you are, Mr. Strip-a-gram."

"Too bad. You just ruined another fantasy I had about you. Black leather bustier, thigh-high leather boots, and a whip," he teased.

"I see you've given this a lot of thought. Have these dreams often, do you?"

"Now that you mention it, yes." He moved closer to her.

"Not going to happen." Cassie pointed at the door. "Go."

"I'll go whip something up for dinner. No pun intended. I already know what I'd like for dessert." Adam was smiling as he left the room.

She removed the gown and hung it in the closet. She yanked open a drawer so hard, it came out of the dresser. She stumbled backward over her shoes and let out a squeal as she landed on her bottom.

The drawer crashed against the wall, and its contents flew all over the room.

"Cassie!" Adam rushed into the room. He stopped in his tracks when he saw Cassie sprawled on the floor, clad only in a pair of white bikini panties. He eyed her lithe body in appreciation. Her breasts were magnificent.

She grabbed a top and held it in front of her. It did little to hide her abundant charms.

He quickly figured out what had happened as he took in the scattered clothing. Kneeling down, he picked up the red lace thong panties and held them up. The price tag dangled from his hand, which assured him that Monica wasn't fighting fair. Cassie did not look pleased at her sister's choice in underwear.

"Very appetizing. When do you model these for me?"

She lunged for the panties, and he held them out of reach. He dodged as she threw a sneaker at him.

"I guess I can take that as a no. If you change your mind, just whistle. You do know how to whistle, don't you?"

"Get out!" Cassie screamed, throwing the other sneaker at his retreating back. When the door closed behind him, she vaulted to her feet. She slipped on a pair of sweats. It was a lot less than what she usually wore in this kind of cold, but at least she was sufficiently covered, or so she thought. She could only sulk and pout for so long before hunger took control.

Adam looked up when she came into the kitchen, but he didn't stop what he was doing. "I hope you're hungry." He was dishing up plates of food. "I made chicken fettuccine, garlic bread, and salad. We also have a nice chilled bottle of wine."

"I'm starved," said Cassie, taking the seat across from him. "I hope it tastes as good as it looks."

"I'm starved as well." He handed her a plate. From the look in his eyes, she knew he was not referring to food.

She watched him devour his food. *I guess kidnapping makes him hungry.* Picking up her fork, she began to eat. The meal was delicious. The chicken was tender and spicy, and the garlic bread practically melted in her mouth. The wine added a nice touch.

After dinner Cassie helped Adam clean up the kitchen before following him out to the cozy living room. He sat down on the sofa and watched her pace like a caged animal.

"You're making me dizzy. That's a lot of pent-up energy you have. Do you want to go on a hike, or stay here and exert it with me?"

"Why don't *you* go take a hike? I'm glad I'm making you dizzy. Why did you bring me here, and how long am I required to stay?" She watched him shift uncomfortably under her heated stare.

"I was trying to save you from yourself, but apparently, I didn't have to bother. You came to your senses before it was too late."

"Why do you care who I marry?" she asked, turning on him. "You didn't want a relationship with me. You only wanted a bed partner. You're the man who's afraid of commitment, remember?" He flinched and she smiled nastily. "So tell me, Adam, do the words *commitment* and *marriage* make you break out in a cold sweat? Do your hands shake when someone tells you they love you?"

"There's only one way to find out. So tell me you love me, and we can test your theory," he challenged. "I care very much. The thought of you with any man drives a knife through my heart."

"I'd like to drive a stake through your heart, you selfish, heartless Neanderthal, but you don't have a heart. Who do you think you are to play God with my life? You have no right to interfere. You gave up that right when you walked away from me. I want to go home, and I want to go now."

"I told you it's not an option," he stated, crossing his arms over his chest and turning on the television. He leaned back on the sofa with the remote in his hand.

Cassie grabbed the remote from him and turned the television off. "What exactly does 'not an option' mean? Take me back, or so help me, I will have you arrested for kidnapping. My family is probably worried sick about me."

"No, they are not. You left them a note. Wasn't that thoughtful of you? You said something along the lines of you realized what a mistake you were making and couldn't go through with the wedding. You don't love Trent, and you can't marry him. You're still in love with me. You're taking a trip to get your head together."

"I guess you thought of everything." She picked up a pillow from the sofa and threw it at his smiling face. He caught it and placed it behind his back. Vaulting to his feet, he advanced on her.

"Stay back!" She backed away from him. "Don't come any closer!"

"Or what?" Adam asked. "You might not be able to control yourself? You might strip me naked and have your way with me? I'd let you."

His arm whipped around her, and he drew her against him. His head swooped down, and his mouth covered hers in a hungry kiss. His tongue demanded entrance, and her lips parted to allow him access. He deepened the kiss, pulling her even closer into the circle of his arms. His hands moved up to cup her breasts. Her nipples turned to pebbles under his caressing hands.

Cassie moaned and her arms went around his neck as she returned his kiss. Her tongue mated with his, playing a game of cat and mouse. Her hands moved under his shirt to caress his bare flesh. She was startled when Adam pulled his mouth from hers and gently pushed her away from him.

"I know you don't love Trent. I can see it in your eyes, sweetheart. You love me. Cassie, I didn't need you to protect me. You didn't have to marry him to save me."

She sat down on the sofa and leaned back against the sofa cushion. Picking up her wineglass, she took a sip for courage. He removed the wineglass from her hand and set it back on the coffee table. Cassie got to her feet and went to her room. She wasn't ready to admit anything to him. Admitting the truth would give him the power to hurt her again.

She felt him behind her, but she refused to move away or turn around to face him. Cassie jumped when his hands came down on her shoulders. With firm, caressing fingers, he began to massage the tightness from her shoulders. Her head rolled to the side, and she shivered when she felt his hot breath on her neck. When his lips did make contact with her heated flesh, she almost leaped out of her skin. She took a deep breath to clear her head. The smell of the man behind her was intoxicating, and her body caught fire.

"What do you think you are doing?" she asked breathlessly, moving to the other side of the room to escape his nearness.

Adam followed her in hot pursuit. "I'm trying to help you relax. You are way too tense." He caught her arms and pulled her against him. His lips touched her neck and his hands cupped her breasts through her shirt. Instantly, her nipples hardened in his palms.

Gathering all the willpower she had left, she turned around to face him. His mouth covered hers, and she returned his heated kiss and swayed into him.

"Adam," she whispered, breaking the kiss and fighting desperately for control of her body and her emotions.

"Yes, my sweet?" he answered, lowering his head to hers once again. His lips touched hers lightly, tentatively. "Your wish is my command."

"Get out of my room," she said softly against his lips. She moved out of his arms and walked over to the door. Opening it, she waved for him to leave. "Good night and good riddance."

Laughing, he walked over to her. He leaned over and dropped a light kiss on her parted lips. "If you don't want to sleep alone, don't bother to knock. Just come in. As you recall, I sleep naked."

Letting out a squeal of exasperation, Cassie slammed the door shut behind the insufferable man. She heard Adam's laughter all the way from the living room.

Chapter 14

Cassie woke with a start. Something was wrong. She sat up in bed and looked around the room. She couldn't see anything in the dark, but it was freezing in her room. Her teeth were chattering as she hopped up from the bed and went to check the thermostat in the hallway. Her feet bare, she danced from foot to foot on the cold hardwood floors. She turned the gauge up to eighty degrees, but the heat still didn't kick on. Cassie hit it with her hand, but still no results.

"Great. It's not working." She went back to her room, took a pair of socks out of a drawer, and slipped them on. Grabbing her pillow and comforter off the bed, she headed for the living room.

The huge fireplace cast a soft, inviting glow over the room. There was no need for her to turn on the lights. Cassie dropped her bundle on the sofa and added two logs to the fire. Settling down on the sofa, she drifted off to sleep listening to the sounds of the crackling fire and the howling wind.

The next morning she dragged herself off the

sofa. Every muscle in her body ached from the uncomfortable sofa. She stretched and groaned as her muscles protested.

I should have let the bed out. Who am I kidding? It's probably so old, it won't fold out. Oh, well, it's my turn to cook breakfast. I might as well hop to it.

Shivering slightly, she walked into the kitchen and flipped on the light switch. When the lights didn't come on, she frowned.

The bulb must be out. I'll have Adam take a look at it as soon as he gets up.

She washed her hands in the semidarkness. Cassie found the matches and lit the oven. She left the oven door open to help warm the room. Opening the refrigerator, she discovered the light was also out in it.

No. It can't be.

She ran to the living room, picked up the television remote, and hit the power button. Nothing happened.

This is not happening. This is a bad dream. It has to be.

"Great. We have no electricity."

With a sinking feeling, she walked to the front door and opened it. Cassie stared in horror at the foot of snow, which must have fallen last night.

It was not only freezing outside, but the snow was coming down hard and heavy. She could barely make out the SUV. Closing the door, she ran to Adam's room.

"Adam Hart, you are dead! Get your butt out of bed, now!"

Barging into the room, she came up short and a loud gasp filled the air. Her face turned crimson as she found the man she was searching for. Her eyes moved over him in slow deliberation from head to toe and back up again.

Adam stood before her in all his naked glory. Her breath caught in her throat at the sheer masculinity of him. Thick, brown, bulging muscles begged to be caressed. His stomach and chest had muscles on top of muscles. Strong, hard thighs rippled as he moved. His body was superb. Her eyes were drawn back to that part of him that had first made her a woman. His body reacted to hers, and her eyes grew round as saucers.

No need to ask if he's happy to see me. I'm doing it again. I'm talking to myself. I guess I'm okay as long as I don't start to answer my own questions. Okay, now I'm rambling nervously. Shut up, Cassie, and back out of the room slowly. Put your eyes back in your head, and close your mouth.

Backing out of the door, she allowed her eyes to meet his. His were smiling, while hers were embarrassed. There was no mistaking the hungry leer in her eyes as they devoured him.

Cassie leaned against the closed door, trying to steady her racing heart. When she closed her eyes, visions of a naked and sculptured Adam Hart kept creeping into her mind. The heat not only rose to her face but spread to the nether regions of her body as well. She tried to calm the raging fires inside her.

Okay, so no cold- or hot-blooded female would be unaffected by the sight of Adam. He definitely knows how to make a lasting impression. Just what I don't need, a visual of him naked. Cassie, stop it! There are more important things to think about right now. Don't think about how quickly you can remove your clothes and join him in his room. You can't ravish him right now. Why not? I doubt he would resist, but maybe another time. Think about him later. You need to cool off.

She marched over to the front door and opened it. The freezing cold quickly cooled her ardor. Breathing in the frigid air, she shut the door and locked it.

Okay, I'm back. I'm in control again. Bad body! You see a naked man and you go nuts. Okay, so not just any naked man. You see Adam naked and go nuts.

"Why is it so cold in here?" Adam asked, emerging from the bedroom. He went to check the thermostat. He was now clad in a pair of jeans and a sweatshirt. "Did you try adjusting this thing?"

She ignored him as she walked to the kitchen. She searched through the cabinets and pantry looking for a portable radio. Cassie smiled when she found one. Now the search was on for batteries. Cassie found a pack of AAs and brought her bounty to the table. Slipping the batteries into the back of the radio, she prayed they were still good and the radio worked. She turned the dial, hoping to find a weather station. Any station would do in this weather.

"Cassie?" He came to the table and sat down across from her. "What are you doing? What's going on here?"

"Shush." She held up her hand to silence him when he was about to speak again. "I'm listening for a weather report. We need to know the forecast."

"Why? It's not like we're going anywhere." He smiled. The teakettle whistled, and he got up to turn off the burner.

"Why?" she asked, glaring at him. "Because we have no electricity. The weather was obviously something you neglected to think about in hatching your kidnapping scheme with my sister."

"How did you say all that without taking a breath?" he asked under his breath. "You tired me out just listening to you."

"Take a look outside, genius," growled Cassie, glaring at him. "Tell me what you see. Tell me what's different about today."

Adam walked to the door and opened it. His mouth dropped open in surprise. The ground was covered with snow, and it was still snowing very hard. Shivering, he quickly shut the door.

"Okay. That could be a problem." He came back to the table and collapsed in a chair across from her.

"No kidding, Sherlock. I guess from the troubled look on your face, this wasn't part of your plan. Well, you know what they say about the best-laid plans."

"We interrupt this program to bring you a special weather report. The worst blizzard in history has hit the city of Palestine and the surrounding areas. Overnight, we were blanketed with a record thirteen inches of snow. This storm has taken the city by surprise. For safety reasons, all major roads are shut down. We expect another twelve inches or so by tomorrow morning. For your safety, we urge everyone to remain indoors until this storm passes. All schools are closed until further notice. There have also been several power outages reported. Let's just pray that everyone has at least a fireplace or gas stove. The temperature is about five degrees below zero and dropping. We won't get out of these freezing temperatures for at least another couple of days. Be warm and be safe.".

"Great kidnapping job, Doc. Next time be more thorough and listen to the weather forecast. You might learn a thing or two."

"Princess, look on the bright side. We have everything we need right here. We have food, a gas oven, a fireplace, a generator, six bottles of wine, bottled water, and plenty of body heat."

"Sounds like the perfect seduction to me," she snapped, crossing her arms over her chest. "Did you also remember to bring the condoms?"

"Ribbed or glow in the dark?" he asked, winking at her.

"You arrogant, conceited, conniving swine," hissed Cassie, coming to her feet. She walked over to the refrigerator. Taking out eggs, bacon, biscuits, and butter, which were still cold, she set them on the counter. Her body tensed when she felt him behind her.

He turned her around to face him. His head lowered to hers. At the last possible moment, she turned her face from his. His lips landed harmlessly on her flushed cheek. She took a step back from him.

Cassie had to be strong. She couldn't let his nearness affect her sound judgment. She had to keep a cool head for both their sakes.

Adam was not to be deterred. He pulled her flush against him. His mouth covered hers in a hungry kiss. He devoured her as his hands molded her to him. His tongue slipped between her parted lips, and he deepened the kiss. Moaning in surrender, she placed her arms around his neck. Her tongue mated with his, and she responded with a hunger to match his.

She stared at him through passion-glazed eyes. His mouth touched hers again and again. Slowly her sanity returned, and she pulled back.

"I was kidding about the condoms, Cassie. I have only two in my wallet." His hand brushed a strand of hair from her flushed cheek. "After that, it would be Russian roulette. We both know that with us twice is never enough. I'm willing to risk it. Are you? Do you think you can handle being tied to me for life?" He dropped a soft kiss on her cheek and walked away.

Why do I already feel tied to you for life? You are my first real love and my first real lover. I'm sure I can handle it, Adam, but can you? Are you still gun-shy about commitment?

Cassie listened to his retreating footsteps as he left the room. She knew they were in big trouble. This was an impossible situation. There was no way they could share a cabin and keep their hands and mouths off each other. The raw sensuality he exuded was calling to her. Her mind was saying no, but her body was saying something totally different.

Her body was getting warm just thinking about him. Cassie walked over to the front door and opened it. Taking a deep, calming breath, she closed the door again and went back to the kitchen.

Okay, that cooled me off for a little while. If I keep doing this, I'll get pneumonia. Okay, Cassie, just take one day at a time, or in this case, one minute at a time.

* * *

Cassie hid out in her room until the cold forced her out of hiding. She sat on the sofa, looking at a magazine.

When Adam moved to the living-room floor to do his nightly exercise ritual, she groaned. Her eyes followed his hands, and he drew the snug-fitting T-shirt over his head and dropped it on the floor. He stretched out on the floor and started his push-ups.

Her eyes followed the rippling muscles of his back as he moved up and down on the floor. She could easily imagine herself beneath him. Heat suffused her face and the rest of her body as her head nodded, simulating his movements.

Now he had one hand behind his back as he pushed up. Taking a deep breath, he stretched out on the floor for sit-ups. He raised his knees and put his hands behind his head. He made his workout look effortless.

She forced herself to breathe in and out slowly as she watched him. His chest and stomach begged to be touched, and her hands were itching to do just that.

His stomach was flat and ripped. There wasn't an ounce of fat anywhere on his gorgeous body. He did five sets of stomach crunches in rapid succession.

"Why don't you join me on the floor?" Adam asked between crunches. They both knew his words held a double meaning.

"I'd rather watch the exhibition than be a part of it, but you go right ahead," she said and smiled.

"Taking off your shirt was a nice touch. You have a great body."

He crawled on all fours over to the sofa. Pinning her there by placing his hands on both sides of the cushion, he stared up at her. "So I make you all hot and bothered?"

His hands moved up her thighs. She caught his hands and moved them from her person. When their hands touched, they both felt the spark. She quickly released his hands.

The heat radiating from his body warmed her. She shifted nervously in her seat. Her body was on a slow burn for his. Cassie leaped to her feet, causing Adam to fall back on his bottom. He looked up at her with a knowing look in his eyes.

"I'm going to go shower," said Cassie, rushing from the room.

"Was it something I said?" The laughter in his voice followed her out of the room.

She trembled as she leaned against the bathroom door. Her hands were shaking as she turned on the shower. Her body was craving a man, but not just any man. She wanted the man in the next room. They were good together. Adam was an unselfish lover. He took his time and made sure she was fulfilled again and again before he found his own release.

I've got to stop thinking about him like this. We've only been here a few days, and I'm ready to jump him.

She stripped and stepped under the cool spray of the shower. She thoroughly washed her body. Cassie took a quick short shower. She was afraid to let the water run any longer. Adam still needed to shower. During her brisk shower, she cleared her mind of all thoughts of the handsome man in the other room.

Stepping out of the shower, she grabbed a fluffy navy blue towel and dried the moisture from her body. She closed the toilet seat and sat down. Opening the cap on her favorite lotion, she applied the decadent-smelling balm to her arms, legs, and hands. She slipped on her red cotton pajama bottoms, pulled the top on, and buttoned the four buttons down the front. She hung the towel over the shower stall to dry. Turning off the light in the bathroom, she left the room.

Cassie stared in surprise when she walked into the living room. Her steps faltered as she neared the sofa. Adam had rearranged the room. The coffee table was now against the far wall. The sofa sleeper had been let out, and the bed was made.

Her eyes narrowed on his smiling face. It was nice of him to let out the bed for her, but why were his pillow and blanket on it? Surely, he didn't think she would share the bed with him. No way! There was absolutely no way she was sharing a bed with him.

Adam walked toward her, smiling. He was carrying a pair of purple paisley silk pajama bottoms, and a towel was draped around his neck. "Why don't you warm up the bed for me?" He winked as he passed her. She was scowling as he closed the bathroom door.

Warm up the bed for him! I'll warm it up for you all right, you pig! If you think I'm sleeping with you, you have another thing coming, mister.

A wicked smile parted her lips as she marched into the kitchen. Opening a cabinet, she found the ziplock bags she was searching for. She took two out of the box and closed the cabinet.

As the shower came on, she quietly walked over to the front door. Easing it open, she kneeled down and picked up two handfuls of snow. She placed the snow in the bags, sealed each one, and closed the door softly behind her. With an impish smile on her face, she placed the bags under the sheet on Adam's side of the bed. She placed one at his back and the other at his feet.

"That should cool you off, Dr. Hart," she whispered to the empty room. She walked to the fireplace and warmed her freezing hands, then went to the bed and slipped between the covers, turning her back to Adam's side. She couldn't look at him, or the smirk on her face would give it away.

As she lay listening to the water running, visions of Adam naked kept popping into her head. Rolling over, she punched the pillow. She closed her eyes as she imagined the rivulets of water coursing down his sculptured chest. The water would continue a path down his rock-hard stomach, following the dark trail of hair until it reached that part of him that brought her so much pleasure.

Okay, enough of that! Think about something else!

She threw the covers off and got up. She was pacing the room when she heard the shower stop. Slipping back into bed, she waited for Adam to come out of the bathroom. She didn't have long to wait.

Her eyes strayed to his bare chest. She noticed how low his pajama bottoms rode on his hips. Her face was flushed when she turned away. "Good night," she mumbled, feigning exhaustion. "Sweet dreams." She rolled over onto her side and bit her lip to keep from laughing.

She felt the bed dip as Adam's weight pressed on the mattress. He let out a yelp and vaulted to his feet. Turning to face him, she smiled innocently.

"What the he . . ." His voice trailed off as he pulled back the sheet. "Very funny."

"So is the temperature to your liking?" She laughed, rolling onto her back. "Should I adjust the heat for you? Do I need to turn up the heat?"

"If I were you," said Adam, tossing one of the ziplock bags in the air with one hand and catching it, "I'd get out of bed before it becomes a bed of snow."

"You wouldn't." The smile left her face. She knew him well enough to know he definitely would. "You would." She scrambled off the bed, with Adam in hot pursuit.

He caught her before she made it to the bathroom. Pinning her body between his and the bathroom door, he smiled wickedly at his prey. He opened the ziplock bag and held it over her head. "Give me one good reason why I shouldn't give you a cold shower." His hand brushed a strand of hair from her flushed face.

"This," she said, her breathless reply surprising both him and her. She tiptoed and wrapped her arms around his neck. Pulling his head down to her, she planted a ravenous kiss on him. She put all the need in her body over the past two years into one single kiss.

His lips parted eagerly in response, and her tongue slipped between them. The bag of snow fell to the floor as he took her in his arms. Catching her tongue, he gently sucked until she moaned in pleasure. His hands moved up her rib cage to cup her breasts. Her nipples became hard pebbles in his hands. Her body craved his touch.

Cassie was in heaven as his mouth left hers to explore her neck. She didn't even realize her top was undone until he flicked her pert nipple with his tongue. She gasped as he drew the hardened pebble into his mouth.

"Oh, Adam." The words came out in a rushed whisper as she held his head to her throbbing breast. His head moved back up to capture her mouth. When his mouth left hers to draw a breath, sanity returned.

Embarrassed by her response to him, she pulled her top together. She had no idea when her mind had lost control of the situation and her body had taken over. Her body was quivering in need, but she fought the urge to step back into his arms. Shaken by the kiss, she turned and walked to the bed and lay down.

This can't happen. I can't let this happen. Keep your distance, Cassie. You have to keep a clear head. Don't let him get to you.

Pulling the comforter to cover her, she turned her back to him. She willed herself to go to sleep and not think about the man who would be sleeping next to her.

Adam followed her to the bed. Without a word, he climbed in beside her. She heard him curse and then remembered the second bag of snow. She had forgotten about it until now.

"I think you need to cool off as much as I do," whispered Adam next to her ear. Cassie was not prepared for what happened next. Adam dumped the bag of snow down her pajama bottoms. He quickly moved out of harm's way.

Cassie let out a bloodcurdling scream as the snow hit her bottom and nether regions. She jumped out of the bed and danced around the room. Adam's laughter only intensified her anger. He was lying back on the bed, laughing his head off at her expense.

She marched over to the front door and yanked it open. Making a snowball, she threw it at Adam's head. He dodged it, and it hit the wall.

"Close the door, Cassie. It's freezing out there."

"It's also going to be freezing in here. You put snow down my pants," she said, glaring at him. "You declared war, mister."

"You started this, sweetheart. You put snow in my bed. You can dish it out, but you can't take it. I'd say now we're even."

"We're not even," she promised, shaking her leg. "We're not even close. I'll get you when you least expect it, Adam Hart. I owe you one."

"I guess this means I should sleep with one eye open tonight." He propped her pillow behind his head.

"If I were you, I'd sleep in the other room for your own safety. I really don't trust myself not to harm you."

"Nice try, but the answer is no. I'm not you, and it's freezing in there. You are welcome to sleep in there if you like, but I'm staying right here. I'll even give you a blanket."

"Fine." She walked over to him and snatched her

pillow from behind his head. "If I freeze to death, it's on your head."

His hand snaked out and grabbed her wrist. He gave a hard tug, and she fell on top of him. The air left his lungs with a whoosh as she landed on him. Her eyes became large brown pools of panic owing to their precarious position. Her breathing became labored as she saw a sparkle in his eyes.

He rolled them over, reversing their positions. She was flat on her back, and he was peering down at her. "Now we've come full circle. Good night, Cass. Sweet dreams." He planted a soft kiss on her forehead, as though she were a child. He lifted himself off of her and moved away. Turning his back to her, he settled on his side of the bed. Minutes later his even breathing assured her he was asleep.

How dare he fall asleep? The two of us are sharing a bed, my hormones are raging out of control, and he falls asleep.

She lay there staring at his bare back and broad shoulders. Her hand itched to reach out and touch him. Instead of giving in to the temptation, she rolled away from him and snuggled down beneath the covers.

Sometime during the night the fire died down, and for warmth, they moved toward each other. Cassie ended up in the safe haven of his arms. Their arms and legs were entwined as they slept. At one point Adam untangled his limbs from hers and eased out of bed. Padding over to the fireplace, he added two more logs to the fire. He looked in the corner and noticed the low wood supply. In the morning he had to go scrounging for wood. Their survival depended on it.

He got back in bed and pulled Cassie back into his arms, where she belonged. In the morning she would recoil from him, but tonight he would hold her. Adam fell asleep with a satisfied smile on his face.

They awoke early, and after breakfast Adam went out to chop more firewood. Cassie wanted to accompany him, but he refused. He insisted she stay where it was safe and warm. Cassie called him a male chauvinist, and he didn't refute it. He went out the back door when she went to the bathroom. He wanted to leave before she could argue with him.

He found a chainsaw in the shed out back. He prayed that it worked. He pulled the cord, and it came on. He hadn't been outside more than a few minutes, and he was already freezing. He knew with the temperature so cold, he had to move fast. He frowned when he saw a tarp covering something right outside the shed. Removing the tarp, he said a silent prayer and turned off the saw. There were a couple cords of wood. They wouldn't even use half of it before the weather broke.

Picking up an armful of wood, he carried it to the back door and stacked it in a pile. He repeated this several times, until he thought they had enough wood to last for several days. He went back to the shed, covered the wood with the tarp, and closed the door to the shed.

Chapter 15

When he opened the back door, he heard the front door close. His arms were loaded with wood, so he kicked the back door shut with his foot. His eyes narrowed on Cassie, and she shifted uneasily under his stare. Cassie stood there guiltily in one of his jackets and warm-up pants. They were way too big for her, and she looked ridiculous. He carried the wood to the fireplace and placed a few pieces on the rack.

"Going somewhere?" Adam asked as he placed two pieces of wood on the low-burning fire.

"I was coming to find you," she confessed softly. She walked toward him, happy to see him safe and in one piece.

"Then your sense of direction is extremely skewed. I went out the back, not the front. It's way too cold outside to be playing in the snow today. I wouldn't relish having to search for you and rescue you, or prevent you from breaking your neck."

"I'd rather freeze than have you rescue me. I'd never live it down or hear the end of it," she fired back. "You were out there a long time, and I was worried about you."

"I'm touched by your concern. Should I take this to mean you still care?"

She made no comment but blushed under his astute observation.

"You were supposed to stay put, remember? But then, you've never done what you were told or listened to reason. If you want to give me a hand, I have some wood by the back door. We need to fill this rack."

She followed him out the back door. She shivered and her teeth chattered. It was freezing outside. Together, they quickly filled the wood rack and closed the back door.

Cassie removed his jacket and laid it across her arm. She reached for the one he was wearing as well and hung them both in the closet.

She joined Adam in front of the fireplace to warm her hands and the rest of her. Adam squatted down in front of the fireplace, holding out his hands.

"You'd better get out of those damp clothes before you catch a chill. You look like a Popsicle," she said.

"Does that mean you're going to lick me?" he teased as he watched the color seep into her cheeks. "Still trying to get me out of my clothes, princess? All you have to do is ask."

She hid a smile. "I'm being realistic. I don't want to have to nurse you back to health if you become ill, Doc. Don't argue with me. Go change. And before you ask, no, I won't do it for you."

"You're no fun." Adam was smiling as he came to his feet. He kicked off his soggy sneakers and proceeded to pull the snug-fitting T-shirt over his head.

Her eyes strayed to his chest before she lowered her gaze. "I've been told something along those lines repeatedly over the past couple of years. I'll make you a cup of hot chocolate."

"With two marshmallows, please."

"If you're a good boy, I'll give you three marshmallows. If you promise not to get sick on me, I'll add whipped cream to it."

"I'm always good, but save the whipped cream for another time," he teased.

She ignored his suggestive comment and walked into the kitchen. Filling the kettle with water, she placed it on the burner and turned it on.

Adam left the room, taking his soggy clothes with him. He was shivering when he returned to the living room. He was dressed in a red track suit and a pair of socks. He walked over and kneeled down in front of the fireplace.

"What's wrong?" Cassie asked, setting the two cups of hot chocolate on the coffee table. "You don't look so hot."

"I can't seem to get warm." His teeth were chattering as he got to his feet. "I think I was outside too long." He swayed on his feet, and she ran to him. He put his arm around her, and she helped him to the couch.

Panic set in at his confession, and she sprang into action. Cassie went to the other room to get a blanket. She wrapped the blanket around him and handed him the cup of hot chocolate. His hand shook slightly as he took the cup.

"Drink up. You are not to move from that spot," she ordered.

She watched him as he finished the hot chocolate. Taking the cup from his hands, she set it on the table. Cassie stood up and patted the spot for him to put his legs up. Adam did so without arguing, which was a bad sign. He held open the blanket for her to join him. He saw the indecision on her face as she weighed her options. Against her better judgment, she went to him. She told herself it was because he was cold. The truth was she needed to be held as much as he needed her warmth.

She wasn't sure about him, but she knew her body immediately warmed up when she lay down next to him. Her head rested on his chest. Within a matter of minutes she watched the even rise and fall of his chest. Cassie was worried as she watched him sleep. She touched her hand to his forehead and was relieved he wasn't running a temperature, yet.

When she tried to ease off the sofa, his arms tightened around her. She relaxed against him, and she, too, drifted off to sleep. She woke a little later and eased out of Adam's arms. She put her lips to his forehead and was relieved his temperature was still normal.

She let him sleep through the afternoon. Cassie sat at the kitchen table, sipping hot tea. From time to time, she walked over to check on Adam. He was sleeping like a baby. She prepared an early dinner of baked pork chops, green beans, potatoes, and corn on the cob. The meal was the extent of her culinary talents. She hoped it was at least edible.

Cassie was setting the table when Adam awoke and sat up slowly. His head was pounding as he swung his legs to the floor. He had put in a lot of hours the past few weeks going over his inheritance, but he hadn't expected it all to come back and knock him on his butt. A lot of people were depending on him. Adam didn't know the first thing about running a multimillion-dollar corporation. He had a lot to learn, and he didn't know if he was up for the job. He had no idea if he would or could go back to the hospital.

He had personally paid to settle the lawsuit. It wasn't an admission of guilt. He just didn't want the hospital to get all the bad press Trent was sending their way. Now Trent had his own problems to worry about. When Adam was finished with him, Trent would wish he had never tangled with him.

He got unsteadily to his feet. Regaining his footing, he made his way to the bathroom, with Cassie watching his every movement. He washed his face and took a couple of aspirin.

"Sorry for crashing on you," Adam said, coming into the kitchen. He sat down at the table across from her. "Dinner smells wonderful. I'm starving."

He started to rise, and she put her hand on his shoulder to stop him. She massaged his stiff muscles.

"That feels wonderful," he moaned as he moved his head from side to side.

"I'll fix your plate, but don't get used to this. You get only one massage a night."

He returned her warm smile.

She filled his plate with what she hoped was a masterpiece. She set the plate in front of him. Going to the refrigerator, she took out juice and brought it to the table. Cassie fixed her own plate and sat down. They said grace silently before eating.

"This is pretty good," Adam said diplomatically. "It needs a little more seasoning, but it's not bad." He sliced his pork chop, and she watched a morsel disappear into his mouth. He chewed with relish.

"If you eat my cooking, I guess you really are hungry. I'm just glad it's edible. Maybe you can teach me to cook during our extended stay."

"I've been told on more than one occasion, I'm a great teacher."

Their eyes met. Hot color suffused her cheeks, and she lowered her eyes. Cassie tried to block out the memories, but she couldn't.

"Cassie, there's something I have to tell you. I guess I'll start at the beginning. I'm not sure if you've heard of multimillionaire Wade Kirkland. About eight months ago he was in town and had an accident. He was rushed to the ER, and I saved his life. He crashed twice, and I brought him back. I ordered a full set of X-rays and a CAT scan on him, only to discover he had a brain tumor. He was from Los Angeles and didn't want his family to know. He and I clicked, and I invited him to stay at my home while he underwent his chemo treatments. I was with him every step of the way during his chemotherapy treatments. He had only a few of them before we realized it wasn't helping. The radiation wasn't shrinking the tumor. The doctors told him there was nothing else they could do, so he went home. He and I stayed in constant contact. I went out to visit him regularly and got to meet his family. Now I understand why he didn't want them to know. Instead of worrying about him, they were counting the silver. Wade had no wife or children to leave his fortune to. He had two brothers, a niece, and two even greedier nephews. One of them actually moved into the mansion with him before he died. Wade knew it was only for the money. They were all trying to get into his good graces. Well, the joke was on them. Wade had the last laugh. He named me as his heir. He left seventy-five percent of his fortune to me, fifteen percent to his grandniece Lauren, and the other ten percent was to be equally divided between his two brothers and two nephews."

"I'm sorry about your friend," Cassie said and covered his hand with hers. "Fortune and mansions. Wow."

"Therein lies the problem. Two weeks ago I signed all the paperwork transferring everything into my name. So now you see why I said you didn't have to protect me from Trent. I could buy and sell your ex without blinking an eye. I can buy anything I want, but I can't have the one person I want." Their eyes met. "I was happy just being a doctor, and now I have thousands of people depending on me to make decisions about an international company I know nothing about. I'm a doctor. It's what I do. It's who I am."

"Adam, are you thinking about giving up medicine? The world needs great caring doctors like you. You have a gift. Everything isn't about money. Don't lose yourself in what you now have."

They talked for hours about possible options for him to choose. Cassie knew how much medicine meant to Adam. Walking away from medicine would take a piece of his heart. After their conversation, Adam realized leaving medicine was not what he wanted to do at the present time. He still wanted to be a doctor, and he wanted Cassie by his side.

* * *

Cassie was sitting on the sofa bed, writing in her journal, while Adam prepared dinner. The wonderful aroma of food drew her attention away from her troubles. The smell of Southern fried catfish filled the air and beckoned her to the kitchen. She followed the heavenly aroma out to the kitchen.

"Do you need some help?" Cassie asked, walking up behind Adam. "Nice apron. Kiss the cook. Not very original." She reached past him to the plate of mouthwatering hush puppies.

"We'll have none of that," Adam scolded, swatting her hand and making her drop the coveted morsel. He stepped back from the stove. "You can check the casserole in the oven. It should be almost ready."

Cassie opened the oven to survey another of his culinary masterpieces. The casserole looked delicious with its golden brown potatoes and melting cheese.

"It looks heavenly. I think it's almost ready." She closed the oven and moved to the refrigerator. "I'll toss a salad to go with dinner."

They chatted easily as they worked side by side to finish the dinner preparations. The confines of the kitchen were small. Their hands and bodies brushed innocently and often. The room was charged with sexual energy as their eyes devoured each other. Cassie turned off the oven and took the casserole out. Adam removed the last of the fish from the deep fryer and turned to face her.

Cassie had her back to him, but she could feel his eyes on her. She was busy setting the table and trying not to look at him. She fanned herself with her hand. She looked up and saw raw hunger sparkling in his brown eyes. His desire mirrored hers, and it terrified her. In three strides, he was standing in front of her. Taking the plate out of her hand, he set it on the table, then caught her hand and led her into the living room. Talking was not exactly what she had in mind, not unless they were going to use body language. They sat on the sofa bed.

"I never should have walked away from you, Cass," he admitted, bringing her hand to his mouth.

Her eyes flew to his in surprise. She fought for control of her spiraling emotions. She fought the urge to pull her hand from his. His lips on her fingers was almost her undoing.

"I'm asking for another chance. I know I hurt you, and I'm sorry. I want the chance to make it up to you. I know somewhere deep inside you want that, too, at least I'm hoping you do."

She pulled away from him. She couldn't take being hurt by him again. He was only telling her what she wanted to hear.

Will he change his mind once the snow melts? Will his feelings last past a night of intense lovemaking? I can't take the chance. I can't do this again.

"I can't do this again, Adam." She turned to face him. His hand touched her face, and she caught his hand.

He intertwined his fingers with hers and drew her closer. Adam leaned in and placed a tender kiss on her lips. When she didn't pull away, his lips brushed hers again and again.

Cassie removed her hand from his and got to her feet. Adam followed her. She needed some distance between them. She tried to slip past him, but his arm snaked out to stop her. Looping it around her waist, he pulled her against him. Cassie could feel every inch of his flesh pressed against her back and thighs. She shivered when he pulled her hair away from her neck. She felt his warm breath on her skin before his lips touched her burning flesh.

A soft moan escaped her lips, and she swayed into him. Strong, firm hands moved from her waist slowly upward. His hands cupped her breasts, and her eyes closed in pleasure.

With slow deliberation, he removed the straps of her tank top from her shoulders. Stepping back, he let it fall down her shoulders and slip unhindered to the floor. His mouth moved down her throat to her bare shoulder. He licked and then nipped at her sensitive skin. His hands moved back around her and up to her breasts. Nimble fingers covered her firm breasts.

Cassie turned in his arms. Her sultry eyes closed as she pulled his head down to hers. Their mouths fused in a tender kiss. Her toes curled and she moaned in pleasure as heat suffused her body. Her mouth left his long enough to pull his shirt over his head. She tossed it somewhere in the direction of the living room. His mouth covered hers again, and her tongue mated with his. He lifted her up, and her legs wrapped around his waist. Without breaking the kiss, he carried her to the sofa bed.

"See, aren't you glad you listened to me and left the sheets on?" he asked.

"Dr. Hart, you talk too much," she said, falling back on the bed and holding out her arms to him. "Shut up and make love to me."

"That's a foregone conclusion," he said in a sexy voice, kneeling at her feet. He removed her socks one at a time. Strong, sure hands moved up her legs, which were clad in warm-up pants. Catching the waistband of the pants, he peeled the offending material down her shapely legs.

She giggled as his tongue followed the descent of the pants.

"You're not supposed to laugh," he teased. "You're supposed to be moaning and panting. I'll have to work on my technique."

"I find absolutely nothing wrong with your technique," she said and smiled up at him. Holding her arms out to him, she welcomed his weight as his body covered hers. Her legs tangled with his, and she enjoyed the rough, hairy texture against her smooth skin.

"I'm glad. Tonight I intend to taste every inch of your delicious body. If I miss a spot, be sure to let me know."

A rosy blush colored her cheeks. She opened her mouth to speak, but his mouth drowned out whatever it was she was about to say. Cassie forgot her train of thought as he took control of her mind and body.

Hours later the rumbling of their stomachs forced them from the bed. They were both reluctant to move.

"I'm starving," said Adam, dropping a kiss on the top of her head. "We forgot about dinner."

She smiled up at him. "I know. We went straight to dessert. We can heat everything up again." She tried to get up, but he stopped her by tightening his arms around her. "Come on. Let's eat." She reached up and kissed him.

They laughed and talked while they dressed. Adam withheld her panties, stating they blocked his easy access. She retaliated by telling him if she had to give up something, so did he. Moving closer to him, she pulled his shirt over his head. Cassie would never tire of looking at his bare chest.

Together, they warmed up dinner. Sitting at the table, they laughed and talked about everything under the sun. The walls between them were gone once again.

After dinner they cleaned up the kitchen together. They adjourned to the living room, where they lay on the bed and talked most of the night. Still clothed, they fell asleep in each other's arms.

The next day they prepared breakfast together. Cassie stared out the window. The snow was beginning to melt away. They were no longer trapped in their snowbound paradise.

Adam moved behind her, kissing her neck and putting his arm around her waist. She turned in his arms and kissed him.

"The snow is finally starting to melt," said Cassie, snuggling against him. "I don't want to leave here."

"Neither do I." He kissed her cheek. "You've given me some wonderful new memories. This place has always been special to me, and now you've made it even more special. This has been my sanctuary for so many years. When my parents were alive, we came here at least two to three times a year. My dad called it 'getting back to nature.' We would hunt, fish, hike, and go sailing. It was a great life. It all changed when my parents died."

"I know," she said softly, lacing her fingers through his. "Let's go out for a while."

They put on jackets and gloves and went for a short hike. Cassie was admiring the beauty of the countryside when the first snowball hit her in the back. Turning to face Adam, she couldn't believe he had hit her.

A wicked gleam lit her eyes as she leaned down and picked up a handful of snow. Packing it into a ball, she let it fly in his direction. He ducked and fired again, hitting her on the thigh.

The fight was on. For the next thirty minutes they threw snowballs at each other. He let Cassie catch him and tackle him in the snow. He fell back and rolled to break her fall. Laughing, she landed on top of him. The fight was forgotten as she stared down at him with love shining in her eyes. Her mouth lowered to his. He framed her face in his hands and pulled it down to his.

She felt the rising need of his body pressed against her thighs. Her temperature went up an octave lying so intimately against him. Her arms went around him.

I probably shouldn't do this to him, but he does need to cool off a little. We both need to cool off. I still owe him one. I did warn him to expect it when he least expected it.

Cassie's hand slipped from his jacket to grab a handful of snow. Breaking off the kiss, she pulled back his warm-up pants and dumped the snow down the front.

Adam let out a startled yelp, and she tried to scramble away. She tripped and fell, and he caught her by the ankle with one hand while removing the snow from his warm-ups with the other hand. He pinned her down and covered her in snow, then released her and jumped to his feet at a run. Adam knew Cassie would retaliate. He ran inside the cabin and waited for her.

Cassie was squealing as she danced around to get the snow out of her clothing. She stomped toward the cabin with bloody murder on her mind.

The door banged against the wall as she glared at the man she loved. She stomped the snow from her shoes. Shaking her head, snow flew everywhere. She took off her gloves one at a time and threw them at Adam. He caught them both. He whistled for her to continue her striptease routine and yelled for more.

Hanging her jacket in the closet, she walked to the fireplace and sat down on the floor. Adam wrapped her in a blanket and sat down behind her. He pulled her against him and held her. She relaxed against him, and his arms helped to warm her. Her arms covered his, and she hugged them to her. Cassie turned in his arms and kissed him.

"Thank you for today," she said, smiling up at him. "Not the covering me in snow part, but the rest of it."

"The day is not over." He kissed her lightly. "Cassie, this is only the beginning for us. We have the rest of our lives to get it right this time."

Chapter 16

No words were spoken between them as they got ready for bed. They were both deep in thought. Cassie turned her back to him and lay there, staring up at the ceiling. She wanted nothing more than for him to take her in his arms and hold her.

They both turned at the same time and ended up facing each other. Adam moved with lightning speed before she could turn away. His mouth touched hers in a light, questioning kiss. She didn't pull away, but she didn't respond, either. He kissed her again. His mouth was light as a feather as it brushed over hers. His tongue traced the heart-shaped outline of her lips.

She tried to fight the rising tide of emotions inside her, but to no avail. Her lips parted, granting him access to her mouth. His tongue slipped inside her mouth, stroking, searching, teasing, and taunting her. She retaliated in kind, and her tongue traced his lips and then explored the sweet haven of his mouth.

Cassie was grateful he wasn't rushing her. The

only part of their bodies that was touching was their mouths, which were fused together.

With much regret, he withdrew his mouth from hers. His lips touched her cheek, and he rolled over onto his back. He stared up at the ceiling, trying to regain control of his emotions. He wanted Cassie. His body craved her, but he wanted her to know that what they shared was more than physical. He knew he had to take things slow for both their sakes. This time around he would do things right. He would court her and treat her the way she deserved to be treated.

Cassie turned her back on him. She was dazed and confused by his kiss. If Adam had wanted things to go further, she wouldn't have protested. She would have made love with him. Her body was tingling with need. She took several deep breaths to calm her racing heart. Her fingers touched her lips as she closed her eyes and relived the pleasure of the kiss.

So why did he stop? Why did he pull away? Was he having second thoughts again? Was he getting ready to bolt again?

Cassie spent a restless night trying to figure out the male mind. She was no closer to comprehension when she finally drifted to sleep in the wee hours of the morning.

She was still sleeping when Adam got up and put another log on the fire. Returning to bed, he lay on his side, staring at her while she slept. Sometime in the night she had turned to face him. He resisted the urge to touch her because he didn't want to wake her. She looked so peaceful sleeping. He watched her move to her back and smile in her sleep. He was glad at least one of them was having a pleasant dream.

He reached out and lightly caressed her cheek. When she didn't stir, he moved closer and placed a soft kiss on her lips. "I'm not letting you go this time, princess," he whispered softly against her lips. "I can't lose you again."

Adam rolled onto his back and stared up at the ceiling. He wondered briefly what she would do if he made love to her while she was sleeping. Would she respond, or would she wake up and slap his face for trying to take advantage of her?

Cassie moaned softly and turned. She snuggled suggestively against him, wrapping her leg around his. It was obvious she was dreaming about a man. "Adam." The name was a bare whisper as it slipped past her lips. "Make love to me, Adam," she whispered.

Adam did a double take. No need to wonder what she was dreaming about. She had just told him. *Okay, time for a cold shower.* He got up from the bed and went to the bathroom. The shower helped some, but he still wanted her. He wanted her more than ever.

As he eased into bed, she rolled over and snuggled up against him. Adam froze against her. This was pure hell. Cassie moaned softly, and her lips touched his chest. She took his hand and placed it on her breast.

If he didn't know any better, he'd swear she was purposely torturing him. Adam gave up trying to resist and pulled her into the circle of his arms.

I'm glad one of us is getting a good night's sleep. What did I do to deserve this kind of torture? Was I that bad? This is payback, right? This is a test for me. I accept the challenge. I can do this. I have this lovely creature in my arms, and I can't make love to her.

By Saturday the snow had almost melted away. The weather was cold, but not unbearable. That evening the electricity came back on.

With much regret, Cassie took the sheets off the sofa sleeper and carried them back to her room. She had gotten used to sharing a bed with Adam. Tonight she would be back in her own room, in her own bed.

A few seconds later she heard the shower come on. She immediately closed her eyes and pictured Adam naked in the shower.

Okay. Stop. Think about something else, anything else, other than the man in the next room. He's not the one. Don't do this to yourself. Forget the night of incredible passion you shared.

She took a sip of wine and leaned back against the cushion of the sofa. She turned on the television to take her mind off the man in the next room. The shower stopped. Now she could picture him stepping naked out of the shower. His biceps would bulge as he picked up a towel to dry himself off. He'd start with his arms. Placing the wineglass on the table, she shot to her feet. Cassie paced the room like a caged animal.

After dinner they cleaned up the kitchen and then adjourned to the living room to watch television. They were watching a romantic movie when Cassie got up and left the room. The love scene had gotten to her. She had to get away from Adam. Cassie got ready for bed.

Cassie didn't leave her room the rest of the night, which gave Adam a chance to put his plan in motion. Adam had no decorating skills whatsoever, but he was willing to try to make this day special for Cassie. He covered the dining table with a white lace tablecloth. He went out to the Jeep and took out a large box from the trunk.

Adam was up bright and early the next morning. He made breakfast for Cassie and placed it on a tray. He wanted her in her room as long as he could keep her there. He carried the tray to her door and knocked softly. Balancing the tray in one hand, he opened the door and carried the tray in to her. "Good morning, sunshine."

Cassie sat up in bed. "Why are you in my room? What are you up to now?"

"You are so suspicious." He dropped a kiss on her forehead before setting the tray on her lap. "Eat up. We have a busy day ahead of us."

Cassie took a bite of the crispy bacon. "What are we doing today?"

"A little of this. A little of that," hedged Adam. "Call me when you are done, and I'll take your tray."

Cassie watched him suspiciously as he left the room. Something was going on with him. She knew he was up to something.

After breakfast she called to Adam and he came to take the tray away. She hopped out of bed and followed him to the living room. The sight that greeted her took her breath away. The room was decorated all in white, and there was an arch in front of the fireplace that made her take a step back. It almost looked like a setting for a wedding.

Adam heard Cassie's loud gasp and turned to see her standing behind him. He quickly placed the tray on the counter and went to her. This was not how he wanted to do things, but now the cat was out of the bag. Kneeling down on one knee, he caught her hand and brought it to his mouth. "I never thought I would be at this point in my life, but here I am. I love you, and I want to spend the rest of my life with you. Cassandra Mancini, will you marry me?"

Cassie stared at Adam in shock and disbelief. She almost forgot to breathe as her eyes met his. Her mouth dropped open, but no words would come out.

I'm hearing things. He didn't ask me what I thought he asked me! This is only a dream! No, it's a fantasy! The Adam Hart I know would never do this. He doesn't want to get married!

She closed her eyes and shook her head as if to clear it. When she opened them, Adam was still staring up at her with eyes filled with love. She wasn't dreaming or imagining things. Adam had asked her to marry him. She opened her mouth again, but again, no sound came out. Biting her lip, she gazed down at him. All the old doubts kept popping into her head.

Is he doing this only because he knows this is what I want? Or is he doing this only to keep me from marrying Trent? This is what I want, but I am also afraid. Can I trust him not to hurt me? Can I trust him to love only me and to be faithful to me? Do I want him to be the father of my child and my future children? The man you love loves you, he is offering you everything you have always wanted, and you are afraid to reach out and take it.

Silent tears rolled down her cheeks. "We need to talk." Cassie sat down on the sofa, and Adam followed suit. "When Trent and I were first married, we were so happy. Every time I brought up the subject of children, he would change the subject and say he didn't want to talk about it right now. He just wanted it to be the two of us. I wanted children, and he didn't. After our first divorce he told me he had changed his mind, and we remarried. I was too stupid to hear the warning bells going off in my head. He wanted me, but he really didn't want a family. I listened to my heart and not my head. I see myself doing the same thing with you. I tried to change you into the man I wanted you to be. I wasn't even listening to you. I had it all figured out. I thought I knew best. I thought I could make you want all the things I wanted." Cassie got up from the sofa.

"I am not Trent, Cassie. I do want TJ and other children, if we are fortunate enough to have them. I want a family. I want everything you want. I want your dream for us. We have both earned the right to be happy. I love you." He took a step toward her, and she quickly moved away from him.

"I'm not going to make the same mistake again. I can't marry you," she whispered.

He pulled her into the circle of his arms and hugged her tightly. His arms loosened when he felt her tremble against him. She was stiff in his embrace, and silent tears ran freely down her pale cheeks. He raised her chin, and his mouth touched hers lightly. When she didn't resist, he deepened the kiss. Her lips parted tentatively under his, and then ever so slowly her arms went around his neck. Then without warning, she pushed him away and ran back to her room.

I love you, too, Adam, but I can't be with you. I don't trust you not to break my heart again.

Adam was not willing to let the subject drop. He followed Cassie into her bedroom. "Let's me see if I've got this straight. You are willing to marry a man you despise to save me, but you refuse to marry me. How in the hell does that make any sense to you?"

"I'm not discussing this with you. Please, just get out," said Cassie, getting off the bed. Cassie couldn't explain it to herself. Adam was right. She was willing to marry a man she didn't love to protect the man she loved. But when the man she loved proposed, she turned him down. "I don't know what to say."

"Then start by admitting the truth to me. You love me, and you were willing to sacrifice yourself to save me."

"Fine. I admit it. Trent told me if I married him, he would make sure the lawsuit against you was dropped. I knew how much your career meant to you, Adam. You could have lost everything, or so I thought at the time."

"You mean more to me than my career. Forget Trent, and forget the damn lawsuit. I love you, and you love me. Stop making excuses for why we shouldn't be together, and think about all the reasons we should be. Honey, I know we don't have a perfect or even an ideal relationship, but we have the love and we have the passion. We have our whole lives to work out the rest. I want another answer, and I want it right here and right now. Yes or no? For the last time I am not Trent Mancini. I am not just telling you what you want to hear. I want you and TJ. I want us to be a family. If you don't have any trust or faith in me, then your answer should be no, and rightfully so. I can't promise you I will be the perfect husband, or I would be lying, but I will love you the best way I know how. If the answer is no, then I will walk out of your life forever. We can't go on like this. It's either all or nothing, Cassie. The decision is yours. I'm waiting for your answer."

Tears blurred her vision as she gazed at the man she loved with all her heart. *Can I really trust you, Adam? Can I believe in your love?* In her heart she believed him, she believed in him, but her head wasn't so sure she could.

Time seemed to stand still while Adam waited for her to answer. She closed her eyes against the hurt and pain in his eyes. When seconds ticked by without any response from her, Adam left the room. He went to his room and took the cell phone out of the drawer. Walking outside with the phone, he moved around in the yard until he got a signal. Shawn had warned him he was taking a big risk planning a wedding without Cassie's knowledge.

Adam had no idea what he was going to do now. He had gambled and lost. He had been sure that once he proposed, Cassie would accept and marry him. Why wouldn't she? She loved him. So much for well-made plans.

He hit the speed-dial button on the phone as he

got into the Jeep. "Shawn, it's me. You can cancel the wedding plans. She turned me down."

"I'll take care of everything," said his friend. "I'm sorry. I was sure she would accept."

"You and me both," said Adam sadly. "We'll be back tomorrow, at the latest. I'll talk to you then." Adam disconnected the call and dropped the phone on the seat beside him. He got out of the Jeep and just started walking. He needed some time alone to think.

Cassie heard the Jeep door open and close. Walking to the cabin door, she watched Adam take off down the dirt road. She walked outside and peered inside the Jeep. When she spotted the phone, she opened the door and picked it up. Cassie quickly dialed Monica's cell phone.

"Adam, are you nuts planning a wedding without first asking the bride?"

"It's not Adam. It's Cassie."

"Hello?" Monica said, yelling into the phone. "We have a bad connection. Hello?" She crushed something for noise.

"Don't even try it," warned Cassie. "I know you helped with this little kidnapping scheme. I'm also sure Trent was furious."

"He was at first, but Trent has more pressing problems to deal with at the moment. He's busy trying to save his company from a hostile takeover. Doesn't that just warm your heart? It couldn't happen to a nicer guy."

"I don't even care. How's TJ? I miss him. Can I speak to him?"

"He went out with Shawn. Your intended has been a busy boy. He has Trent shaking in his

loafers. Oh well. Gotta go. I'll see you soon."
Monica hung up the phone.

"Monica!" Cassie stared at the phone in her
hand. Her sister had hung up on her. When she
called back, it went straight to voice mail. "Great."
Cassie carried the cell phone inside and set it on
the coffee table.

It didn't take a rocket scientist to figure out that
Adam was going after Trent where it hurt the most,
his company. She couldn't blame him for wanting
revenge. Trent had tried to ruin his career. Cassie
made the wise decision not to get caught in the
middle again. She would stay out of it.

Cassie put pork chops and potatoes in the oven
to bake for lunch. By noon, when Adam hadn't returned, she began to worry. She turned the oven
down and left the cabin in search of Adam. She
had walked a little over a mile when she spotted
him headed in her direction. She stopped and
waited for him to catch up to her. Adam walked
past her, not saying a word. Cassie had to almost
run to catch up to him.

"Adam. I was worried about you."

"No need," he said, not slowing his pace. "I'm a
big boy, Cassie. Despite what you may think, I can
take care of myself."

They were both silent the remainder of the walk
back to the cabin. Once they were back inside,
Adam washed up while Cassie finished getting
lunch ready. She watched him warily as he sat down
at the table.

"We will head home in the morning. Can you
be ready by ten?" asked Adam, loading his plate

with food. "I figure the sooner I'm out of your life, the better."

Cassie laid down her fork. Adam was on the defensive, and she couldn't blame him. She knew she had hurt him. "I'll be ready," she replied softly. *What else can I say under the circumstances?*

After eating Adam rinsed his plate and went to his room. He fell onto the bed, closing his eyes. Hopping up from the bed, he packed his clothes. *Why put off till tomorrow what you can do today?* He packed his bags and carried them out to the living room.

Cassie was lying back on the sofa with her eyes closed. He watched her wipe the tears from her cheeks.

"We can leave whenever you are ready," said Adam, disturbing her thoughts. She jumped guiltily to her feet.

Adam carried his bags out to the Jeep and stored them. He went back inside and bagged up the leftover food and took the garbage out.

Cassie was an emotional wreck as she packed. As much as she missed her son, she would treasure her time here with Adam.

The silent drive back to Dallas was the longest one of both their lives. They were both lost in a haze of pain, deep in thought, and the miles seemed to slip by. They were both relieved to see the city limits sign.

Thirty minutes later Adam pulled the Jeep into the driveway at her house. Cassie said nothing as she hopped out of the SUV. She was almost at the door when she realized she didn't have her keys.

She stared on in surprise as Adam took her house key off his key chain and handed it to her.

Their fingers brushed and her hand shook as she took the key. Cassie quickly unlocked the door.

Adam carried her bags inside and sat them by the door. While she disabled the alarm, he made his exit. There was no reason for him to stay. There was nothing left to be said. He wouldn't say good-bye to her again.

Cassie stood by the door and tears streamed down her face as she watched him drive away. She closed the door and leaned against it for support.

After Adam dropped Cassie off, he drove home. He packed a bag and made flight arrangements to Los Angeles. He was leaving, and he had no idea when he would return. There was no time like the present to go see his new house in L.A.

He hit the speed-dial button on his phone for Shawn. The call went straight to Shawn's voice mail. "Shawn, it's me. I'm heading to L.A. for a while. I'm not sure when I'll be back. Talk to you soon." He hit the speed dial again. This time for Gloria. "Hey, Gloria. How are you?"

"A million times better," she said and laughed. "Thank you for the money. I called Shawn, and he told me the story. My big brother is moving up in the world."

"You're welcome. Hey, I'm headed off to L.A. I just wanted to touch base with you before I left. Take care of yourself, sis." He disconnected the call and stuck the phone in his jacket pocket.

Chapter 17

Cassie called the head nurse and was reinstated at the hospital. She was put back on the schedule the following week.

After her shift on Friday Cassie was getting into her car when she heard someone calling her name. She stopped when she saw Roger sprinting toward her.

"Hi. Have you heard the latest news yet?" he asked breathlessly, stopping in front of her. She frowned as she watched him try and catch his breath. "I've got to get in shape."

"Yes, you do if that little sprint winded you. What is the latest news?" she asked, puzzled, but not really interested.

"Have you talked to Dr. Hart recently? Did something happen between the two of you today? I hear he's moving to Los Angeles."

Cassie stared at him in total disbelief.

"Dr. Sinclair is leaving at the end of the month to be the new chief of staff at a new hospital opening in L.A. He offered Dr. Hart a job a couple of months ago. Dr. Hart turned him down, saying he had ties here in Dallas, but for some reason, he changed his mind and accepted about an hour ago."

Cassie closed her eyes as her heart sank. She was the reason he had changed his mind. Because of her, Adam was leaving town.

"Thanks for telling me, Roger. I didn't know," Cassie said sadly, getting into her car. "I'll talk to you later."

On impulse, she drove to Adam's house. She rang the doorbell several times before it was finally yanked open. Cassie took a step back as she stared up into Adam's angry face. His shirt was off, and he was furious.

"What do you want?" he asked bluntly.

Cassie looked past him to see a woman lying back on the sofa in a bathrobe. She felt like a knife had been plunged into her heart. She took a deep breath before brushing past him and walking into the living room.

The woman came to her feet smiling at Cassie. "I'm Gloria," said the woman, extending her hand. "You're Cassie, right?"

Cassie was confused as she stared at the woman's outstretched hand. She didn't know what to think about the woman smiling at her. Cassie finally took her hand. "I'm Cassie Randall."

"I've wanted to meet you for a long time," said Gloria.

"Gloria, can you wait upstairs for me?" said Adam, cutting her off.

"Been there. Done that. Not doing it again. Tell her the truth or I will," replied Gloria.

Cassie stared from Adam to Gloria in confusion.

"I'm all talked out," said Adam, putting his arm around Gloria and kissing her cheek. "I have other things on my mind right now."

Gloria elbowed him, and he shot her a murderous glare. Cassie didn't move as she stared at them. Something wasn't quite right, but she couldn't put her finger on it.

"Gloria, I know how insatiable you are, but can you give us two minutes?" asked Adam.

Cassie looked on with a heavy heart. "I heard you accepted Dr. Sinclair's offer and are moving to L.A. Please tell me you are not leaving because of me."

"I see good news travels fast. I think it would be best for both of us if I left. Besides, my business is there. Will you tell TJ for me? It might be easier coming from you. Being as creative as you are, I'm sure you can come up with a good explanation. Time's up," said Adam, walking over to the door and opening it for her.

She stepped outside and flinched when the door was viciously slammed shut behind her. *Let him go, Cassie. Just let him go.*

During the following weeks, Adam did some soul-searching, and two weeks later, at what was supposed to be his going-away party, he announced to everyone that he had reconsidered and he was staying. According to Roger, the hospital had made him a counteroffer he couldn't pass up. Cassie knew it had nothing to do with money. Adam had plenty of money, thanks to his inheritance.

Cassie had just walked in the door when her

phone rang. Sitting her purse on the coffee table, she picked up the phone.

"Cassie, hi. It's Shawn," said her brother-in-law.

Cassie frowned at the receiver. *Why is Shawn calling me?*

"How are you?" he asked.

"I'm fine. Since I know you didn't call me for idle chitchat, what's up?" she asked, dropping down on the sofa. "Is everything okay with Monica and the baby?"

"Fine," he said hesitantly. "Cassie, the reason I'm calling is Adam." That much she had guessed. "His birthday is next week, and I'm planning a birthday party for him. Can you pass the word around at the hospital?"

"No problem," she said, toying with the phone cord. "When, where, and what time?"

"Saturday, Have Hart, about nine o'clock," he said in rapid succession. "Can you make it?"

"Shawn, I'll let everyone know, but I'm not sure I'll be there. Adam and I are not exactly friends anymore. I haven't seen or talked to him in weeks."

"Then think about it," he insisted. "Adam has been flying back and forth to L.A. since you got back from the cabin."

"I guess that explains his continued absence from the soccer team," said Cassie, biting her lip. "I hope things work out for him."

True to her word, Cassie passed the word around at the hospital about the party. Biting her tongue, she even told Zack and Rafael and the rest of the ER gang.

She and TJ went out shopping for a birthday present. TJ wanted to buy him something special.

They ended up compromising on a Mickey Mouse tie and matching suspenders.

The rest of the week flew by. On Friday Rachel agreed to be the designated driver and drop Cassie off at home in case she needed a few drinks to get through the evening with Adam so close at hand.

Cassie was dressed in a black, sleeveless, formfitting minidress and matching black pumps. The dress stopped just above her knees. Leaning her head down, she brushed her hair and then threw her head back. This gave her hair added body and bounce. She put on very little makeup, finishing it with a single coat of red lipstick.

Cassie made it to the club before eight to help Monica and Shawn get things ready for the party. This was Adam's thirty-fifth birthday party, and she wanted him to enjoy himself. So what if it meant she had to spend an evening gazing at him from afar and wishing things had been different for them?

Her stomach muscles tightened when he walked in the door an hour later. Her heart fluttered at how handsome he looked in a two-piece black Italian suit. He walked toward her slowly, ignoring everyone else as they patted his back and wished him happy birthday. Adam stopped a few feet in front of her.

"Hi," they chorused and then smiled at each other.

"Happy birthday, Adam," said Cassie, kissing his smooth cheek. He turned his head at the last possible moment, and her lips touched his. Her eyes widened in surprise. She felt a tingling sensation in the pit of her stomach.

"I'm surprised you came," said Adam, breaking the silence. He resisted the urge to pull her into his arms.

"I surprised myself. TJ wants you to come by the house. He bought you a birthday present, and he wants to give it to you personally."

"I'd love to come. I haven't seen him since we got back from the cabin. How is he?"

"He's fine. He doesn't understand what happened and doesn't really care as long as I'm not re-marrying his dad." She wrung her hands nervously. "Let's not talk about this right now. This is your birthday party. I'll let you go mingle with the rest of your guests," Cassie said, walking away from him.

Cassie found Roger and Rachel and sat at the table with them. When the waiter came to the table, she ordered a margarita swirl. She had taken only a few sips when Roger pulled her out onto the dance floor. Her step faltered only slightly when they passed Adam and Gloria on their way back to their table. Adam's and Cassie's eyes met briefly before Roger and Gloria pulled them toward one another.

Alone again, Cassie and Adam looked at each other uncertainly. Cassie sat back down and quickly downed her margarita and ordered another one as Adam took a seat directly across from her. After they exchanged several glances, Adam got up, with his drink in hand, and moved over to sit next to her.

"I can't believe things have come to this," Adam said quietly, tapping his drink glass. He took a sip and set the glass down.

"Same here," she agreed. "There was a time

when we had a lot of fun together. We could talk about almost anything with each other. What happened to those times?"

"I don't know. Would you like to dance?" He smiled. He held out his hand, and she took it. They both felt the spark as their hands touched.

"I'd love to dance." She stared up into his handsome, smiling face.

They danced to several fast top ten songs. When the music slowed down, Cassie tried to leave the dance floor. Adam caught her hand and pulled her into his arms. Slowly, they moved around the dance floor to the beat of the music. Her head rested comfortably on his chest, and she breathed in the scent of him. Her heartbeat quickened when she felt his lips in her hair. At the end of the song, she pulled away, embarrassed by her response to him.

Back at the table she picked up her margarita glass and emptied it. Fanning herself, she ordered another one. Two had always been her limit, but right now she needed a third to calm her.

"You'd better take it easy with that stuff," suggested Adam, indicating the empty glass in her hand.

"I can handle it, Adam. It's just a little warm in here," she insisted. "Can I have a sip of your drink until mine gets here?"

"Not a good idea," he warned, moving his glass out of her reach. "It's a little strong for your taste."

"Try me."

His eyebrows rose suggestively, as if to say "I already have."

She held out her hand for the glass. "It's just rum and Coke, isn't it?"

Smiling, he gave her the glass. "Sip it," he instructed. "Don't gulp it."

Ignoring him, she turned the glass up and took a big swallow. Coughing and sputtering, she wheezed and tried to breathe. Tears ran down her cheeks, and her face turned red.

Adam quickly went to the bar to get her a glass of water. "Drink this."

"What are you drinking? Rocket fuel?" Cassie managed to ask while still gasping for air. She gratefully took the glass of water and took a big swallow. She looked up at him with accusing eyes.

"Close." He laughed. "It's Bacardi one-fifty-one and Coke. I told you to sip it. Some people are just too stubborn for their own good."

"I hope you weren't too attached to your date." Cassie smile. "She seems to prefer Roger's company to yours."

"So it would seem." Adam laughed. "About that. She's not exactly my date."

Cassie stared at him, waiting for him to explain. "Gloria is my half sister." Reflex sent Cassie's water in Adam's face. "I guess I deserved that," Adam said, picking up his napkin and wiping his face. He knew he deserved it for letting her believe he and Gloria were lovers.

Cassie couldn't leave her seat, because Adam was blocking her in. His confession had hurt. He was playing games with her again. Cassie was furious. "Let me out."

"Not until you calm down."

"This is as calm as I'm going to get," she assured him. "Move, or I will scream." She opened her mouth to scream, and his mouth covered hers. He buried his hand in her hair as he plundered her mouth. Cassie tried to resist, but Adam was relentless. Her resolve weakened, and she returned his passionate kiss.

"Get a room, you two," joked Roger as he and Gloria took the seats across from them.

Adam regrettably pulled his mouth from Cassie's. "That's a great idea."

"Cassie," said Gloria, "did Adam finally tell you the truth about us?"

"What truth?" Roger asked, looking from Adam to Gloria. "I thought everyone knew you were his sister."

"Everyone but me obviously," said Cassie. "Adam just filled me in. You have my sympathies. Can I get out now?"

Adam eased out of his seat and let her pass. For the next hour Cassie and Adam exchanged glances at least a dozen times. They kept a close eye on each other, but each refused to make a move toward the other. Whenever she danced with someone, Adam always mysteriously ended up dancing next to her.

"It's time to slow the music down a little," said the DJ. "I have a special request. This song is dedicated to a very special woman from the man who loves her. You know who you are."

When the music started, Cassie's eyes darted around the room looking for Adam. She jumped when a hand touched her shoulder.

"Sorry. I didn't mean to startle you. May I have this dance?" Adam asked, holding out his hand to her.

Hesitating only for a moment, she took his hand

and let him lead her to the dance floor. Cassie was stiff in his embrace, and then, after a while, she began to relax and melt in his arms as he slowly twirled them around the dance floor. She rested her head on his chest and moved with the music.

"I believe in this song, Cassie. I never thought in a million years I would be here. I never thought I would love anyone the way I love you."

She didn't respond; instead she just held on to him for dear life. She shivered when she felt his lips in her hair.

When the song ended, she should have pulled away, but Adam raised her chin and his mouth covered hers lightly. Putting her arms around his neck, she returned his kiss.

Breathless, they both pulled back, and Adam caught her hand and pulled her with him to his office in the back of the club. She was in his arms before the door closed behind them. Her mouth met his in a hungry kiss.

"Come home with me tonight," whispered Adam, planting hot kisses on her face and throat. "God, I've missed you." His hands slid up her hips to caress her throbbing nipples through the material of her dress. Cassie moaned in response and pressed her body closer to his. "I want to make love to you right here, right now."

"I'd let you, but Mama Rosa is out of town," groaned Cassie, pulling his head up to fuse his mouth with hers again. "I have a babysitter tonight. I have to go home. Come home with me," she added, surprising herself.

"What about TJ?" he asked between kisses. His

mouth moved down her throat, and she moaned in pleasure.

"We'll set the alarm clock," she gasped as his hand slid up her thigh, "so you can be up and out before he wakes up in the morning. If you keep this up, we won't make it out of this room."

"That's not a bad idea. I can lock the door." Adam smiled. "I don't like to rush, so let's go." Catching her hand, he led her out the door. They almost made a successful escape, but Shawn and Monica caught them slipping out the front door.

"You haven't even cut the cake yet," scolded Monica, folding her arms over her chest and blocking their exit.

"Fine, Monica," said Adam, taking the cake knife out of her hand. "I'll cut the damn cake. Then we are out of here."

Cassie suppressed a giggle as her sister winked at her.

Everyone gathered around the table as Adam cut the cake. He speared a piece of chocolate cake with his fork and popped it into his mouth. He repeated the act, this time putting the cake to Cassie's lips. She slowly opened her mouth for the cake. Adam leaned over, licked the icing off her red lips, and then kissed her. Shawn uncorked a bottle of champagne and began to fill glasses.

"Speech! Speech!" yelled Roger, clapping his hands. They all raised their glasses and waited expectantly.

"The best is yet to come," said Adam, gazing into Cassie's smiling face. Only she knew the true meaning behind his words.

Staring hungrily at each other, Adam and Cassie

both downed their champagne in one gulp and left the party holding hands. When they got to her house, she paid the babysitter and rushed her out the door. She was in Adam's arms the minute the door closed. Between passionate kisses, they tore at each other's clothes in haste. Clothes went everywhere on their sojourn up the stairs to Cassie's bedroom. By the time they made it there, they were both completely naked.

They fell back on the bed in a tangled mass. They were both ready as an erect Adam slid smoothly into a wet, warm, and waiting Cassie. She met him eagerly, thrust for thrust. She urged him on and then had to bite Adam's shoulder to keep from screaming out in sheer bliss. Their lovemaking was fast and furious, and Cassie was not a bit disappointed. Afterward, they fell asleep in each other's arms.

Chapter 18

Cassie was having the most sensual dream. She moaned and arched into the body above her. Adam was doing all sorts of wonderful things to her body. Her eyes fluttered open as he slipped inside her. This was no dream. The man above her was very real. This time there was no rush. They made love slowly. Sleep soon followed their explosive climax.

The next morning Cassie was slowly brought out of her fog of sleep by a knock on the door. She sat up slowly, and the sheet covering her slipped down to her waist. Remembering the night before, she smiled and pulled the sheet back up to cover her breasts. Adam bolted into an upright position at the next knock. He stared at Cassie and then fell back onto the bed, laughing.

"Ssh! Just a minute, sweetie," said Cassie, pulling the covers off of Adam. "Go into my bathroom," she whispered, pointing to the bathroom door.

She jumped out of bed and went to her bureau. Taking out a gown, she dropped it over her head.

When the bathroom door closed softly behind Adam, she opened the door.

"Morning, Mommy. You overslept. I'm hungry," TJ announced, still dressed in his favorite Spiderman pajamas.

"I'm sorry. Go back to your room. I will be there in a few minutes, and I'll fix you something to eat."

"I'll be glad when Mama Rosa comes back. She never oversleeps," mumbled TJ, running back down the hall.

"That was too close," said Cassie, closing the door behind him. The bathroom door opened, and Cassie stepped inside. Ignoring Adam, she turned on the shower.

"We've got to shower and get you out of here. TJ is a bright child, Adam. I don't want him to see you here."

"A shower with you sounds very stimulating." He reached down, pulled the gown up and over her head, and tossed it aside. He leaned over, and his tongue flicked her pert nipple.

Trembling, she pulled his head away from her throbbing breast. "Adam. We don't have time for this," she scolded, trying to disengage herself from his grasp. "I have to fix breakfast for him."

"He can wait five minutes," whispered Adam, pulling her into the shower with him. "I can't."

Smiling, she put her arms around his neck and brought his head down to hers. "You have five minutes, Dr. Hart. Make it worth my time," Cassie whispered breathlessly against his mouth.

Adam reclined on the bed, with a towel draped around his waist, as he watched Cassie get dressed. She put on a T-shirt and a pair of shorts. He stared at the woman before him as she brushed her hair and applied a dab of perfume to her wrist.

"You stay here, and I'll go get our clothes. We'll tell TJ, if he sees you, you dropped by to have breakfast with him. Got it? Good," said Cassie, opening the bedroom door. To her horror, her son was standing there. He was holding their discarded clothes in his small hands. She stood frozen as he peered past her and ran to Adam.

"Adam! Adam! Did you sleep over?" TJ called.

Cassie closed her eyes in mortification, while Adam laughed out loud.

"Wait until I tell Grandma and Grandpa!" TJ exclaimed.

Cassie's eyes flew to Adam's, and he burst into a fit of laughter. She groaned, rolling her eyes at Adam's laughing face, then dropped down to the bed, beside TJ, and pulled him into her arms. How was she going to get out of this one?

Over breakfast, it took her almost half an hour to explain Adam's presence and to get TJ to promise not to tell anyone about Adam sleeping over. TJ wanted to know if she and Adam were getting married. An uncomfortable silence followed the question. She proceeded to tell him no but assured him that they were friends again, sort of, anyway.

Adam was thrilled with the tie and suspenders TJ had bought him. To appease the rambunctious five-year-old, Adam put them on.

Cassie was putting the dishes in the dishwasher when Adam walked up behind her and put his arms around her waist. TJ was upstairs, watching cartoons in his room. She purred when she felt his lips on her neck. She closed her eyes and gave in to the onslaught of feelings his mouth was causing. Strong hands cupped her breasts through the thin material of her T-shirt before sliding up under it. She trembled, and her nipples hardened in response. Turning in his arms, she kissed him. Cassie was the first to pull away. She moved away from Adam. He was not going to like what she was about to say.

"Adam, I want us to make peace. I don't want to fight with you anymore. I don't want us to be enemies. I want us to be friends."

"So you want to be friends." He laughed without humor. "We care too much about each other for it to be possible. Cassie, how can we be friends when we can barely be in the same room with each other without wanting to tear each other's clothes off? What happened to friendship last night? What was that, Cassie? Friends with benefits, or was it just birthday sex?"

She flushed hotly under his heated gaze. "Maybe we can't fight the attraction between us, but we should be able to deal with it. We are adults, right? We can do this, Adam. We don't have to let sexual attraction guide us to the bedroom. We should be able to fight certain urges we have."

"We should," said Adam softly, moving toward her. Cassie trembled at the blatant look of desire in his dark eyes. He stopped only inches from her. "But can we? I want you, Cassie, but not without strings. It's funny, but eight months ago I would have jumped at a relationship like this, but now I want more. I want a commitment from you. I want to know one day you will be my wife. I want your dream, Cassie. It's all or nothing."

She watched sadly as he walked away and closed the door behind him. "I want it, too," Cassie whispered to the closed door, "but I'm afraid of those strings. I can't make the same mistake again. I can't do that to me or to you. I have to be sure."

Cassie was hesitant when Monica invited her and TJ for dinner. She was sure Monica was trying to play matchmaker again. Her sister assured her she was out of that business.

She and Monica were laughing and chatting in the den when the doorbell rang. Shawn and TJ went to answer it. They returned with Adam in tow. The smile left both of the sisters' faces. Two pairs of brown eyes turned toward Adam and then accusingly toward Shawn.

"There's been a slight mix-up," said Shawn, peering intently at his wife. "I didn't know you had invited Cassie to dinner. I invited Adam."

"I'll leave," said Cassie, coming quickly to her feet. "Come on TJ. We can come back some other time."

TJ ran to Adam. Adam swung him up in his arms. "No, Mommy," pleaded TJ. "Adam just got here. I want to stay with Adam. I miss him. Don't you miss him?"

Yes, I do, Cassie's heart cried out.

"You two stay," said Adam, turning to leave the room. "I'll see you some other time, TJ. I promise." He set the disappointed little boy on his feet.

"Good grief," said Shawn, frustrated with both his best friend and his sister-in-law. "You two are adults. Can't you stay in the same room with each other for more than two seconds without one of you leaving? You two work at the same hospital. What are you going to do? Avoid each other the rest of your lives?"

Cassie and Adam stared at each other in silence. Slowly, they both sat down. "No. I guess it would be a bit ridiculous," Cassie agreed, looking directly at Adam, who nodded in agreement.

Dinner was tense, at best. Cassie and Adam avoided conversation with each other. She could feel Adam's eyes on her most of the evening, but she refused to make eye contact with him. Instead she kept her eyes downcast.

After dinner Cassie and TJ made a hasty exit. She told Monica that she would phone her later in the week. She hugged Monica and Shawn but couldn't meet Adam's eyes as she left the house. Maybe it would have been better for them all if he had accepted the job in Los Angeles.

That Sunday Cassie and TJ went to church with Peter and Karen. After church they all went out to lunch. She and TJ spent a good part of the day with Peter and Karen. After lunch they went by to see Monica and Hope. Cassie, Mama Rosa, and TJ spent a quiet night at home.

Cassie had not seen or heard from Adam in the two weeks that followed his sudden departure from her house. She had called his home twice but had hung up when he answered the phone. What was the point? A relationship between them was hopeless, anyway. Adam wanted her commitment, her hand in marriage. This was something she didn't think she could ever give to another man after Trent. Trent had been mysteriously quiet, which made her uneasy. She hadn't spoken to him since she'd left him standing at the altar. He didn't know Adam had whisked her away, and Cassie had no plans to tell him.

Cassie was surprised to get a phone call from Mark, Shawn's brother. He invited her to a promotion party at the radio station where he was a DJ. Cassie was glad to hear from him and agreed to go. Because Mark had to be there early, he couldn't pick her up. She had to meet him there.

The day before the party, her babysitter called to cancel. Mama Rosa was spending the weekend with some relatives. So, Cassie called Monica to see if she could keep TJ. She already had plans. Cassie's last hope was Peter and Karen. They were also busy that night. On impulse, she called Adam. He agreed to look after TJ, but only if she agreed to have dinner with him one day next week. Cassie was furious that he was blackmailing her, but she agreed to his terms.

The evening of the party Cassie was getting ready when her doorbell rang. She opened the door to a smiling Adam. She blushed furiously under his close scrutiny. The red dress she was wearing hugged almost every curve of her body. It didn't leave much to the imagination.

"Wow!" Adam whistled as he walked into the room. "You never dressed like this for me. I doubt we would have left the house," he noted, making Cassie blush more. "So who is the lucky guy?"

"Mark," she answered, turning away from him.

Taking a tube of plum lipstick out of her purse, she applied it to her lips.

"Shawn's brother Mark? You're dressing like this for a DJ? I'm a doctor, and I could barely get you out of warm-ups and jeans."

"Mark and I are friends."

His eyebrows arched in question. His look asked the question, how good friends are you? He waited for her to continue.

"Friends without benefits," Cassie amended. She rolled her eyes at him and took her perfume out of her purse. She sprayed her wrists. She sprayed some in the air and walked through it.

"New fragrance?" he questioned. "It smells as appetizing as you look."

"Adam!" TJ yelled, running down the stairs and throwing himself in Adam's arms. "Are you babysitting me? Can we watch a movie?"

"You bet we can," Adam said, lifting the smiling boy up into his arms. "Say good night to Mom."

"Good night, Mom," repeated TJ, leaning over to hug and kiss his mother. Her face was only inches from Adam's as their eyes met over her son's head.

Unnerved by Adam's nearness, she took a step backward. "I'll be back around twelve thirty," said Cassie, turning away from his penetrating stare. She rushed out the door. Closing the door behind her, she leaned against it and took several deep breaths.

The party was already in full swing when she got there. Cassie had a wonderful time. Mark was always fun to be around. He had a happy, infectious personality. They laughed, talked, and danced the night away.

During dinner he tried to steer the conversation toward her past relationship with Adam. Cassie was having none of it. She evaded all his questions and changed the subject several times. Finally, Mark took the hint and let the subject drop.

At the end of the event, he walked her to her car and kissed her cheek. They agreed to do dinner and dancing some time in the near future.

Mark was a great guy, but Cassie didn't want to give him any false hope. She now knew the complications of becoming involved with someone close to her family. Monica and Adam were not on the best of terms because of her.

When she returned home, she found Adam sound asleep on the sofa, with TJ lying on his chest. Smiling at the picture they presented, she hated to wake either one of them. She quietly took out her cell phone and snapped several shots of them. Cassie laid the phone on the coffee table. She turned off the television, throwing the room into semidarkness.

"Adam," she whispered as softly as she could. She shook him lightly, but he didn't budge. Straightening, she left the room. *Okay, I'll go shower and get ready for bed before I wake him.*

Refreshed from her shower and clad in a two-piece cotton shorts sleep set, she pulled on her robe to cover herself. Adam and TJ were still asleep. Lifting her sleeping son from Adam's chest, she carried him to his room. She laid him between the sheets and leaned over to kiss him good night.

Returning to the den, she found Adam still asleep on the sofa. Leaning over him, Cassie let out a startled gasp when strong arms went around her and she landed on top of him. Cassie tried to get up, but he wouldn't release her.

"Don't run from me, Cassie. Not anymore." Passion-glazed eyes gazed up at her in hunger. "Give in to your feelings. Don't think with your head. Think with your heart and with your body. Let me love you tonight."

She was under his magical spell as her mouth lowered to his. Strong, sure hands massaged her back and thighs, and she melted against him. Slowly, Adam sat up and laid her on the sofa without breaking the kiss. Quick and nimble fingers divested her of her robe without her even realizing it. The rest of her clothing soon followed his to the floor.

When his mouth covered her breast, Cassie closed her eyes in pleasure and moaned. Her legs parted when his hand slid down her stomach to cover the most sensitive part of her. Rising up, she watched with heavy lids as Adam's mouth moved down her breast to her stomach. Her heart slammed against her ribs when his mouth replaced his hand. Her body quivered uncontrollably under his mouth. She had to bite her lip to keep from screaming out. One explosive climax followed another as he drove her wild.

Cassie was weak and trembling with the aftershocks of her climax. He moved briefly away as he grabbed a condom from his wallet. When his body finally covered hers, he slipped easily inside her. Lifting her lower body, he drove deeply into her.

Cassie gasped and felt her body coming to life again. Hugging him to her, she met him thrust for thrust until she felt him tense above her. He buried his face in her neck to keep from crying out himself.

Afterward, they both lay trembling and a little surprised by what had happened. Adam rose up to gaze down into her hot face. When he saw the tender expression in her eyes, it made his heart soar. She still loved him. No matter how many times she denied it or said they were finished, he knew she loved him. He knew where there was love, there was hope.

"I love you, Cassie." He put a finger to her parted lips. "You don't have to say anything. I . . ." The rest of the statement was lost as the phone began to ring. He lifted himself off of her so she could get the phone before it woke TJ.

"This is Dr. Hart's answering service," said an authoritative female voice. "May I speak with him please?"

"Sure." Turning around to face Adam, she held the phone out to him. "It's your answering service." She slipped her robe on and tied the sash.

"This is Dr. Hart." She saw Adam tense and then grip the phone tightly. "Where is she?" Silence. "How is she?" Silence again. "I'll be there as soon as I can." He replaced the phone and silently began to put on his clothes.

"Adam, what's wrong?" she asked worriedly as she watched his hurried movements. "Is it one of your patients?"

"Gloria was involved in a hit-and-run accident. They took her to County General Hospital. I have to go. I'll call you later," said Adam, closing the door behind him.

Adam made it to the hospital in record time. He parked and rushed through the emergency-room doors.

"I'm looking for Gloria McCullough," said Adam, rapping his hand on the counter. "Do you know what room she's in?"

"They took her down for X-rays a few minutes ago," said Rachel. "She should be out in a few minutes. She's a little banged up, but other than that, she seems to be doing all right."

"Thanks." He looked up to see Gloria being wheeled their way. "Excuse me." Going to her, he dropped down on one knee in front of her and hugged her to him. "Are you okay?"

"Yes," Gloria said, returning her brother's warm embrace. "Just a bit sore. They want to keep me overnight for observation."

After looking over her chart, Adam said a silent prayer. *Thank you, God, for not letting anything happen to her. She is the only family I have left.*

It was late when Gloria was moved to a room. Once she was settled, Adam hit the speed dial on his phone and called Cassie. "It's me," he said softly. "Gloria's okay. I'm spending the night at the hospital. I just wanted to let you know."

"I'm glad she's okay, Adam. I'll talk to you soon."

Adam returned to Cassie's on Sunday. He surprised Cassie when he showed up to go to church with her and TJ. They went out to eat afterward with Shawn and Monica. They spent a quiet evening at home playing games with TJ and keeping him entertained.

After putting him to bed, they sat on the sofa and talked. They shared their fears and discussed the past, the present, and the future. Adam assured Cassie he wanted her to be a part of his future.

Chapter 19

Cassie was a nervous wreck as she paced the living room. She still couldn't believe she had let Adam talk her into going away with him for the weekend. Cassie admitted that she didn't want to face a future without him. They agreed to give their relationship another chance. She didn't know where they were going, and she was even more nervous about spending the weekend alone with him. They were still on shaky ground. She had promised him a date, which he'd quickly maneuvered into an entire weekend.

TJ ran down the stairs and straight to his mother. Cassie kneeled down and hugged him. "When are you coming back?" he asked, smiling.

"We will be back on Sunday. Be a good boy for Mama Rosa."

"Does this mean you and Adam are back together?" he asked.

Cassie smiled at her son. "Yes, it means Adam and I are back together."

"Yippee!" he cheered excitedly. "Then maybe he can still be my dad."

The doorbell rang, preventing Cassie from answering.

"Can I open it, Mom?"

"Yes, you can." Cassie got to her feet and followed him to the door.

"Adam!" TJ yelled when he opened the door. Adam swung him up in his arms. "Mom said you guys are back together."

"She did, did she?" Smiling, Adam leaned over and kissed Cassie. "What else did Mom say?" Adam set TJ on his feet.

"I said for him to be a good boy while I'm gone." She wiped her lipstick from his mouth, and he caught her hand and kissed it.

"TJ is always a good boy. If he's really good, I might bring him back a surprise," Adam replied.

TJ's face lit up with excitement.

"Are you ready to go?" asked Adam.

Ready as I will ever be. "Yes," said Cassie, smiling at him. "Come give me another hug, you."

TJ went to his mother and hugged her.

"I thought I heard the doorbell," said Mama Rosa. "Hello, Dr. Hart."

"Hi. We are heading out." Adam picked up Cassie's bags. He watched her hug TJ again. "Cassie, we have to get going."

They drove to the airport. Cassie was speechless when Adam assisted her into the private plane. He was full of surprises. She learned on takeoff that they were en route to L.A.

When the plane landed, a white limousine was there to drive them to their destination. It still had not dawned on Cassie where Adam was taking her. She leaned back in the limo to enjoy the ride. Adam had been on the phone from the moment the plane touched down. Cassie hoped this was not how they were going to spend the whole weekend. L.A. had one of the home offices for the company Adam had inherited. She prayed this wasn't a business trip but a time for them to reconnect.

Peering out the window at the countryside, Cassie was amazed that people actually lived in the homes she saw. Most of them sat back from the road and had electrical fences. When at last the limo turned off the main road, Cassie stared in shock as the driver stopped at a gate and put in a code. The gate opened, and they drove through it. The limo rolled to a stop in front of a grand mansion straight out of a Hollywood movie, then pulled into the circular drive. The driver got out and came around to open the door for Adam, who helped Cassie out of the car.

"Oh, my," said Cassie, looking around in wonder.

The front door opened, and they were greeted by a full staff.

"Welcome home, Dr. Hart," said a middle-aged woman, smiling. "We have everything prepared that you requested. Welcome, Ms. Mancini."

"Thank you, Mrs. Tate. Did Bill Kirkland and his wife vacate the premises?" asked Adam, leading Cassie inside.

"Yes, sir, and not a moment too soon," Mrs. Tate smiled. "Ms. Lauren is out for the evening. She said she would see you both tonight. Would you like for me to show Ms. Randall her suite?"

"No. You can put her things in my suite. I'll

show her the way after I give her the tour. Thanks, everyone."

Catching her hand, Adam led Cassie through the house, giving her a tour. She was beyond amazed. The house contained six bedrooms, five bathrooms, a media room, a game room, a ballroom, a huge kitchen, a formal dining room, a den, and a formal living room. Out back were a pool, a tennis court, a basketball court, and a pool house. She followed Adam up the winding staircase. He opened the huge double doors to the master suite.

Wow! Cassie stepped inside the suite. It was bigger than the whole downstairs of her house. The room was decorated almost entirely in black. She smiled. No need to wonder whose idea that was. That was Adam's signature color.

The large wood king bed had tall posts that were larger than her body. The bed came to her waist. There were steps leading up to the mattress on both sides and at the foot of the bed. The bed faced a large plasma television. There was a black leather love seat near the double doors leading out to the balcony. He opened another set of double doors, and she walked into the master bath. To the right was a large beveled-glass shower made for two, and beside the shower was a Jacuzzi tub big enough for four adults. Behind a closed door was the toilet. Across from the shower and Jacuzzi were his and her sinks. At the end of the room were his and her closets.

"Now I know how the other half lives," said Cassie, slowly spinning around the room. "Your home is incredible."

"Thank you. Come here. Let me show you something." He held out his hand to her. Cassie caught his outstretched hand, and he pulled her out onto the balcony. They could see the L.A. sky-line in the distance.

"What an amazing view!" Cassie said, leaning against him. His arms were around her waist.

"I'm glad you came with me, no questions asked."

"I trust you." As Cassie said the words, she knew she meant them in her heart. She did trust him. She hadn't thought she would ever be able to trust anyone again after Trent, but she did. She trusted Adam. She turned in Adam's arms. "I trust you," she repeated.

Adam's heart soared. He knew he had broken down the last wall between them. His lips touched hers lightly. "We'd better get moving. We have plans for tonight. Tonight is a business dinner with the Kirkland board of directors. It's a formal affair. I hope you don't mind, but I took the lib-erty of picking out a couple of gowns for you to choose from. Tomorrow and tomorrow night are strictly ours."

"You have excellent taste in clothing, Dr. Hart. I can't wait to see what you picked out for me."

He led her down the hallway. Opening the door to a bedroom, he waved for her to go in. On the bed were several gowns. He had picked semiformal and formal gowns of varying styles and colors.

"Did you have to buy out the shop?" she asked, picking up a gorgeous purple off-the-shoulder formal gown. She held it in front of her.

"Only the best for my girlfriend," he teased.

"Take a few of them into the bathroom and try them on, or you could do it here. Better yet, I could help you." His hands went to the buttons on her blouse, and she swatted them away. He dropped down on the bed and waited.

"Your *girlfriend*. I like the sound of that. I've been dressing and undressing myself for years. I don't need any help. I'm going to surprise you. You won't see me in the gown until I walk down the stairs to greet you, my handsome prince." Cassie fingered the dress. "Who is Lauren?"

"She's Wade's grandniece. She and her husband live in the pool house. Lauren will be at the dinner tonight. You'll like her. She reminds me a lot of you."

Cassie smiled at the whistle of appreciation she received as she came down the stairs. She should look dynamite since she was wearing a gown that cost more than her car. Her sandy brown hair swirled around her face and accentuated her bare shoulders. Around her neck she wore a diamond necklace, and her ears sparkled with matching diamond earrings, which Adam had had Mrs. Tate deliver to her. She looked stunning in a red, form-fitting, long, sequin gown with almost a thigh-high split in the back.

Adam almost forgot to breathe as he watched her descend the stairs. She was magnificent. His eyes devoured her. He knew he would have to fight the men off tonight to keep them away from Cassie.

Tonight he would introduce Cassie to a new world, a world that he was now a part of. Adam had made the decision a few days ago to move to L.A. Now he had to convince Cassie to marry him and move with him.

Adam looked very distinguished in his black tuxedo. As usual, he looked like he had just stepped out of a fashion magazine. He caught her hand and spun her around before pulling her into his arms.

"You look amazing. Words fail me when looking at you. Are you ready?" he said.

"I'm a little nervous," she admitted.

"So am I, but together, we can pull it off," he assured her. With her arm through his, he led her out the front door to the waiting limousine.

When Adam and Cassie entered the party, a hush fell over the room and all eyes turned in their direction. This was Adam's first function outside of the one board meeting he'd attended a month ago.

Adam's arm was around her waist for moral support. "Relax. You look fantastic," he said, kissing her cheek. "Together there is nothing we can't do, remember."

Adam introduced her to several people, but she knew she would never remember all their names. Most of them were warm and friendly. A few of the wives were snooty and snubbed Cassie for the outsider she was. Cassie took it all in stride. Their rudeness didn't even bother her.

Cassie moved gracefully around the room. She chatted with several people before finding a semi-secluded spot. Without Adam by her side, she felt like a fish out of water. Her eyes scanned the room. Adam had left the room a few minutes earlier with a man named Greg Norris. He was acting CEO of Kirkland.

"Hi," said a young woman, popping up beside her.

Cassie turned to face her. She was young, about nineteen or twenty. Her long blond hair hung down her back in a mass of curls. She wore a blue silk off-the-shoulder gown.

"I'm Lauren Bryant. You must be Cassie."

"Lauren, hi," said Cassie, taking her outstretched hand. "It's nice to finally meet you. I've heard a lot about you from Adam."

"Same here. The people here are harmless. They are all quaking in their five-hundred-dollar loafers, afraid Adam is going to get rid of them, my father, brothers, and uncle included. They all work for Kirkland."

"That must put you in an uncomfortable position, especially living in the pool house."

"Not really. I learned early on what motivated my family. Money. I'm twenty-one. I've been living in Uncle Wade's pool house since I turned eighteen. We are house hunting, by the way. Now that I own fifteen percent of the empire, we can afford it. See the man in the black suit staring intently at us? He's my father, and he wants my voting proxy. I'm not sure why, because Adam owns sixty percent of the stock. Uncle Wade wouldn't give up controlling interest in the company he started. There is nothing anyone can do to remove Adam. He's majority owner. Enough business talk. Come on. I can't wait to introduce you to my family."

"Why do you say that with a smile?" asked Cassie, following her. Cassie grabbed a glass of champagne from a passing waiter. "I have a feeling I'm going to need this."

Cassie regretted the moment she met the Kirkland clan. Within minutes she was ready to find Adam and leave the party. They were what she'd expected and more. Adam swooped in and rescued her.

"Sorry about that," he whispered. "I guess you couldn't avoid them forever. Let's go find our table. After dinner there is dancing. I know this isn't what you signed up for, but I promise to make it as fun as possible for you. We don't have to stay long."

Her hand squeezed his. "It's okay, Adam. It's really not that bad."

"Thanks." He leaned down and kissed her.

"Stop it, you two," said Lauren to their left. "Hello, stranger."

"Hello, yourself," said Adam, releasing Cassie and hugging Lauren. "I didn't expect to see you here. Where's Reggie?"

"He had an emergency. Someone's pooch is at death's door or something. A veterinarian's work in L.A. is never done. I think we're at the table up front."

Adam and Cassie followed Lauren. He pulled a chair out first for Cassie and then for Lauren. He sat between the two women.

"You should have seen the look on everyone's face when you two walked in. I recorded it on my phone to show Reggie later. It was priceless," Lauren told them.

After dinner Adam held out his hand to Cassie, pulled out her chair, and led her to the dance floor. They moved beautifully together to the music. They danced to several songs before calling it a night.

The limo driver was outside waiting for them. Adam instructed him to drive them through Hollywood. He wanted Cassie to see it lit up at night. He opened the moonroof and stood up. Cassie kicked off her sandals and joined him. The night was clear and cool. She shivered, and Adam took off his jacket and put it around her shoulders.

After their tour of Hollywood, the limousine headed for home. Hand in hand, they walked upstairs to Adam's suite. He walked out onto the balcony while Cassie got ready for bed. She washed her face free of makeup and slipped into a purple pajama short set. She climbed up the steps and got into bed.

Minutes later, when Adam came in, she was sound asleep. He slipped off his clothes and climbed into bed. He touched Cassie's face, and she moved into his arms. A feeling of peace came over him and he drifted off to sleep.

On Saturday they ate breakfast at home and ditched the limo for the Bentley. The driver took them to Rodeo Drive and then to Beverly Hills. Adam treated her to a shopping spree, and they ate lunch at an elegant seafood restaurant. The food was good but way overpriced.

They went back home to rest up for the night ahead. Adam had a special night planned for them. While Cassie was sleeping, Adam eased from the bed. He went downstairs to check with Mrs. Tate to make sure everything was ready. She assured him the night would be perfect.

Adam went back upstairs and eased back in bed. He leaned over and kissed Cassie's closed eyelids "Sweetheart, it's time to get up."

Cassie yawned and stretched like a cat. "I was having the most wonderful dream." She snuggled closer to Adam.

"Was I in your dream?" he asked, dropping a kiss on her head.

"Most assuredly." She smiled up at him. "And you were naked."

Adam pulled the covers off her. "Up you go." He got up from the bed and hopped down. "Come on." He reached for Cassie. She let him lift her down from the bed. "That purple gown will do nicely."

After Cassie left the room, Adam quickly showered and dressed. He went downstairs to check on the progress. He walked out onto the patio and smiled. The patio and the backyard were lit up like Christmas. A white lace–covered dining table held two candles and champagne flutes. A bottle of champagne was in an ice bucket by the table. He waved to the small band, which had set up in a corner. Adam gave them a list of songs to play.

Cassie showered and dressed in record time. She went to the master suite, looking for Adam. When she found the room empty, she went downstairs to find him.

"Adam," Cassie called, going into the kitchen. "Hello, Mrs. Tate. Have you seen Adam?"

"Yes, madam," said the housekeeper. "I think he's out on the patio. It's such a beautiful night."

"Thank you," said Cassie, gathering the hem of her gown. She walked over to the patio door, opened it, and stepped outside.

Adam turned as the door opened and stared at the vision in front of him. Cassie looked even more beautiful than the night before, if that were even possible. Her hair was pinned on top of her head with combs and flowers. The purple gown hugged her body and moved with her.

At Adam's signal, the band began to play "Unforgettable." Adam held out his hand to her. Smiling, she walked toward him and took his hand. Adam pulled her into his arms, and they danced around the patio.

"You are full of surprises," said Cassie as Adam twirled her around the patio. "Lucky for you, I like surprises."

"I know." He smiled as his lips touched hers. "This is only the beginning." When the song ended, he led her over to the table and pulled out a chair for her. "I hope you're hungry."

Mrs. Tate appeared with two appetizers. Cassie smiled as she looked down at the oysters on the half shell. She waited until Mrs. Tate was out of earshot.

"I'm not eating that," said Cassie, wrinkling her nose in displeasure. "I don't eat raw seafood. So I hope she's not bringing out sushi next."

"Cassie, sweetheart, where's your sense of adventure? Try it. You might like it. I dare you. Watch."

She watched him curiously as he used a fork to dislodge the oyster. Raising the shell above his mouth, he tilted it and the oyster slipped into his mouth.

"I'm not doing that," Cassie blurted, shaking her head. "I'm not sure I want to even kiss you now."

"Oh, really?" he teased. "Care to put that to the test."

She laughed with him.

"Here. Try it." He squeezed a wedge of lemon on the oyster for her. "Now try it."

Sighing in resignation she picked up the oyster and the tiny fork. Mimicking his movements, she raised the oyster shell to her lips and let the oyster slip into her mouth. "Now what?" she mumbled past the cold, clammy morsel in her mouth.

"Don't talk with your mouth full." He laughed, shaking his head. "Chew it and swallow."

"Ugh," said Cassie as the oyster slid down her throat. "Please open the champagne quick."

Adam popped the champagne cork. Picking up her flute, he tilted it and filled it, then filled his own. "To us." He raised the flute to her.

"To us," she repeated as she touched her flute to his.

A man whom Cassie had never seen before came out of the kitchen with two plates. He set before them grilled lobster tails, shrimp skewers wrapped in bacon, steamed vegetables, and wild rice.

"It looks delicious," said Adam as he picked up his knife and fork. He cut a piece of lobster and held it to Cassie's lips.

She took the offered morsel and moaned in pleasure. "It's wonderful."

Adam nodded to the chef, who smiled and walked away. He took a bite of his lobster. "You're right. It's delicious."

Dessert consisted of strawberry cheesecake covered in fresh strawberries. Cassie was stuffed from dinner, but she forced herself to have a small piece of the cheesecake. She wasn't disappointed. It was heavenly.

After dinner they danced the night away. Cassie

smiled as she watched Adam walk over to the band. When the band began to play "Endless Love," Adam picked up the wireless microphone. Her mouth fell open as he began to sing to her. Adam came to her and caught her hand. Her heart melted, and tears misted her eyes as she stared at the man she loved. At the end of the song he kissed her tears away.

"I love you, Cassie Randall. Despite the hell you have put me through, I love you. I want to spend the rest of my life with you. I am not the same person I was eight months ago. You taught me how to love and to accept love unconditionally. I love your smile, your laughter, and your delectable body. I love everything about you. Will you marry me?" Adam kneeled down in front of her and opened a ring box.

Cassie gasped as she stared at him and the ring. Their eyes met and held for what seemed like an eternity. She smiled through her tears as she pulled him to his feet. "The answer is yes! Yes!" she repeated loudly. "I will marry you!"

Neither one of them paid any attention to the applause around them as Adam slid the ring on her finger and kissed her. The large marquis diamond engagement ring sparkled on her finger. It was at least four carats, with baguettes on both sides.

His mouth covered hers passionately, and she returned the heated kiss with all the love she had in her heart for him. When her feet finally touched the ground, Adam kissed her again and again.

"You crazy man," she whispered through her tears, kissing him. "I can't believe you did this. I love you."

He kissed the ring on her finger. "I bought this for you about two months ago. I debated about taking it back to the jewelry store. I'm glad I didn't."

"So am I. It's beautiful," said Cassie, holding out her hand to look at the ring. "You have exquisite taste, Dr. Hart."

"I'm glad you approve. I was kind of hoping you would like it."

"I like the ring, and I love you." Throwing her arms around him, she hugged him to her. This was her dream. Correction. Adam Hart was her dream. All she had ever wanted was to be loved and accepted for who she was.

Cassie was so touched by his love and thoughtfulness, she started to cry again. *He went through all this just for me. I can't believe this is happening.*

They made love until dawn. Afterward, they fell asleep in each other's arms. They slept late on Sunday. Instead of calling her family with the news, they wanted to tell them in person. Adam called Shawn and asked him and Monica to meet them at Cassie's place at five o'clock.

Chapter 20

They ate brunch on the private plane as they discussed the future. Cassie reluctantly agreed to move to L.A. after they were married. Adam made it clear to her that he didn't believe in long engagements and wanted to marry within the next few weeks. He jokingly told her that he would plan the wedding if she didn't think she could pull it off in such a short time. She threw a pillow at him and told him she would make the arrangements.

Cassie couldn't wait to tell TJ the news. He would be ecstatic that they were getting married. It was what he'd always wanted.

When the limousine pulled up in front of Cassie's house, she frowned when she saw not only Shawn's car but also her father's car. "Dad's here."

"I can't wait to see his face when we tell him the news," said Adam. "Should I call him Dad or Pops?"

Cassie elbowed him. "Be nice. We can't pick and choose our in-laws."

Catching her hand, he helped her from the limousine. When the front door opened, she immediately knew something was wrong. Monica's face was a dead giveaway. Cassie brushed past her sister.

"TJ!" Cassie called as panic set in. She rushed through the house, looking for her son. "Where's TJ?"

"Trent took him," said Monica quietly. "I don't know who he bribed, but he somehow got temporary custody of TJ. He left this note."

Cassie reached for the note.

"It's not for you. It's for Adam." Monica handed the envelope to Adam.

"He what? How can he get temporary custody?" Cassie asked. "I have full custody. This is not happening. We have to get him back."

"We will get him back," Adam promised as he tore open the envelope. He scanned its contents quickly. He gripped the note so tightly, it crinkled in his hand. He took out his cell phone and dialed.

"Adam, what's going on?" asked Cassie anxiously. "What did it say? What does Trent want from you?"

He handed her the note.

"What does this mean? You have something he wants. What did you do to put my son in the middle of your fight with Trent?" Cassie sputtered.

"Cassie, calm down," said Adam quietly. "I will take care of it." He dialed the phone number on the note. "It's Adam Hart. When and where do you want to meet?" Adam hit the speaker button on his cell phone so they could all hear the call. He put his finger to his lips to keep Cassie quiet.

"Dr. Hart. I was expecting your call. Is my runaway bride with you? Hello, Cassie. You should have known your little exit wouldn't be the end of it. I always have the last word."

"Trent, where is TJ? I want my son," said Cassie,

unable to remain quiet a moment longer. Trent knew he could goad her by using TJ.

"This isn't about you anymore. This is between me and your boyfriend. Hart, you have something I want, and I have something you want," Trent replied.

"Really? And what would that be?" asked Adam, baiting him. They both knew he was referring to the stock Adam had purchased.

"You have controlling interest in my company, and I have TJ. I'll make a deal with you. You give me back my company, and I give you the boy," said Trent.

"I guess this means you won't win Father of the Year," Adam sneered. His hatred for this man knew no bounds. He was using TJ to hurt Cassie and to get back at him. "Where is TJ? Is he okay?"

"Of course he's okay. I wouldn't hurt my own kid," Trent muttered.

"No, but you would use him as a bargaining chip. What a great guy! Where and when do you want to meet, Mancini?"

"Tonight. The sooner the better. He's whining for his mother. You have a pen?"

Adam wrote down the address.

"I don't want it all, Dr. Hart. I just want controlling interest back, which adds up to ten percent of my company stock."

"It's not like I carry it around with me."

"I'll take a letter of intent. Since your lawyer friend is probably there, too, have him draft up a legal and binding document. Once my attorney looks over it, I will turn over the kid. If you try any tricks, I will send him out of the country so fast, Cassie will never see him again."

"I don't want just TJ," said Adam. "I want you to sign a legal and binding document giving up all parental rights and visitation. You will also sign adoption papers giving me the right to adopt TJ. We will have them signed, notarized, and filed with the courts. Once you sign those papers, you are out of their lives forever."

"You get your wish, Doc. I'll see you in an hour." The phone clicked as Trent hung up.

Cassie was furious at her ex-husband. He was using their son as a bargaining chip. She wanted to call the police, but Adam wouldn't let her. Instead, he persuaded her to let him handle Trent. She had major reservations about it, but in the end she relented. Cassie made Adam promise her that after they got TJ back, he would bury Trent.

Cassie, Monica, Peter, and Karen waited at home while Adam and Shawn went to meet Trent. Cassie thought up a million and one ways to make her ex-husband suffer for taking their son.

Her father assured her Adam would get TJ back. Peter had done a complete turnaround after finding out that Adam, along with Monica and Shawn, had kidnapped Cassie from her wedding to Trent. Peter had gained a newfound respect for him. It also didn't hurt when Peter learned that her boyfriend was worth millions of dollars.

Shawn drove to the hotel while Adam made several phone calls. Adam hung up the phone with a smile on his face. He had gotten the remainder of the shares of Mancini Industries that he'd needed.

Trent was about to be outsmarted and beaten at his own game.

"I got it," Adam said, dropping the phone in his shirt pocket. "Mancini won't know what hit him."

"It couldn't happen to a nicer guy," Shawn noted, laughing. "I wish I could see his face when he finds out about your little surprise."

Adam and Shawn met Trent and his attorney in the hotel lobby. Adam fought the urge to slug Trent on sight. Instead, he sat down at the table and finalized contracts. Adam signed ten percent of his Mancini Industries shares over to Trent. In return Trent relinquished all rights to TJ and promised in writing that he would never contact him again, or the shares in Mancini Industries would revert back to Adam. Trent also signed adoption papers, giving Adam the legal right to adopt TJ once he and Cassie were married.

"Nice doing business with you, Dr. Hart. Look at it this way. You didn't lose. You get the girl, the kid, and the house with the white picket fence, or in your case, the mansion." Trent made a call on his cell phone. "You can bring him down." He disconnected the call. "Take care of them."

"Count on it," said Adam, getting to his feet. "I'll make you another promise, Mancini. Come near my family again and I will take you apart piece by piece and no one will ever find those pieces."

"I got what I wanted," said Trent, glaring at him and holding up the documents. "You are welcome to them."

"Adam!" TJ yelled excitedly, running to him.

Adam met him in the middle of the room and swung him up in his arms.

"I knew you would come. I knew it. Where's Mom?"

"She's at home, waiting for you," Adam said, hugging him. "Let's go home."

"What about him?" TJ asked as he watched his father exit the hotel.

"He won't be bothering us again. I promise."

Adam phoned Cassie and gave TJ the phone. After TJ finished speaking with her, Adam took the phone and let her know they were on their way.

Forty-five minutes later Adam unlocked the door, and TJ dashed inside the house, searching for his mother.

"Mom!" he cried and ran into Cassie's open arms. Cassie enfolded him in her arms and hugged him tightly before covering his face with kisses.

Adam and Shawn stepped inside, closing the door behind them. Adam lovingly watched the reunion of mother and son. Cassie released TJ long enough to go to Adam. She threw herself in his open arms and kissed him. TJ ran to them, and Adam hugged both of them.

"Have I told you today how much I love you?" asked Cassie, smiling up at Adam through her tears. She twirled the engagement ring right side up on her finger so everyone could see it. "I think it's time we let everyone in on our little secret. We have an announcement to make." Cassie held up her ring finger. "Adam and I are getting married."

"Yippee!" TJ yelled, dancing around. "Adam's going to be my dad!"

Cassie wiped at the tears streaming down her face and removed her wedding gown from the plastic bag. Letting out a gasp of pleasure, she touched the gown. It was the most beautiful gown she had ever seen. It was a combination of pearls and white lace. The front was low cut, with three strings of pearls across it. The waist was fitted, and so was the rest of the gown until it flared out slightly at the bottom. She held the gown in front of her and smiled, then hugged it to her breast as she said a silent prayer of thanks to God for sending Adam to her.

"I can't believe this is happening," Cassie said to Monica. "Adam and I are actually getting married today. This is not a dream. Tell me I am not imagining any of this. It's really happening."

"Yes, it's happening," said Monica, smiling. "Your groom is already here and already dressed, if you can believe that."

"I'm going to miss you," said Cassie, hugging her sister.

"I won't be that far away. We're coming with you."

Cassie's look was incredulous. "What? You guys are moving to L.A.?"

"Shawn is Adam's attorney. He's going to be heavily involved in the company, and it makes sense for us to be there. I hope you don't mind, but we will be staying with you guys for a little while before we get our own place. Lauren and her husband found a house, and the pool house is now vacant."

Cassie hugged her sister again. "This is great news. I can't believe it!"

An hour later Cassie stood before the floor-length mirror, admiring herself. Adam had picked out the perfect gown for her. It hugged every curve of her body, without being tight. She looked like a fairy princess now that Monica and Karen had finished doing her hair and makeup. Raising the white rose bouquet to her nose, she sniffed the heady aroma. She turned at the sound of the door opening and smiled at the sight of Mama Rosa.

"Mama Rosa, where have you been? I've been looking for you."

"I wanted to give you some time with your family. You look absolutely breathtaking, Cassie. I am so happy for you," said Mama Rosa, wiping the tears from her eyes.

"You are also my family," said Cassie, hugging her. "Don't ever forget it. I depend on you. I don't know what I would do without you."

"You have Dr. Hart now. You, TJ, and the doctor will be a family now. I think it's time for me to go back to New York."

"You can't," cried Cassie, squeezing her hands. "We will still need you. You are coming to live with us. You are part of our family, Mama Rosa. We want you to stay with us. TJ would be lost without you."

"We'll talk later, dear," Mama Rosa said, wiping Cassie's tears away. "You are going to ruin your makeup. Be happy, daughter." They embraced each other warmly.

"Cassie, they are ready for you," said Peter, sticking his head in the door. "You look breathtaking. Good luck, honey." Peter kissed her cheek. "I wish you all the best." Cassie hugged him, and he kissed her cheek again. "I'll see you both inside. Be happy, sweetheart."

"I am happy," whispered Cassie, fighting back her tears. "I have everything I've always wanted, a family who loves me."

"Mommy, you look beautiful," said TJ, squeezing through the door and peering up at her.

She smiled down at him. "Are we ready to marry Adam?" TJ asked.

"Yes, we are," Cassie replied, taking in his brushed hair and his black tuxedo. She leaned over and dropped a kiss on top of his head.

As long as she lived, Cassie would never forget the look of love and pride on Adam's face when she and TJ walked into the chapel. Their eyes met and held as she walked slowly down the aisle. She was soaring so high, she never wanted her feet to touch the ground.

When they were pronounced man and wife, a smiling Adam gently pulled Cassie into his arms and kissed her full on the lips. Laughing and crying, she parted her lips beneath his, and her arms went around him.

"That's enough," the minister declared and laughed. The crowd laughed, too. "I now present to you Dr. and Mrs. Adam Hart."

Beaming with happiness, Cassie and Adam turned to face the crowd, and everyone applauded. The chapel was packed. The door to the chapel was open, and the majority of the hospital staff was lining the hallways to see them.

"I love you, Mrs. Hart," said Adam, smiling down at his blushing bride. His lips touched hers in a gentle kiss.

"I love you, too," repeated Cassie, smiling up at him, with all her love for him shining in her eyes. "Adam, why the hospital chapel?" she asked, puzzled. "Of all the places to get married, this is not one I would have thought of."

"None of the hospital staff would have believed it if they didn't see it for themselves." He winked. "I wanted everyone to be a part of our new beginning. I also wanted them to know how much I love you and how committed I am to you. Actually, the real reason is this is where I was when I finally realized I loved you. The realization of it almost knocked me off my feet. I didn't want to love you. I didn't want to love any woman. But somehow you wiggled your way into my life and into my heart before I even knew what hit me. Because of you, I was able to come to grips with my parents' deaths and get on with my life. I love you, Cassie Hart. You are the best thing that has ever happened to me. I thank God for sending you to me. I may not be the best or the most perfect husband for you, but know I love you more than any man possibly could. You are my destiny, and I am yours."

"Congratulations, you two," said Roger, hugging Cassie and shaking Adam's hand. "I wish you the very best." He turned to walk away and then stopped. "By the way, Dr. Hart, the fifty dollars you owe me, you can keep as a wedding gift," he said, winking at them.

"This is one bet I don't mind losing," said Adam, kissing his confused bride's parted lips. "Hey, Roger, this is for you." Adam reached in his coat pocket and took out a set of keys. He tossed them to Roger.

"What's this, Doc?" Roger asked, confused.

"I no longer need Have Hart. Cassie has the key to my heart." The look on the other man's face was incredulous as Adam kissed his smiling bride.

Epilogue

The board meeting of Mancini Industries was called to order.

Trent came in late. He was furious. "What is the purpose of this meeting, Hart? I know you are the one who called it, but guess what? Your plan to remove me, or whatever it was, has failed. I'm the majority stockholder again. I still own thirty-five percent of this company. You can't touch me."

"You are right," said Adam, winking at Cassie. "I can't touch you. There is one little thing I forgot to tell you. I gave Cassie my twenty-five percent as a wedding gift."

"She is even less of a threat than you are. What does Cassie know about business?" Trent sneered, laughing. "She can barely balance her own check-book."

"Maybe not, but I think it's time she learned." Adam squeezed Cassie's hand. "There's one more detail I forgot to mention. I purchased an additional twenty-eight percent of stock in Cassie's name. She now has controlling interest in your company."

Cassie's eyes grew round as saucers as she stared at the man she loved. She couldn't believe he had done this. She was now majority owner of Mancini Industries. She turned to Trent and laughed at the look on his face. He could not believe that Adam had outsmarted him. He had lost his company and any hold he had on Cassie when he signed the papers agreeing to let Adam adopt TJ.

Cassie was smiling when she got to her feet. "I make a motion to remove Trent Mancini as president and CEO of Mancini Industries." She looked around the room for a second motion.

"I have worked my butt off for my company. I have sacrificed everything for my company. You are not getting me out of this company without a fight!" yelled Trent.

"Let's talk about sacrifice, Trent. You sold your son to gain ten percent of Adam's stock. What kind of person does that? What kind of father? You are finished here," Cassie remarked.

"I second the motion," said Valerie Burkes, the second vice president of Mancini Industries. "It's time for a change. Trent has strong-armed us long enough. We need new leadership and new ideas. I nominate Cassandra Randall Hart as CEO and president."

"The motion is carried," said George Rogers, the first vice president of Mancini Industries, standing up. "Mr. Mancini, clean out your office and be off the premises within the hour. A security guard will go with you to your office to collect your belongings. Any property or possessions you purchased in the company name will remain with the company, which includes your home." He buzzed the secretary. "Please send security up."

"Thank you for the offer, but I must turn it down," Cassie said. "We can start the interview process to find a qualified replacement. I live in L.A. with my husband and son. With twins on the way, I won't have time to run a company."

Want more Sylvia Lett?
Turn the page for a sizzling excerpt from
Take Me Down

Available now wherever books are sold!

Chapter 1

Stephanie looked over the impressive résumé of her next interviewee. She had posted a position for a security consultant three weeks ago. So far only amateurs had bombarded her.

What Stephanie needed was a professional. Someone who knew all the ins and outs of hotel security, and could hire and train a staff of security guards for the hotel chain. She wanted limited involvement in the process.

Jackson Kaufman appeared to be the man she was looking for. At least on paper. He had an engineering degree and experience, which gave him a leg up on the competition. His last two jobs were with Fortune 500 technology companies. Jackson had worked as a security consultant for both of them. He was also an ex-Navy SEAL. His expertise was weapons and hand-to-hand combat. He possessed a black belt in tae kwon do and judo, too.

The only thing that bothered Stephanie was the two-year gap between the navy and Jackson's first consulting job. If he could give her an acceptable answer—one that he could prove—she'd hire him on the spot.

She looked down at the thin gold watch encircling her wrist. Jackson was due to arrive in about ten minutes. "I guess we'll see if the man measures up to the résumé," she said aloud. "God, I hope so. I am so tired of interviewing."

There was a brief knock on her door before it opened suddenly and her mother came breezing into the room. Stephanie rolled her eyes heavenward. She was not in the mood for her mother today or any other day.

"Hello, dear. Sit up straight. You'll ruin your posture," chided Mildred Mason as she closed the door behind her. "That color looks dreadful on you. You really should take me or your sister shopping with you."

"Thanks, Mom," Stephanie said, pasting on a smile. "Seeing you always manages to brighten my day. I'm busy and I don't have time for fashion tips. What are you doing here? Shouldn't you be out shopping or looking for a husband for me? That does seem to be your favorite pastime lately."

"You know me too well, darling." Mildred sat down in the vacant black leather chair across from her daughter's desk. She held out her hand, inspecting her perfectly manicured red fingernails. "You received an invitation to the Waterfords' party on Saturday night. I accepted on your behalf."

Stephanie shot her mother a murderous glare.

"Now, don't be like that."

Stephanie laid her head down on the desk. *Why me? What did I do to deserve a social-climbing mother?*

"Mom, why did you do that? You know I hate those things. I specifically told you I didn't want to attend this one. I had plans to curl up with a good book and a glass of chardonnay."

"Why snuggle up to a cold book when you can have a hot-blooded man? Honey, you could have your pick of men. You have a smorgasbord to choose from. Try a few different tasty morsels before you settle for the main course."

Stephanie's eyes narrowed on her mother. "Why do I even bother? I talk. You don't listen. Some things never seem to change. I give up."

"Don't give me that look. I listen sometimes. You can't snub the Waterfords. It's simply not done. They are one of the most powerful families in the state of Texas. I'll go with you. It'll be fun, just us girls. There should be tons of eligible bachelors. Maybe you can make a connection with one of them. Who knows? Maybe I will."

"I wish you would. My bank account would thank him." She smiled. "I am not looking for a connection. It will be another boring dinner party with old lechers pawing at me. I always feel like I'm an appetizer or something. I hate it. I wish you would stop accepting invitations for me. I don't need a man in my life to be happy."

"You've proven that, dear, by dating Stanley," Mildred replied smugly. "You can be miserable with one or without one, but everyone needs companionship. Men have their purpose."

"Yeah, they are strong enough to hold all your shopping bags. I have companionship. I have Stanley." The words sounded lame even to her ears. Stephanie regretted them instantly.

"Stanley is not a companion. Stanley is your lapdog. You say jump and he asks how high. Honey, there is no fire, no spark, no nothing. He's too boring. You need excitement. You need romance. You need someone other than that limp biscuit. You are not going to find the right type of husband if you don't get out there and mingle with the right people."

Picking up her gold pen, Stephanie jotted down the date and time of the Waterfords' party in her monthly planner without giving it any thought. Despite her mother's plans, she had no intention of attending. Laying her pen down, she looked up at her mother. "You mean Stanley's not rich, don't you? Why is everything about money with you? Stanley is not exactly destitute. He owns an accounting firm. He does very well for himself."

"Yes, dear, but you can do much better than Stanley. If you can't bring yourself to sleep with the man, then what would be the point of marrying him? He's boring and has the personality of pocket lint. Expand your horizons, dear. Reach for the stars. The sky is the limit when you're sitting on a gold mine. You are worth a fortune. The rich marry rich. That's how they stay rich."

"No, Mother, I'm not rich, but you seem to have selective memory when it suits you. I'm a pauper. Christina is worth a fortune."

"You could be too if you knew how to manage her inheritance. You could pay yourself a high six-figure salary and wouldn't have to drive a five-year-old SUV. You could buy yourself a nice Mercedes or BMW. I saw a black two-seater the other day I simply fell in love with. It would be perfect for me. I mean you."

"Mother, I am not having this conversation with you again. Listen closely. Christina's money is Christina's. Yes, I'm her mother, but the money is hers. I'm not touching her inheritance and neither are you. I used it to buy our house, but there is no need to use it again. I make enough money to buy a new car, if I wanted one. At this particular time in my life, I don't want a new one. Besides, there is nothing I can do with a two-seater. I like my SUV. It's roomy and it's comfortable." Stephanie had never divulged the will to her mother. She let her believe everything went to Christina. If she knew that half of everything went directly to Stephanie, there would be no end to her greed.

"Well, I could certainly use a new car." Mildred looked down at her fingernails again. "My transmission seems to be acting up again."

"Mother, the car you have is only two years old. You wouldn't know the transmission from the battery. If something is wrong with it, take it to the dealership. It's still under warranty. If you just have to have a new car, then get a job and buy one yourself." Stephanie was quickly losing patience with her mother. "I am not buying you another car."

"You expect me to get a job?" Mildred gasped in outrage. "I gave your father and you girls the best years of my life. Is this how you repay me? Your father walks out on me and you suggest I become a common laborer. Children are so ungrateful these days." She stormed out of the office, leaving the door wide open.

Coming to her feet, Stephanie rounded the desk to slam the door shut. She let out an exasperated growl. To her horror, it was that particular moment Jackson Kaufman chose to knock on her opened door. He smiled and she turned red in embarrassment.

Stephanie stared openly at the man in front of her. She wasn't sure what she was expecting, but this wasn't it. He was tall, a little over six feet with broad shoulders. His eyes were light brown with gold flecks shimmering in them. His skin was the color of smooth rich copper. His mouth was sensual, with full, inviting lips. The mustache and goatee gave him an almost sinister look. He was a handsome, but dangerous-looking man. He was dressed impeccably in a black suit, blue shirt, and tie. His feet were enclosed in designer shoes. Everything about him screamed *trouble* and *raw sexuality*.

In the same few seconds, Jackson appraised her from head to toe and back again. Until now he had only seen her from a distance; up close she was even more beautiful.

Stephanie stood about five-seven. Her skin was a soft honey color. Her eyes were a dark brown. Her small heart-shaped face was perfectly made up. Her lips were formed in the same heart shape. Her long sandy brown hair was pulled back from her face with a clip. Her body was incredible. She was clad in a dark blue pantsuit. Her jacket was open and she wore a silky red camisole. What a pair of breasts. He guessed around a 36-D at least. Being a breast and leg man, Jackson knew he was pretty close in his estimation.

Stephanie had to tear her eyes from him as she moved back behind the oak desk and sat down.

She felt safer putting some distance and an obstacle between them. She flushed under his direct gaze and quickly regained her composure.

"I growl sometimes too, but I don't bite, much," he teased, breaking the uncomfortable silence.

Her face turned a darker shade of red. *For some reason I don't believe that. You are anything but harmless.*

He smiled as if reading her thoughts. I like a woman with fire.

"Please come in. I'm Stephanie Mason," she said, holding out her hand to him. She tried to shake off the feeling of intimidation as she met his bold eyes.

He closed the distance between them in long powerful strides. "Jackson Kaufman. Call me Jack," he said in a deep, professional voice that did little to hide its sexiness. When his hand caught hers, they both felt the spark. Their eyes locked in silent communication.

Stephanie slid her hand back quickly and momentarily broke eye contact. She mentally counted to five and tried to compose herself. No man had ever rattled her the way this one had in less than five minutes. "Mr. Kaufman, please have a seat." She sat down and he followed her lead. "You have quite an impressive résumé. Can you tell me a little about what you did at each of your past jobs?"

"I was a Navy SEAL. I reenlisted when my time was up. After the navy, I took some time off and did some traveling. When I was ready, I put my training to good use. I became a security consultant. I had multiple duties with various companies. I hired and trained the entire security staff. I traveled from state to state recruiting and training. The chosen ones, I trained them in everything from recognizing a possible problem to hand-to-hand combat. They also had lessons at a firing range. I made sure every person carrying a gun was comfortable and capable of using one. My program included putting them all through a two-month rigorous training regimen. I shocked upper management by hiring a few ex-cons. The old saying is definitely true. Crooks do make the best security people, present company excluded. They are suspicious by nature and know the signs to look for. It was a win-win situation."

"Interesting philosophy. It makes perfect sense in a strange way, but I'm not sure I agree with it. How did you solicit these companies' business? Some of them are Fortune 500 companies. How did you get past the front door?"

"I had them put their money where their mouth was. They bragged about their wonderful security guards and their new security system. I told them I could not only break into their building, but I could make it all the way up to the CEO's office without being caught. The CEO laughed and told me I was crazy. He said if I could make it past the third floor, he'd hire me for double what I was asking." Jack smiled and Stephanie had already guessed how the story ended.

"And you of course made it all the way up to the CEO's office." She leaned back in the overstuffed leather chair fingering the gold pen in her hand.

"After observing and monitoring his security guards and hacking into his security system, I was sitting at his desk enjoying a glass of his hundred-year-old brandy when he came to work a week later. He gave me the bottle and hired me on the spot. Miss Mason, I'm the best at what I do."

"I'm sure you are. Tell me about the two-year gap between the navy and your first consulting job. You stated you took some time off and did some traveling. You don't seem the type to take a two-year sabbatical. What did you do in those years?" She laid her pen on the desk and folded her hands together. Leaning in, she waited for his answer.

"Are you sure you want to know?" *Don't do it, Jack. Don't tell her. You will send her running for cover. She's ready to bolt right now. She can't handle it. Make something up. You have this job in the bag. Don't blow it now. You have this job in the bag.*

"I think I need to know if you want to be considered for this position. I'll be honest with you. Your résumé is very impressive, but I get the feeling you are not being straight with me. I can't hire a man I don't trust. Were you in prison or something?" His reluctance to tell bothered her. She had a feeling that whatever he was hiding would be a bombshell. Maybe some things were better left unsaid.

"No, I wasn't incarcerated. After I left the navy, some friends and I went down to South America to work as soldiers of fortune. It was dangerous and exciting at the same time. The pay wasn't bad either." He saw her freeze up right before his eyes. He knew it would shock her. The truth would shock anyone. This was why he chose not to reveal his former line of business to many people. Men were envious of his daring escapades, but women were sometimes turned off by his past. He didn't need to be told which one Stephanie would be. He could see it in her eyes and her body gestures that she had become uncomfortable.

Stephanie was speechless at first. Her brain could

not form one coherent thought. "You were a mercenary?" she asked tightly, folding her hands in front of her. Stephanie was aghast as she stared at him. This man was a gun-for-hire. She had read somewhere that mercenaries were loyal only to the highest bidder. She couldn't believe there was one sitting in front of her, applying for a job at her hotel. Yet there he sat.

"Yes," he answered, meeting her startled eyes. He watched her eyes twitch. "You wanted the truth. I gave you the truth. Ms. Mason, I'm the best man for this job. My past is my past. I'm no longer in that line of work. My résumé speaks for itself. You won't find anyone as qualified as I am."

That might be true, but Stephanie couldn't hire him. She would not subject the rest of the employees to him. She would continue her search. The interview was over. "Mr. Kaufman, thank you for coming in. I'll be in touch when I make my final decision." She came quickly to her feet and bumped the desk in her nervousness. The glass of water teetered and he caught it before a drop spilled. His hand moved so quickly, Stephanie thought she had imagined it. She watched as he set the glass upright.

Jack followed her lead by coming to his feet. He took two steps toward her, and Stephanie backed away cautiously, then eyed the door. Jack stopped when he noticed the alarm in her eyes. He smiled warmly. "I was only going to shake your hand and say thank you for your time. Thank you for the interview and your open-mindedness," he said as his eyes raked over her. "I hope you find what you're looking for. Have a good day, Ms. Mason. Good luck."

Stephanie felt foolish as she watched Jack back out of the office with his hands raised in front of him. He was sending a message. But Stephanie knew she wouldn't change her mind. She couldn't hire someone who'd preyed on the weak—even if it was a lifetime ago. And her attraction to him didn't help matters. No, she definitely couldn't hire Jack Kaufman.

Confident that she'd made the right decision, Stephanie took a deep cleansing breath and stared at the résumé one more time, and dropped it in the wastebasket.